Titles by Anthony Horowitz

Alex Rider
Stormbreaker • Point Blanc
Skeleton Key • Eagle Strike
Scorpia • Ark Angel
Snakehead • Crocodile Tears
Scorpia Rising • Russian Roulette
Never Say Die • Secret Weapon
Nightshade • Nightshade Revenge

The Power of Five
Raven's Gate • Evil Star • Nightrise • Necropolis • Oblivion

FOR YOUNGER READERS

The Devil and his Boy
Granny
Groosham Grange
Return to Groosham Grange
The Switch
Scared to Death

The Diamond Brothers
The Falcon's Malteser • Public Enemy Number Two
South by South East • The Blurred Man & I Know What You
Did Last Wednesday • The French Confection & The Greek Who
Stole Christmas • Where Seagulls Dare

ALEX RIDER

ACTION
ADRENALINE
ADVENTURE

NIGHTSHADE REVENGE

ANTHONY HOROWITZ

WALKER
BOOKS

For Guy Burt, who brilliantly
adapted Alex Rider for TV. With thanks.

First published 2023 by Walker Books Ltd
87 Vauxhall Walk, London SE11 5HJ

2 4 6 8 10 9 7 5 3 1

Text © 2023 Stormbreaker Productions Ltd
Cover © 2023 Walker Books Ltd
Cover artwork by Two Dots
Trademarks Alex Rider™; Boy with Torch Logo™
© 2023 Stormbreaker Productions Ltd

The right of Anthony Horowitz to be identified as author
of this work has been asserted in accordance with
the Copyright, Designs and Patents Act 1988

This book has been typeset in Officina Sans

Printed and bound by CPI Group (UK) Ltd, Croydon CR0 4YY

British Library Cataloguing in Publication Data:
a catalogue record for this book is available from the British Library

ISBN 978-1-4063-9122-0
ISBN 978-1-5295-0793-5

www.walker.co.uk

MIX
Paper | Supporting
responsible forestry
FSC® **C171272**
FSC
www.fsc.org

CONTENTS

THE INVISIBLE BULLET

The three-headed dog was sitting on the corner of Times Square in the middle of New York.

As he climbed out of the subway and caught his breath, Steven Chan got the sense that the dog was searching for him. It would have the advantage, of course. With its twisting necks and its six smouldering red eyes, it could look in three directions at once. Had it actually seen him? The dog was built like a Dobermann but it was several times larger, looming over the traffic that was snarled up in the surrounding streets, the swarms of yellow cabs all blaring their horns as if that would actually help them find a way through the tangled knot of cars, delivery vans and open-top tourist buses.

It was a bitterly cold February evening. Although it was only five o'clock, the sky was already slate grey. The neon advertisements all around the square seemed to be fighting with each other: NBC, Pepsi, Levi's, *The Lion King*, *The Phantom of the Opera*. Clouds of steam and smoke were rising into the air, spilling out of the various braziers cooking hot dogs, burgers and candied nuts, or billowing through the manholes, escaping from the miles of service pipes below the pavements.

Steven Chan tightened the hood of his silver-grey puffer jacket and hurried along Seventh Avenue, trying to lose himself in the crowd. He was in his twenties, Asian an, with a round face, black hair and haunted eyes.

s in danger and he knew it. Had he really allowed himself to fly almost three thousand miles, from West Coast to East Coast, simply to walk into a trap? For that was what New York had become. The whole city. And he was already wondering how he was going to get out alive.

He should have known better.

Chan wasn't exactly a private detective. His friends would have laughed if he'd called himself that. But he was most certainly an investigator, working in the closely related fields of computer fraud, identity theft and industrial espionage. His job had often brought him up against people who were as wealthy and powerful as they were dangerous, and he knew how to look after himself. After all, he had worked for three years as a field agent with the CIA. Trained in the use of firearms, he had a licence to carry the SIG Sauer P226 pistol, which was his weapon of choice. Right now he wished he had brought it with him. He would have liked to have felt the weight of it, tucked into his waistband. But it was too late now. He had to find a way out. He had to get home.

He glanced back. The dog was still there. One of its three mouths was hanging open, revealing a drooling tongue and impossibly sharp teeth. The crowds of pedestrians were passing by on either side. Nobody else seemed to have noticed it.

As he urged himself on, Steven Chan thought back to the moment, two hours ago, when his nightmare had begun.

He had come to New York to meet the one man who could help him with his investigation and tell him everything he needed to know. He had managed to piece it all together for himself, but the truth was so shocking, so unbelievable, that he needed proof. That was what Paul Shaffer had promised to give him.

The two men couldn't have been more careful. They had only ever spoken using "burners": cheap cell phones that they used once and then destroyed. They had sent disposable emails that self-destructed the moment they were read. And Shaffer had been clear about the arrangements for the meeting.

Come alone.

Tell no one.

Don't be late.

Chan had obeyed all three instructions. His plane had landed exactly on time at LaGuardia Airport and he had taken a taxi straight to SoHo, a smart area much loved by writers and artists at the southern end of Manhattan. This was where Shaffer lived. The taxi had pulled up in front of a tall, red-brick structure in Mercer Street, a warehouse that had been converted into a handful of spacious apartments. As he paid the driver and got out, Chan had wondered how much it would cost to buy a place like this. Five million dollars? Ten?

Shaffer would easily have been able to afford it. He was one of the most famous video game designers in America, the man behind *Zombie Nights 1, 2* and *3*. He had joined Real Time, one of the biggest tech companies in America, and had helped them create the shooter *Trigger Happy*, which had sold half a million copies in the week following its launch. Most recently, he had been the guiding force behind the creation of *Eden Fall*, the augmented reality game that had taken the world by storm. Many people were saying that it was going to be as big as *Pokémon GO*. Real Time boasted that it already was.

Chan had walked up to the door and rung the bell. Nobody had answered. Should that have warned him that something was wrong? Would it have made any difference if he had turned round and left, there and then?

But this is what had happened. As he stood at the entrance, wondering what to do, the door had opened and one of the other residents had come out: a woman in a fake fur coat with a large handbag. Chan had smiled at her as if he had just been buzzed in and walked past her before she had a chance to question him. He found himself in a gloomy hallway with a lift on one side, but he had been trained to avoid lifts whenever possible. To any field agent, a lift was a small room with just one metal door and no other way out. He took the stairs.

Paul Shaffer owned the penthouse, six storeys up. When Chan reached the top of the stairs, he saw that the door was ajar, and that should have been another warning, but it was too late to go back now. He knocked and waited. Then, with a rising sense of dread, he pushed the door open and went in.

He continued along a wide corridor with a polished wooden floor and brightly coloured Marvel posters – originals – on the walls. One door opened into a kitchen, old-fashioned but full of modern gadgets; the next led into a bathroom. Chan didn't call out. He moved carefully, making no sound. The instinct that he had developed as a CIA agent told him that he was alone in the apartment, but he couldn't be sure. Once again, he thought of the SIG Sauer P226 that he had left behind. He missed the cold comfort of the metal in his hands. As he entered the living room, he felt completely naked.

The living room was huge, with double-height ceilings and four oversized windows with views stretching out over West Broadway. The day was already nearing its end, but Chan didn't reach for the light switch. There might be someone watching the flat. Why advertise that he was here? His eyes took in expensive furniture, a jukebox, shelves jammed with photographs and awards, a long metal table surrounded by chairs, a Persian rug. No sign of any computer equipment. Shaffer must work somewhere else. A spiral staircase led to a gallery with more doors at the back. Chan climbed up.

The man he had come to meet was in the bedroom. Paul Shaffer was lying on his back, wearing a black T-shirt and jeans, his bare feet sticking out. He was staring at the ceiling with eyes that no longer saw anything. It was impossible to say how the games designer had died. It could have been natural causes: a heart attack or a stroke. But Chan knew otherwise. The meeting had been planned very carefully. The stakes could not have been higher. It was too much of a coincidence that Shaffer should have chosen this moment to pass away in his sleep. He had been murdered, and Chan realized that he had to get out of this place as quickly as he could if he didn't want to be next.

He was about to leave when he noticed that the dead man was clutching something, holding it against his chest. It was a pair of goggles, the sort of thing a skier or a motorcyclist might wear. They had large lenses, a thick frame made out of black, moulded plastic and a wide strap that went over the ears and all the way round the head. Chan would have recognized them instantly, even without the Real Time logo of a miniature clock face and the letters RT printed on the side. This wasn't just a headset; it was one of the most advanced computers on the planet, battery-powered and stuffed with state-of-the-art processors, 3D sensing modules, high-resolution displays.

More than that, it was Paul Shaffer's headset. He could have left a message inside it. He could have left the entire story of his life. The headset connected Chan with all the information he needed about Real Time. He knew at once that he had to take it and, leaning forward, he prised it loose from the dead man's grip.

The fingers had not yet become stiff and offered no resistance. That told him that Shaffer had been alive only a short while ago.

All the more reason to get out fast.

Holding the headset, Chan hurried into the kitchen. He had noticed the fire escape before he entered the building and now he used it, zigzagging down to the narrow alleyway that ran along the side. He pulled his hood over his head, then, walking more slowly, slipped out into the main street. He had already worked out what he had to do. The first thing was to find a place of safety as far away from the apartment as possible. There was no point trying to go back to the airport. If anyone was following him, that was the first place they would look. He needed to surround himself with people. No more alleyways. No parking lots. Nowhere that he could be picked off on his own. He would take the least obvious way out of New York. He might travel by train from Penn Station to Boston or Washington, for example. Or he could take a Greyhound bus all the way to California. Chan was carrying two thousand dollars in his wallet. He would pay in cash. Any form of electronic or Internet banking was out of the question.

He followed the crowd along Canal Street. It was mainly workers leaving their offices, but there were tourists and early-evening shoppers too. Safety in numbers. It felt good being surrounded. He came to a subway entrance and, without thinking about it, plunged down the narrow staircase, disappearing underneath the street. This was the fastest way to get uptown, and the further he was from SoHo, the more anonymous he would become. The New York subway system was more than a hundred years old and felt like it, with old-fashioned tiles and a meshwork of grimy steel girders. But it was efficient. Chan had only been on the platform for a minute before a train came grinding in. He climbed inside and sat down, relieved when the doors slammed shut behind him.

As the train thundered through the darkness, Chan examined the headset he had taken. Should he put it on? No. Not down here. There were too many people watching. But once he reached the surface, it might actually be useful. The headset would have a map with street directions built into it, and the simple truth was that Steven Chan didn't know New York all that well. It would provide him with bus routes, train stations and timetables, distances, news reports and more, all of them projected directly into his eyes. That was how augmented reality worked. It was like an overlay. A whole world of games and information printed on top of the real world.

He looked up. A young woman was staring at him from the other side of the carriage. She had a headset folded around her neck. She could have been completely innocent, a gamer on her way home, but why had her eyes locked into his? Suddenly, Chan was worried. Perhaps it wasn't so good being surrounded, not when he was trapped underground. The train slowed down and pulled into a station: Times Square/42nd Street. Making an instant decision, Chan got up and left the train.

As soon as he had climbed up into Times Square, he slipped his own headset on and everything changed. At once he was surrounded by information he didn't need. Ticket prices for the Shubert Theatre. Ripley's Believe It or Not! opening times. The weather forecast: snow expected tonight. The words were floating in rectangular boxes, suspended in the air. He turned his head, and that was when he saw the three-headed dog, sitting on the pavement. For a brief moment, Chan was jolted. The dog looked so real, as if it had stepped out of a Greek myth. But of course it didn't exist. It was computer-generated and presumably belonged to *Eden Fall*. Steven Chan had to smile. Paul Shaffer was a real genius. Working with maybe a hundred or even a thousand programmers, he had first created the monster and then placed it in the middle of New York.

As he continued up Seventh Avenue, Chan saw a horned owl perching on a fire hydrant and a huge snake slithering underneath a parked car. Overhead, three winged pigs flew above the traffic. A number 17 bus went past with a naked pink demon sitting, cross-legged, on its roof. There were creatures everywhere and as Chan continued moving, he couldn't help noticing that they were taking more and more of an interest in him. None of them approached him, but their heads turned in his direction. The owl smiled at him. An octopus, wrapped around a lamppost, smoking eight cigarettes, pointed one of its tentacles at him and laughed as if at some private joke.

The headset was feeding him information too. **Traffic accident ahead. Snow expected at 10.15 p.m. Police officer approaching: identified as Jim Fletcher, Midtown South Precinct.** And so on. Line after line of data was being thrown at him from every direction.

He had travelled ten blocks, reaching 55th Street with the dark emptiness of Central Park ahead, when a man stepped in front of him. At least, it was a man as far as the shoulders. It had the head of an enormous rat.

"You don't think you're going to escape us?" the creature asked.

Chan stared at the black eyes, the twitching nose and lips, the brown hair brushing over the collar. He realized he was hearing the words through speakers hidden in the wrap-around bands of the headset. They were being fed directly into his ears. He saw something out of the corner of his eye and, despite himself, ducked down. One of the pigs had dive-bombed him.

They can't hurt me, he told himself. *They're not real. They don't exist.*

The rat grinned, showing two rows of vicious little teeth. It was almost as if it had heard what he was thinking and wanted to prove him wrong.

On the other side of the road, the octopus let out another burst of high-pitched laughter and slid down towards the ground.

He heard buzzing and saw a swarm of wasps, each one the size of a tennis ball. They had appeared out of nowhere and were circling around his head. Another demon with a trident leaned out of the window, its tail waving lazily above its head. It seemed to be looking right at him.

The headset might be a useful source of information, but Chan decided he'd had enough. He tore if off and instantly all the creatures disappeared and the sounds stopped. Seventh Avenue returned to normal. Chan had played *Eden Fall*. He knew how brilliantly the computer images had been constructed. Some of the figures – Adam and Eve, angels and demons – had been created with so much detail that it was impossible to tell them apart from actual human beings. He also knew they couldn't hurt him. They were ghosts, holograms. But even so, he had been shaken to find himself surrounded by them. Right now, he just wanted to get away.

He hadn't stopped moving, and before he knew it, he had crossed another road and suddenly there was grass beneath his feet. He had entered Central Park! It was another world. The moon had come out and it was reflecting off the grass, which had a coating of winter frost, stripping away every colour apart from the darkest green and white. Leaving the traffic and the crowds behind him, Chan walked into an all-surrounding silence. He could see thousands of squares of light but they all looked the same, and he realized he was lost.

He had to find his way out of here, and there was only one way to do it.

He put the headset back on.

More boxes blinked to life. **Central Park. Created in 1857. 1.4 square miles in size.** He saw that he had just crossed West Drive (six-mile loop, popular for biking and trail running). Signposts sprang up. **This way to the zoo. This way to Lounging Rock. This way to the Pond**. He raised the headset to make sure. The signs existed in the game, not in real life. Well, he could still use them. He would make his way over to the Upper West Side. He would find a taxi and drive to Washington Heights. He had friends who lived there. Why had he allowed a pack of augmented reality animals to unsettle him? They could taunt him and buzz around him, but they couldn't hurt him. He just needed somewhere to hide out.

He stopped.

There were two young girls standing in front of him, both of them dressed in red coats. One had fair hair and looked about thirteen. The other was younger, with pigtails. Chan wondered what they were doing on their own in Central Park at night. He had forgotten he was still wearing the headset. Nothing seemed real any more.

"What do you want?" he asked.

"I'm Amy," the first girl said.

"I'm Jasmine." The second girl smiled.

They were only children. Chan wasn't scared of them. "I'm sorry," he said. "I'm in a hurry. I can't help you."

"We don't need your help," Amy muttered.

"You're the one who needs help," Jasmine agreed.

She had taken a gun out of her pocket. But Chan saw that it wasn't a real gun at all. It was bright pink and made of plastic, the sort of thing you might buy in a toy shop for ten dollars. In fact, he knew exactly what it was. Gamers used weapons just like this in shooter video games. It was controlled by Bluetooth and although it might fire invisible bullets that could bring down an owl or a flying pig, it was useless against him. It wasn't real.

"What are you...?" he began.

They were the last words he ever spoke.

Jasmine pulled the trigger and – through his headset – Steven Chan saw the single word BANG suspended in the air. Despite himself, he smiled. Then something exploded between his eyes. It was as if he had been hit by an invisible bullet. He felt a moment of searing pain before both worlds – real and fake – turned themselves off. The darkness rushed in and he pitched forward, his knees and then his chest plunging into the soft ground. His hands twitched for a moment, but then he lay still. A pool of blood formed itself around his head, almost black in the moonlight.

Although he would never know it, Chan had been doomed from the moment he had taken the headset. The thick black plastic had contained two devices. The first was a micro-locator which had allowed the girls to follow him. The second was much more deadly. A tiny pipe bomb filled with PETN, one of the most explosive chemicals in the world, had been concealed in the crosspiece that fitted above his nose, slanting towards his head. When Jasmine pressed the trigger of her gun, she had sent a radio signal that had set off a firing pulse. The effect had been of a tiny gun firing a tiny bullet that had gone directly into Chan's brain.

The two girls looked at what they'd done.

"You got him," Amy said.

"It was easy," Jasmine replied.

Neither of them showed any emotion, but then they had killed many times. They both worked for an organization that specialized in murder, and they had spent most of their lives learning how to kill people. The organization was called Nightshade and, quite recently, it had sent them to poison a senior and much-respected British politician, with a chocolate muffin filled with cyanide. His death had set off a chain of events that could have led to a major terrorist incident in London.

It had been a lot of fun.

But for now their work was done. Carefully, they removed all that remained of the headset from Steven Chan's head, leaving the body stretched out on the grass. After all, they didn't want the police to find any evidence. Then they turned round and, holding hands, walked back across the park, heading for the bright lights.

SEPARATE WAYS

In a box there are only black balls, white balls, red balls and yellow balls. A ball is taken at random from the box. The table shows the probability that the ball will be red or yellow.

Colour:	Black	White	Red	Yellow
Probability:			0.35	0.20

The probability that the ball will be black is twice the probability that the ball will be white. There are 21 red balls in the box. How many black balls are there in the box?

Alex Rider stared at the exam paper in front of him. With a sinking feeling in his stomach, he realized that it made absolutely no sense at all. Why were there all these balls in a box? What sort of balls were they? Cricket balls? Tennis balls? Ping-pong balls? How could he possibly know how many of them were black and, at the end of the day, why did it matter?

He sighed and forced himself to concentrate. This might be a mock exam, but his maths teacher, Mr Donovan, took it very seriously. GCSEs were only two months away and he had already told Alex that he expected top marks from him. "Goodness knows how many lessons you've missed over the past couple of years," he said to Alex. "But I'll give you credit. You've really applied yourself this term and you deserve your Easter break. Just don't make any silly mistakes."

Silly mistakes. Right.

Alex tried to focus on the page. He was sitting in the front row of the gymnasium, which had been turned into an exam room at Brookland School, surrounded by the rest of Year Eleven, all of them in uniform, trying to untangle the problems in front of them. His best friend, Tom Harris, was two desks away, staring into space with a pencil sticking out of his mouth and a dreamy expression on his face. There was a clock high up on the front wall. In some corner of his mind, Alex knew that the four values had to add up to one. This sort of problem was easy. He'd done it plenty of times. But with the minutes ticking past, his brain was refusing to work.

Instead, he began to drift away until he had arrived at the final moments in St Paul's Cathedral, when he had grappled with Freddy Grey, a fifteen-year-old terrorist who had been sent to take out the entire British government. Once again, he saw himself fighting for the cylinder of deadly VX nerve gas ... enough to kill everyone in the building. As he sat there with the exam paper in front of him, the entire room seemed to tilt and suddenly he was falling, falling with the ground rushing up towards him...

"Five more minutes!" Mr Donovan announced.

Alex closed his eyes and took a deep breath. When he looked again, the room had returned to normal and the black and white balls were still waiting for him to sort them out.

All right.

Alex spent the next five minutes working out the problem and scribbled the answer down just as Mr Donovan called time and began to collect the papers. Over to his right, Tom was slumped back in his chair, his pencil now being twiddled in his ear. Alex looked down at what he'd written. Had he got it right? Did he even care?

Yes. It was important to him. At the end of the summer he was going to be starting sixth form and he had already decided that he wanted to go on to university. Jack Starbright, who had been his housekeeper when his uncle had died and who was now closer to him than anyone in the world, had agreed. He needed to take control of his own life. For too long, he'd allowed other people to tell him what to do.

MI6. Alan Blunt. Mrs Jones.

The worst of it was, as much as Alex wanted to leave all that behind him, it wasn't over yet.

In just two days' time, he was going to be taking the train from London to Salisbury, as he had every week for the last three months. He didn't really want to go. But Freddy Grey, the boy who had come so close to killing two thousand people, was being held prisoner near there and, like it or not, Alex felt responsible for him.

It wasn't Freddy's fault. Ten years ago, when he was just five years old, Freddy had been kidnapped along with twenty-four other children from different parts of the world. They had all been told that their parents had abandoned them. They had been brainwashed and turned into an army that would do anything and kill anyone without a second thought. The children had no names. They thought of themselves only as Numbers: Freddy had been Number Nine and in many ways he had been the most dangerous of them all. Taken prisoner by the Special Operations of the Brazilian police, one of the toughest security outfits in the world, he had managed to kill five men and injure three more while he was trying to break free.

Nightshade had turned him into a monster. There was no other word for it. And Alex couldn't think of the four so-called "Teachers" – who had run the organization – without feeling sick. They had been making millions of pounds by turning children into cold-blooded assassins and then renting them out to the highest bidder. The children didn't care if they lived or died. They just did what they were told.

Thanks to Alex, Nightshade was finished. The four leaders had abandoned their secret hideaway in Crete and disappeared. Freddy, along with two other Numbers, had been arrested in London. All this had happened over five months ago, but Alex was still visiting him because he thought he could help him. Freddy was being held in a maximum-security facility inside a huge army base at Tidworth in Wiltshire. He had a team of doctors and psychiatrists working with him, but none of them thought it would be easy to reverse the brainwashing that had lasted his entire lifetime. What Freddy needed, everyone agreed, was someone normal, a boy his own age who might somehow help steer him back into the real world.

Who else was there but Alex?

Alex had met Freddy's parents – Sir Christopher and Lady Susan Grey – and they too had encouraged him to keep up the friendship. They were visiting their son regularly, but there were times when he still didn't recognize them or refused to believe they were who they said they were. Alex couldn't help feeling sorry for them. First they had thought their son had drowned in a boating accident. Then they had discovered that he was a professional killer with a trail of bodies behind him. How could Alex turn down their request for help?

Perhaps Freddy was beginning to show signs of improvement. Alex couldn't be sure, but every time he had gone back to Tidworth Camp, he had noticed small differences. First of all, Freddy was using his own name and didn't insist on being called Number Nine. He had started reading books and sometimes asked questions about the outside world. When he had been with Nightshade, he had barely been allowed to talk at all. He was smiling more. Very occasionally, Alex felt that he could relax, as if Freddy was just another boy, almost exactly the same age as him, getting better after a long illness.

But always he had to ask himself: was Freddy just faking it? Was he trying to get his guards to relax, waiting for the moment when he could make a break for freedom? It was horribly possible. That was exactly what he had done when he had been held prisoner in Rio de Janeiro. He had pretended to be a little boy, asking permission to use the toilet. But once the door had been unlocked, he had sprung into lethal action, cutting down eight professional soldiers. Freddy Grey was a killing machine and it was impossible to forget it. Alone in the room with him, Alex knew that he was surrounded by CCTV cameras and that there were several panic buttons with soldiers waiting at the door in case of an emergency. He was doing his best to be a friend to Freddy Grey, but he could never be sure.

"Your paper, Alex?"

Alex looked up and saw Mr Donovan, the maths teacher, standing over him. He realized he'd been miles away. "Yes, sir." He handed the paper over.

There were eighteen black balls in the box. There had to be.

Alex got up and followed the rest of Year Eleven out into the sun.

It was half past three and the school day had come to an end. Everyone was buzzing as they hurried through the main gates. The following day was the start of the spring holiday, two glorious weeks without class. Alex himself was heading off for a five-day break with Jack Starbright. The two of them had decided to go hiking in Ireland along the Wild Atlantic Way with perhaps a stop at Dunfanaghy beach in Donegal for some surfing. Jack was also studying for exams – in her case, the Bar Course Aptitude Test that she needed to pass to become a lawyer. They both needed a break.

Alex found Tom unloading his bike from the rack. He was looking exhausted. "How did it go?" Alex asked.

"Maths ... not my strong suit," Tom muttered. "I just about managed to count the pages."

"Was it really as bad as that?"

"I'm finished here." Tom swung his bike round. "I'm not going into sixth form. I don't want to go to uni. I just want to get on with my life."

Alex found his own bike and the two boys walked out of the school gates together. Alex couldn't help feeling a bit sad. He and Tom had been best friends since they were twelve. More than that, Tom was the only boy at Brookland who knew the truth about Alex: that his uncle had been a spy and that Alex had been recruited by MI6 after Ian Rider's death. Tom had become increasingly involved in Alex's adventures, helping to cover for him when he was away from school. He had even been there at the end, when Alex had single-handedly taken on Nightshade at St Paul's Cathedral. It was surprising that Tom had never been made to sign the Official Secrets Act.

But now it seemed that they were going separate ways. If Tom really did drop out of school before sixth form, Alex would spend his last two years at Brookland without him. Of course they would still see each other and Alex had plenty of other friends, but it wouldn't be the same. And what would happen if Tom got a job on the other side of the country or even abroad? He had often talked of joining his older brother, Jerry, in Naples. Tom and Jerry. Neither of them had ever forgiven their parents.

"You still on for skateboarding tomorrow?" Alex asked.

"Sure." Tom didn't sound enthusiastic.

"I thought you enjoyed it."

"I enjoy it when I'm not falling off and breaking both my legs."

This was another recent development. Alex had gone back to the sport at the start of the year. He wasn't sure what had first got him interested, although watching a sixteen-year-old Australian winning gold at the Tokyo Olympics had certainly been part of it. But it was more than that. Perhaps it was all the training he had been given by Ian Rider when he was growing up. There was a part of Alex that always needed to test himself. He also loved the freedom and the sense of exhilaration that came with a sport that had few rules, which demanded skill but very little equipment, and which could cause you serious harm if you made a mistake. When things went right, Alex felt as if he were flying. He could go anywhere he wanted and it was as if London belonged to him. When he made a mistake, he paid for it. Alex had turned up at school with so many bruises that Miss Bedfordshire, the school secretary, had considered reporting him to social services.

Alex had managed to persuade Tom to join him and they occasionally went to Southbank Undercroft, a skatepark underneath the Queen Elizabeth Hall, close to the River Thames. Tom's older brother was seriously into extreme sports, and if the two of them really were going to hang out together in Naples, this would be good practice. Tom had been reluctant to begin with, but he was pleasantly surprised to find that he liked the other skateboarders, particularly some of the girls who quickly latched on to the fact that he was a beginner and fussed over him, offering to help him with his technique.

Alex and Tom might only have another term together at Brookland. Quite soon, they'd have left their childhoods behind them. But they were both determined to enjoy the months ahead. Together, as they had always been.

"You want to come round for supper?" Alex asked. Tom lived up near Earl's Court. His parents had got divorced and now he was on his own with his mother. Alex's journey home would take him in the other direction.

"I can't." Tom sighed. "Dad's taking me out tonight. Fish and chips and two hours of him moaning on at me. It's all Mum's fault. I should move in with him. I'll love his new girlfriend..." Tom got on his bike. "Why are adults so rubbish?"

"They've forgotten they were kids."

"My parents were never young. I think they were born aged forty."

Despite himself, Alex smiled. He had his cycle helmet over his arm and now he pedalled away. "See you tomorrow!"

If Alex had still been working for MI6, he might have been more attentive. Perhaps he had been too occupied by his mock GCSEs. But he hadn't noticed that he and Tom had been followed from the moment they left Brookland.

There were four of them.

The first had been outside the school gates, a Deliveroo driver on a bust-up Honda SFX 50cc moped. He had been idling on the other side of the road, pretending to look for directions on his mobile phone. A few minutes later, a girl on a rented electric scooter had swerved in behind them, never travelling more than five miles per hour. Like the Deliveroo driver, she was wearing a helmet. This didn't just keep her safe. It concealed her identity.

As Alex and Tom parted company, two cyclists pulled up at the traffic lights ahead of them, both with helmets and sunglasses. They did not turn round but used their mirrors to watch what was happening. They saw Alex go one way and Tom the other. One of them spoke into a concealed throat mic. "Targets separating at Sydney Street. We'll follow Rider. Thirteen and Twenty-Two, you stay with Harris."

Thirteen was the Deliveroo driver. Twenty-Two was the girl on the e-scooter. At once they swung into action, setting off smoothly through the traffic.

Alex was still going over that last question in the maths exam. Eighteen black balls in a box. He saw nothing.

On all sides, Nightshade was drawing in.

FLIPS AND OLLIES

Southbank Undercroft seemed to be hiding from the world. It was a dark, grimy space buried underneath the great bulk of the Queen Elizabeth concert hall, with square pillars holding up the building above it and neon lights burning day and night. The walls were grey cement, all of them covered with graffiti, and there were no signs, no safety instructions, no entrance fee, nothing to suggest who could use it or when.

That was what made it special, a target destination for skateboarders from all over the country. It belonged to the people who used it. British skateboarding was said to have begun here and crowds often stopped on their way along the Embankment, gazing at the variety of blocks, the seven-stair set and the notoriously steep and difficult banks. Maybe they were hoping to see a serious accident. The place could have been designed for teenagers with a death wish.

Alex Rider liked coming here. There was an unwritten law among skateboarders. Everyone helped each other, with the most experienced passing on tips to the rookies, and he had learned a lot of new techniques in this concrete academy. He enjoyed the sense of organized chaos – everyone doing their best not to collide with everyone else – and it said something about the way the sport was run that accidents were very rare. Above all, he never felt he was under any pressure. There was no need to show off. You did what you wanted when you wanted and nobody made any judgements. When you had a wipe-out – another word for a serious fall – people just shrugged. They didn't help – but they didn't laugh at you either.

Alex was standing on the coping, the narrow platform that curved around the edge of the skatepark. He glanced over at Tom, who was wearing sunglasses, jeans and an oversized Hawaiian shirt, chatting to Shanice, a girl he'd met the first time they'd come here. He didn't seem in any hurry to try out his own skills, so Alex left the two of them together and launched himself down the ramp. Dropping In was a basic move, but it was one of the hardest to learn, even if the ramp was only one or two metres high. It just felt dangerous. Alex could still remember the lurch in his stomach when he'd tried it for the first time, the fear that he might be about to kill himself. Now the move came easily to him. He shot down, across the floor, then up a ramp on the other side – Flying Out. For a moment he hung in the air, feeling the lightness in his feet. He sucked his knees in, reaching down to grab the front of the board with his hands. Then he stamped down. The skateboard hit the coping on the other side and stopped. Perfect.

The next twenty minutes passed with that same combination of long, quiet pauses followed by sudden bursts of activity. Alex went through the various moves he'd been practising, including the Nollie Flip, the Switch Ollie, the Pop Shove-It and the (correctly named) Impossible. At the same time, he noticed Tom practising carving, kick turns and foot braking. They were very basic techniques, but they certainly seemed to impress Shanice. She was all over him.

The sun was bouncing off the river and Alex was suddenly thirsty. He shot up another ramp and landed next to Tom. "You want a drink?" he asked.

"Sure. I'll have a Coke."

"Shan?"

"The same." She smiled at Alex. "Thanks."

Alex took off his helmet and knee-pads and left his board with Tom on the coping. Then he climbed over the barrier, making his way through a small crowd of spectators. There was a shop that sold cold drinks and snacks just a few minutes away and he picked up two Cokes, some water for himself, and, because he knew Tom liked them, a bag of chocolate raisins. He lingered on the way back, enjoying the warm sunshine and the feeling that spring had arrived in time for the school holidays. In just a couple of days, he and Jack would be on their way to Donegal for the start of their holiday. He had completely forgotten about his visit to Freddy Grey in Wiltshire. Or perhaps he had deliberately put it out of his mind.

He went back to his board, but there was no sign of Tom. He put on his helmet and knee-pads, at the same time scanning the ground between the pillars. It was very strange. He couldn't see his friend anywhere. He heard the rattle of wheels and suddenly Shanice swept up and then landed beside him.

"Where's Tom?" Alex asked.

"Oh – he had to go."

"Go where?"

"I don't know. He went off with two friends."

That made no sense at all. There was no way Tom would have left without telling Alex. And anyway, they'd agreed to have lunch together on their way back home. "What friends?" Alex asked.

Shanice shrugged. "I didn't really see. There were two of them, about his age. You only just missed him."

"Did you see which way they went?"

"That way!" She pointed vaguely towards another grey concrete building next to the concert hall. This was the National Film Theatre. There was a flight of steps between the two, leading up to Waterloo Bridge, which arched across the river, carrying four lanes of traffic in and out of the centre of London.

Alex had been in danger so many times that he knew the smell and the feel of it. There was absolutely no reason to believe that anything bad had happened to Tom, but there was a sickness in his stomach and, despite the sun, he felt suddenly cold. He snatched up his skateboard, already realizing that he might need it.

Carrying the skateboard, he climbed back over the barrier and ran towards the steps. Somewhere in his head, a voice was shouting at him that this was ridiculous, that nobody had any interest in Tom, who was just an ordinary schoolboy with no secrets. But that wasn't true. He had one secret.

Alex.

He turned the corner into a wide cobbled area, with a row of plastic bins on one side and, on the other, a couple of delivery vans parked in front of the steps. Which way?

When Tom had left, he had been escorted by two friends who were surely no such thing at all. Could they have all gone up the stairs? Or could there have been a car or a third van waiting here? That would make more sense. The service lane continued under Waterloo Bridge and then bent round, continuing past the National Theatre. Even as he made his decision, a dozen other questions were crowding in on Alex. Why Tom and not him? What did they want ... and who were they? How had they made Tom leave with them? Did that mean they were armed? None of this mattered right now. He just wanted to find his friend.

And then he saw it, lying on the ground, under a lamppost. Tom's skateboard. He couldn't have just dropped it. Alex was certain. He must have left it there deliberately, an arrow. Alex knew now that he had been right. Two teenagers had grabbed Tom. A car had been waiting for them around the corner. How long ago had this all happened? Alex had only been away for a couple of minutes and now he remembered what Shanice had said: *You only just missed him*. If he moved quickly enough, there was still a chance that he could catch up.

Alex threw down his skateboard, dropping it under his right foot while his other foot was already propelling him forward. It was a technique he'd practised over and over again, but now, with all his thoughts focused on Tom, it had just happened automatically and he was moving before he knew it, rattling over the cobbles, sweeping round the corner next to the theatre. Skateboarding is all about balance. The rider and the board have to be in perfect harmony and that was exactly how Alex felt as he set off in pursuit. Weeks of practice at Southbank Undercroft and along the roads all around Chelsea had finally paid off. He was in total command.

A wide concrete ramp led up to the main road. Ahead of him, a bright red Honda Civic was just pulling away and he heard the screech of its tyres against the tarmac. That was what had made him notice it. Why would anyone be driving so fast in an area full of pedestrians unless they were desperate to get away? He looked closer and saw someone half-turn on the back seat. For a brief second he got a glimpse of a brightly coloured shirt and black spiky hair. It was Tom!

But he was too late. The car was already speeding into the distance. Even as Alex watched, it reached the end of the road and, without signalling or pausing, swerved right. Alex made an instant calculation. It was lucky that he'd visited the area so often. He knew he couldn't follow the Honda. By the time he reached the corner and made the turning, it would have disappeared from sight and he might never be able to find it. But there were other ways. The road followed the bend of the river, but that was the long way round. If he stayed close to the river's edge, he might be able to get in front. It was a gamble. The Honda could turn left or it could turn right and if Alex made the wrong choice, that would be it. But what else could he do?

He swung round – a perfect kick turn – and pushed off the way he had come. Very quickly he reached the Embankment with its smooth surface and complete absence of traffic. He knew he could move faster than the Honda. He just had to hope he was heading in the right direction.

He sped past the skatepark, weaving his way through the crowd, desperately trying not to crash into anyone. Somebody shouted at him and he glanced round briefly. It was a distraction that lasted no more than a second, but when he looked back he saw with dismay that he was heading straight for a woman pushing a pram. Alex yelled out. There was no time to stop. He stamped down with his back foot, catching the tail of his skateboard and propelling the whole thing into the air. As the woman stared at him, he soared over the pram, then crashed down on the other side. That was the Ollie. He had never done it better.

And the manoeuvre had given him more acceleration. Out of the corner of his eye, he saw the dark green water of the river, two cruisers passing each other mid-stream. He shot past Festival Pier. Hungerford Bridge was just ahead, but Alex knew that it had been built for trains, not cars: there was no way the Honda could cross it. Who was he chasing? It was still a complete mystery. Why would anyone want to kidnap Tom unless it was to get at him?

There was a man walking an Alsatian dog on a lead, the two of them coming towards him. At the last moment, the Alsatian lunged at Alex, barking furiously. Alex bent low and used his heels to perform a carving turn, putting space between himself and the animal, but he still saw the glistening white of the dog's teeth and heard its owner shouting at him. He ignored them both.

The giant Ferris wheel known as the London Eye was ahead of him. This was the bit that he was dreading most. There were already dozens of people waiting to take the ride, with more of them milling around the ticket shop and others queuing in front of an ice-cream van. Alex was forced to slow down. If he slammed into someone – a child, perhaps – he could hurt them badly. There was a large square park on his left and he thought of making a detour across the grass and the play area, but right then he saw the red Honda. It was still travelling up the main road. He was even able to make out four people in the car: the driver, two passengers. And Tom.

They were driving him out of London, heading west. Alex had his mobile phone in his back pocket. Should he stop and call the police? No. By the time he had made the call, the car would have disappeared and, worse still, he had been unable to see the registration number. Even assuming he could make the police believe him, they would have nothing to follow.

He could still beat them. They were approaching the huge roundabout at the southern end of Westminster Bridge and Alex knew that the traffic here always slowed down. He could get in front of them and cut them off. If necessary, he would simply skateboard across their path. They couldn't just run him over! There were more CCTV cameras in London than any other European city and if Tom's kidnappers tried to drive away from an accident, they would be found and stopped within minutes. All Alex had to do was reach the bridge before them.

There were only about two or three hundred people in his way.

Bracing himself, Alex shot forward, his shoulders hunched, searching for the gaps between all the tourists and visitors. He heard voices shouting in several languages. A pair of hands reached out and tried to grab him. But he was moving so fast and with such determination that most of the people preferred just to get out of the way and he was able to steer himself through the empty spaces that opened up in front of him. Even so, Alex misjudged one of the gaps and his shoulder slammed into a man who had just bought an ice-cream cone. The man jerked forward, the ice cream leaping out of his hand as if in slow motion and splattering onto the pavement, where it was promptly eaten by another dog. *Well,* Alex thought, *at least someone's happy.*

The London Eye was on his right, moving so slowly that it seemed to be standing still. There were long queues of people waiting on the two ramps. Alex flew past, swerving to avoid a man in a Union Jack blazer handing out leaflets for a hamburger bar. Did he really look as if he was in the mood for a hamburger? Now the London Aquarium was on his left and the crowds had thinned out. Westminster Bridge was directly in front of him with a wide flight of steps leading up to it from the Embankment. Alex counted about twenty steps. Facing him, a stone lion on a pedestal seemed to be watching out for the red Honda, as if trying to help.

Alex came to a sudden stop, transferring his weight to his back foot and pressing down so that the tail of the skateboard came into contact with the ground. Tail-scraping was dangerous. It was an easy way to fall. But it was also fast. He popped the skateboard into his hand and seconds later he was carrying it up the steps, taking them two at a time.

He was too late. With a sense of despair, he watched the red Honda flash past in front of him. At least he hadn't lost it. The driver had turned right onto Westminster Bridge and was heading towards the centre of town, with Big Ben and the Houses of Parliament on the other side of the river. With his heart pounding and his breath catching in his throat, Alex reached the top step and jumped back onto the skateboard. At the same time, he heard the sound of an approaching siren and for a moment he wondered if the police had somehow learned about the kidnap and were coming to his rescue. But as he joined the road and set off after the Honda, he saw a single police car overtake him and then suddenly swing round at ninety degrees, blocking his way. It was him they were after! Someone must have reported a crazy skateboard rider endangering people's lives on the South Bank. Two police officers got out of the car and held up their hands, signalling to him to stop. On the other side of the police car, the red Honda was getting away.

Alex wasn't going to let that happen. He was almost halfway across the bridge. The skateboard was carrying him ever closer to the officers who were waiting for him to slow down – but at the last minute he carved right, then ollied up between two bollards, shooting back onto the pavement.

The way ahead was blocked!

It seemed as if the whole city was against him. A group of about thirty primary school children was heading towards him in a crocodile, escorted by two teachers. Alex couldn't continue forward. The children weren't going to step out of the way. But nor could he get back onto the road without delivering himself into the hands of the police.

He made an instant decision and ollied a second time, flying diagonally towards the very edge of the bridge as if he intended to hurl himself into the Thames. He had judged it perfectly. He actually landed on the handrail – with the wheels divided on either side. It was a move known as a 50–50 Grind and he'd done it many times. But not like this. Alex was horribly aware of the river, far below. If he lost his balance, he would plunge five or six metres into the water. If the impact didn't kill him, he'd probably drown.

The very thought of it made him shudder and the tiny movement almost finished him, tilting him into the air. Still grinding on the handrail, he fought for balance and somehow managed to find it. With both hands out, he steadied himself and prepared for the next move.

Alex could hear the aluminium trucks on the underside of his skateboard. They were the T-shaped pieces connected to his wheels and they seemed to be crying out in protest. He glimpsed the two police officers staring at him in disbelief. The children were right next to him, chattering excitedly. One of them had his phone out and was trying to take a picture. Alex was slowing down, losing momentum. Time to go. He leaned forward and then jumped back onto the pavement. He had made it! He had got past the crowd of children. The police were scrambling back into their car, but there was no way they could turn round quickly enough. By the time they came after him, he would be gone.

Even so, the manoeuvre had cost him time. The Honda was a long way in front of him, turning into Parliament Square. Alex passed through a set of traffic lights, with Big Ben looming above his left shoulder. Everywhere he looked, there were armed policemen on patrol. He knew that their job was to protect the politicians passing in and out of Parliament, but that didn't make him feel any more comfortable. How many laws had he broken in the last few minutes?

There was a second set of traffic lights in front of him. As Alex approached, they turned red.

He went through anyway. It was too late to stop.

At the very last minute, he saw a black shape bearing down on him. A taxi had come out of nowhere. He couldn't avoid it. It was too close. With a cry, Alex tried one last carving turn, his knees bent, his head low. The taxi filled his vision. He glimpsed the driver, twisting the steering wheel, trying to avoid him. The side of the vehicle hit his arm with tremendous force and at the same moment, the front wheel of the skateboard slammed into the kerb. Alex was sent flying. The whole world corkscrewed around him, and for two or three seconds he was quite certain he was going to die. His last thought was: what will happen to Tom? Perhaps, if Alex was dead, he would be of no use to his kidnappers. Perhaps they'd let him go.

Alex crashed down, landing on his back.

The ground was soft.

Momentarily dazed, he wasn't sure what had just happened. He opened his eyes and saw Winston Churchill with hunched shoulders and a walking stick, looking away as if in disdain. He felt grass under his hands. Slowly, painfully, Alex lifted himself up. The skateboard had crashed into the kerbside and the momentum had sent him hurtling over the pavement and onto the green that covered the centre of the square, close to the statue of the old prime minister. If he had landed on concrete or tarmac, he might have broken his back. He twisted round and saw that the skateboard was finished. The nose had smashed. The wheels were at right angles to each other.

He stood up. A few pedestrians were moving towards him. He saw police officers on the other side of the street. If he didn't want to be arrested, he had to get away.

There was nothing more he could do. The red Honda carrying Tom Harris had disappeared.

DECISION TIME

Jack was already at home when Alex limped in through the front door. She took one look at him and her face fell. "Oh my God. Alex! What happened to you?"

Alex grimaced. "I just need five minutes."

"To call an ambulance?"

"I'd prefer some lunch."

"I'll see what there is..."

Alex went upstairs, threw off his clothes and stood in the shower. The hot water, rushing down onto his head and shoulders, helped to ease the pain, but looking at himself in the mirror, he saw that his right arm was covered in scratches and there was a dark, spreading bruise on his back where he had fallen. Crossing London hadn't been easy either. He was sure the police would be looking for him after what had happened on Westminster Bridge, and the last thing he wanted right now was to get himself arrested.

On the bus home, keeping his head low and trying to avoid the CCTV cameras, he'd received a text on his phone. Three short lines. They'd told him everything he needed to know.

He was in very serious trouble indeed.

Five minutes later, wearing a fresh set of clothes, he came down to the kitchen. Jack had brought out cold chicken, salad, cheese and fruit. She'd been studying for her law exams when Alex came in but now her books were piled to one side. She poured two glasses of orange juice as he sat down, then took her place opposite him.

"So?"

The single word was heavy with anxiety. Like Alex, Jack had believed that he had left the world of espionage, with all its dangers, behind him. But it was obvious that he'd done more than fall off a bike. It wasn't just his injuries, the way he walked. There was something in his eyes that Jack had never seen before. He was afraid.

"Tom's been kidnapped." There was a time when Alex would have tried to hide the truth from Jack. He hadn't wanted her to know when he was being sucked into another mission. But after Jack had almost been killed in Egypt, they had come to an understanding. There would never be any secrets between them.

So now Alex told her everything that had happened since he had arrived at Southbank Undercroft: Tom's disappearance, the chase across London, the crash. Alex felt miserable. Looking back, he was certain he could have done more, but Jack quickly picked up his mood and took his hand in hers.

"Don't you dare blame yourself, Alex," she said quietly. "And don't you worry either. We'll call Mrs Jones right away. She'll find Tom, wherever he is."

"We can't." Alex pulled his hand away. "If we go to MI6, he'll be killed."

"You can't know that."

"But I do." Alex took out his phone and showed Jack the text he had received on the bus. The letters were all in capitals. Somehow it made the message uglier and more menacing.

WAIT FOR US AT HOME.

WE WILL CONTACT YOU SOON.

TELL NO ONE, OR TOM HARRIS WILL DIE.

Jack stared at the screen. With her sprawling red hair and her large eyes, there were times when she could seem comical, even clownish. But now she was totally serious.

"They sent it to me when I was on my way here," Alex explained. "I don't know how they got my number."

"Who are they?" Jack said. "Do you have any thoughts?"

Alex sighed. "I don't think it's Scorpia," he said. "They're finished. There's none of them left."

"Nightshade?"

"I was already thinking that." Alex nodded. "But it could be someone who worked with General Sarov or Dr Grief or Damian Cray. I've got a lot of enemies."

"You've got a lot of friends too, Alex – and we'll find a way to get you through this. Sarov, Grief, Damian Cray ... they all tried to hurt you and look what happened to them!" Jack handed the phone back. "You should eat something," she said.

"I'm not hungry."

"Sitting there, starving yourself, isn't going to help. Are you sure we can't call Mrs Jones? It may be that we need help..."

Alex shook his head. "I can't risk letting them hurt Tom."

The two of them picked at the lunch, but neither of them had much of an appetite. They sat there in silence, Jack's work forgotten. There was nothing else to say. When the phone finally rang, Alex leaped out of his seat as if he had been electrocuted – but it was only Jane Harris, Tom's mother, wondering what had happened to her son. That was something Alex hadn't considered. Eventually, his family would want to know the truth. What was he meant to say?

He played innocent. "The last time I saw him, he was with Shanice," he said. At least it wasn't a lie. "Hasn't he come home?"

"No. I've tried his phone, but it's going straight to voicemail."

"Well, if he gets in touch, I'll tell him to call you."

The doorbell rang.

"Sorry, Jane. I've got to go." Alex hung up and glanced at Jack, who had got to her feet, the colour draining out of her face. They weren't expecting any visitors, not in the middle of the afternoon. The fact that someone had come to see them now could only mean one thing.

Alex went out and opened the door.

Immediately, everything made sense.

There was a man standing on the drive with a gleaming Mercedes S-class limousine parked in the street behind him. He was wearing a well-tailored suit and carrying a leather attaché case. The man was Black with closely razored hair, round glasses and the look of a mourner coming out of a cemetery. When Alex had first met him, he had introduced himself as Brother Mike and, although MI6 and Interpol had spent the last six months searching for him, his real name was still unknown. He was one of the four leaders of Nightshade and his speciality had been martial arts and weapons training. For a moment, Alex's head swam. Brother Mike was one of the most wanted men on the planet. How could he possibly have just turned up on his doorstep in Chelsea?

"Good afternoon, Alex." Brother Mike had a cultivated voice. He seemed to take pleasure in every word he spoke. "Do you think I could come in?"

"Where's Tom?" Alex demanded.

"If you let me in, I'll tell you."

Alex stared at the older man, his face giving nothing away. He let a few seconds pass. Then he stepped back, allowing Brother Mike to enter.

Jack was still waiting in the kitchen. She stared at the new arrival as he walked in but, taking a cue from Alex, she didn't speak. For his part, Brother Mike looked around the room with interest, as if he was admiring the fittings and the furniture. Without being asked, he sat down at the table, laying the attaché case flat in front of him.

"You must be Jack Starbright," Brother Mike said, his voice completely neutral. "I'm—"

"I know who you are," Jack growled.

Alex had told Jack everything about the military base at Kavos Bay in Crete. The four so-called Teachers – Brother Lamar, Brother Mike, Sister Krysten and Sister Jeanne – had set themselves up as the high priests of a religion that they had invented, living in a temple and wearing grey robes and sandals, like modern monks. But everything about them was fake. They had stolen twenty-five children and turned them into a terrorist army. Far from being godly, they were utterly pitiless. And here was one of them, making himself comfortable in Alex's home. It seemed impossible, having him here.

"Then perhaps you know too much, Miss Starbright." Brother Mike smiled at her. "We sent Alex a message, telling him not to speak to anyone. It seems that he has disobeyed."

"I only told Jack," Alex said. "She lives here. We don't have any secrets from each other."

"Even so, your friend, Tom, will have to pay."

"You're going to kill him?" Alex couldn't keep the horror out of his voice.

Brother Mike smiled a second time. "I think we'll give you a pass, Alex. We won't kill him – but I'm afraid he'll have to be punished. I'll have him beaten up. And I'll let him know that it's thanks to you. But if you disobey us a second time, it will be much, much worse."

Jack stared at the man in disgust. "You're a monster," she said. "You've kidnapped a teenage kid. You kidnapped a whole load of kids. You're pure evil. How do you even live with yourself?"

"I think you're being rather childish, Miss Starbright. I've made a great deal of money in my lifetime and I live with myself very easily. If you're going to stand there and throw insults at me, it's only going to make the whole situation more difficult for young Alex."

"What do you want?" Alex asked, with a hollow feeling in his stomach.

"That's much more sensible. A cup of tea would be nice."

Jack flicked on the kettle. There was a kitchen knife lying near by and Alex saw her eye it briefly before she reached for a tea bag. He knew what she was thinking.

Brother Mike clicked open the locks on his attaché case, although the case itself remained closed. "Let me tell you why I am here," he began. "As you can imagine, I put myself at some risk entering this country, although I have to say, your security services are slow and stupid and nobody even asked me how long I intended to stay. I very much dislike England and I look forward to getting far away. In any event, it's worth a little danger to myself to see you again, Alex. I've been thinking a lot about you since we last met. We all have.

"You have done a great deal of harm to Nightshade. You spoiled an operation that had been many months in the planning. We lost an important client thanks to you causing us serious reputational damage. At the same time, you cost us many millions of dollars. But worse than any of this, you were responsible for the loss of three of our best agents, Numbers Nine, Six and Eleven. It has literally taken us a lifetime to complete their training, by which I mean their lifetime. Six and Eleven are out of our reach but in the case of Number Nine, they have made a stupid mistake."

"And what's that?"

"They have allowed you to visit him."

It took Alex a moment to understand what Brother Mike was saying. "You think I can help him escape?"

"That is exactly what we believe. If we didn't, you would already be dead. After everything you did, Sisters Krysten and Jeanne both wanted to terminate you, but I persuaded them that if it was revenge they wanted, there were better ways. We could use you. How do you like the idea of working for Nightshade, this time under your real name? How do you feel about joining us once again?"

"I loathe you," Alex said. "I hate everything you stand for. Jack was right. You're monsters."

"Yes, but we have your friend. So perhaps spitting out petty insults isn't the smartest idea." He paused. "Let me tell you how this works..."

Brother Mike took out his mobile, tapped the screen, then slid it across the table. Alex and Jack looked down at it. There was a photograph of Tom, wearing his Hawaiian shirt, blindfolded, with his hands behind his back. There was a bare brick wall behind him.

"Tom Harris is in a secret location," Brother Mike continued. "Nobody can find him and only you can save him. To do that, you have to obey our instructions to the very letter. There can be no more mistakes, Alex. If you try to communicate with the police or with MI6, if you refuse to do what we ask, if you fail in the execution of our plan, then Tom will die in a very horrible way. Perhaps we will arrange for pieces of him to be sent to you in the post, a new parcel once a week. How would you feel about that?"

"Just get on with it," Alex said.

At the side of the kitchen, the kettle had boiled and clicked itself off, but Jack didn't move. There was no way she was going to make this man a cup of anything.

"We know that you're visiting Number Nine at Tidworth Camp tomorrow. You're going to get him out."

Alex stayed perfectly still. "That's impossible," he said at last.

"If it was impossible, I wouldn't have come here," Brother Mike replied.

"Freddy Grey is being held in a secure unit in a military installation that's home to twelve thousand armed soldiers," Alex explained. He was trying to keep his voice steady. "Delhi Station is surrounded by an electrified fence with just one exit to the main road and this is guarded twenty-four hours a day, seven days a week. The main door is also locked and can only be opened, electronically, by the guards. When I go into the building, I'm searched. Everything I carry – including any food or drink – has to go through a metal detector and an X-ray machine. There are CCTV cameras in every corridor. Freddy and I are never left alone in the room. They have a guard sitting there the whole time. They also lock the door and you need an electronic card to get in or out. When I leave, another guard walks with me all the way to the car—"

"Don't call him Freddy Grey." Nothing else seemed to matter to Brother Mike. "His name is Number Nine."

"It doesn't matter what I call him. He's not going anywhere," Alex said.

Brother Mike looked at him coldly. "I said it wasn't impossible," he went on. "That didn't mean it would be easy." He glanced at his watch as if he was in a hurry to be away. "But if you're telling me you won't even try..."

For a moment, Alex was afraid that Brother Mike was going to walk out. If that happened, Tom was doomed. "I didn't say that," he cut in hastily. "But I can't do it on my own. I'll need help."

"That's why I'm here." The smile was back and somehow

it was even more ghastly than before. "You're talking to Nightshade, Alex. Whatever you may think of us, we are one of the most effective terrorist organizations in the world. The fact that you were able to prevent the operation that we called 'Leap of Faith' was largely down to luck. It was my mistake sending you back to the UK. I should have shot you while I had the chance. That's why I volunteered to come here today. I'm going to enjoy watching you jump through hoops on our behalf."

"I think you've talked enough," Jack said. "How can you help him?"

"If you say another word, Miss Starbright, Alex's friend will have a very unpleasant accident." Brother Mike turned back to Alex. "You're booked on to the eight-fifty train from Waterloo to Salisbury. You arrive at ten twenty-two. We've cancelled the taxi company that usually meets you at the station. Instead, their place will be taken by one of our agents. He will be driving a local taxi. The registration number is NE11 ABC. Nice and easy to remember."

At last, Brother Mike opened the attaché case. "You have outlined some of the difficulties in effecting this escape," he said. "But I have something here that may help you see things in a different light. Do you think we haven't examined every aspect of Delhi Station? You can't tunnel. You can't climb over the fence. Yes, you're hopelessly outnumbered. But the British authorities have almost certainly underestimated Number Nine and this will put the odds back in our favour."

Brother Mike took out a device like nothing Alex had ever seen. At first he thought it was a children's toy. It was made of blue plastic. But examining it more carefully, he saw that it was a gun of some sort, though one that hardly looked lethal, with two large springs connected to the trigger and a clunky grip. Instead of a barrel, the gun had a fat round cylinder, which should have had just one hole for one bullet but instead had six. As Brother Mike swung it round, it took on the look of either a water pistol or something a killer clown might use, performing in a circus.

"This has been created by technicians working for Nightshade," Brother Mike said proudly. "It may look childish, but let me assure you it is anything but. It is a fully working, 3D-printed, semi-automatic pistol made entirely from plastic apart from the single metal screw which is used as the firing pin and, of course, the bullets. You might like to know that it is based on the design of the so-called Yoshee Six Shooter, originally created by a college student. It also incorporates some of the components of the Shuty MP-1, an altogether more lethal weapon, though sadly one that would not meet our needs."

Brother Mike's hands moved swiftly and the gun came apart in front of Alex's eyes. He saw at once that the separate pieces looked nothing like a conventional weapon. It might not be too difficult to disguise them, and most of them would be ignored by the metal detector. But not all.

"What about the bullets?" Alex asked. Jack was standing next to him and, glancing in her direction, he saw the cold fury in her eyes. Alex was being asked to turn traitor. He was being forced into a course of action that could lead to many deaths. But she didn't dare speak, not if it led to Tom being hurt.

Brother Mike produced ten bullets and spread them on the surface of the table. "The gun fires six .22 LR calibre rounds," he said. "One bullet for each barrel. These bullets are used mainly by hunters. Low noise and minimum recoil. They work perfectly with the weapon."

"But they're made of metal."

"Yes. To smuggle them in, you're going to have to swallow them."

Jack opened her mouth to protest but stopped herself at the last minute. Brother Mike produced a tube of Polo mints from his case. "Take one of these when you arrive. They're not Polos. They'll actually make you as sick as a dog almost immediately but some of the bullets will come up again and you'll be able to use them. Not very pleasant, I'm afraid, but there's no other way."

"Won't my stomach set off the metal detector if it's got ten bullets in it?" Alex had already decided that there was no way he was going to adopt this part of the plan, but he was playing along, buying time.

"We've brought you this." Now Brother Mike took out a brace, the sort of thing that many teenagers wore to straighten their teeth. It reminded Alex that the last time he had worn one, it had been supplied by MI6 and contained a tracker device. "The guards will think it's set off their machine," Brother Mike continued. "I don't suppose they'll cut you open."

Alex tried to take all this in. It was just horrible, so cold-blooded ... and so crazy. "So I manage to smuggle in your Toys 'R' Us plastic pistol," he said. "I have to throw up to get the ammunition and that gives me maybe six or seven bullets against twelve thousand armed men and women. Somehow I've got to reach a taxi which is waiting for me outside. What exactly is the plan? Or do I just make it up as I go along?"

"You give the gun to Number Nine. He'll do the rest."

Alex was desperately trying to think of a way out. The whole thing sounded insane and suicidal, but he knew there was no point arguing. From the way Brother Mike was sitting there, calm and confident, it was clear that his mind was made up.

"All right," he said. "You've got a fancy gun. And I presume Number Nine will know how to use it. But what happens if I get killed? I mean, what happens to Tom?"

"I've already told you. Give us Number Nine and we'll let your friend go. If you get yourself killed, we'll consider that a result, too – so you don't need to worry about him. He'll send flowers to your funeral."

Jack couldn't bear any more. She put her hand in the air and asked, "Please, may I say one thing?"

Brother Mike examined her with narrowed eyes. "I think I will give you permission. Yes."

"I really don't want to be rude," Jack said, choosing her words carefully. "But I'd like to know how Alex can trust you. If he manages to get Freddy – I mean, Number Nine – out of Delhi Station, what's to stop you killing him ... and Tom for that matter? You've already said how much you hate him. What guarantee does he have that you'll play fair?"

"That's a reasonable question, Miss Starbright, spoken like the professional lawyer that I'm sure one day you will become. I will give you the honest answer. He has no guarantee at all. He can refuse to do what I ask, in which case Tom Harris dies. Or he can save his friend by delivering Number Nine to us. There is no third option."

He dipped his hand into the case one last time and took out a loose-leaf booklet, written in large letters with coloured illustrations. "This manual will show you how to use the gun, how to break it into pieces and reassemble it. It's extremely simple, but if I were you I'd do some practice. You'll need to move fast." He closed the case and clicked the locks shut. "Do you have any more questions?"

"How do I contact you?"

"You can't. You have no need."

"Don't I need to tell you if I'm going to do this or not?"

Brother Mike got back to his feet. "I think that decision has already been made," he said. The smile flickered across his face. "I'll find my own way out."

He picked up the case and left.

Neither Alex nor Jack said anything for a long time. Outside, they heard the engine of the Mercedes start up and then slowly fade as it drove away. Jack cleared the plates from the table and put the food back in the fridge. Finally, she turned to Alex, but before she could speak he held a finger to his lips, warning her to stay silent. His eyes darted from left to right. The message was clear. They're listening.

"I need to get some air," he said aloud. "I'm going for a walk."

"I feel the same," Jack agreed. "Do you mind if I come with you?"

"All right."

Alex took out his phone and laid it carefully on the table. Jack did the same. Then the two of them left the house. They crossed the King's Road and continued towards Stamford Bridge, the home of Chelsea Football Club. Alex knew exactly what he was doing. He had noticed there were road repairs taking place near by and, sure enough, as they approached, they heard the sound of jackhammers, tearing up the road. They found a bench and sat down.

"The house is bugged." They were the first words he had spoken since they had left home. "They knew everything about you. They knew what train I was booked on to go to Salisbury. They must have been watching us for some time."

"How do you know we haven't got bugs hidden in our clothes?" Jack asked.

"I don't. But that's why we're sitting here."

Jack understood. The noise of the roadworks would hopefully drown out their conversation. It was also the reason they had left their phones behind.

"You know you can't do this, Alex." Jack got straight to the point. "If you give Freddy Grey a gun, he's going to kill people. You'd never be able to live with that. And anyway, the idea of swallowing bullets... I've never heard anything so disgusting." She sighed. "The worst of it is, you know as well as I do, you can't trust these people. They're deliberately turning you against your friends. They're making you into a traitor. This whole thing could be a trap. If it goes wrong, you could spend the rest of your life in jail!"

"Tom's my friend. Are you saying I should just let him die?"

"No. Of course I'm not saying that." Jack glanced away and Alex saw that she was fighting back tears. "I think we have to tell MI6."

"Nightshade will find out."

"They might not."

"We can't take that risk."

Alex was remembering what had happened the first time he'd come up against Nightshade. It turned out that they'd had a double agent working inside the government, telling them everything that MI6 was planning. Who could say they hadn't done the same thing again? He had to assume that everything he and Jack said might be overheard. They could have been followed from the house. There might be someone watching them even now. Showing no expression, Alex looked around him. He saw a man waiting for a bus on the other side of the road. There was a woman talking on her phone outside a clothes shop. A homeless person was sitting with a begging cup and a cardboard sign. Any one of them could be a Nightshade agent. Whatever he did, he had to be careful.

He couldn't go to MI6. He couldn't find Tom on his own. It seemed that he had no choice but to do what Brother Mike demanded. But the situation might not be completely hopeless. There was one thing that Nightshade might have overlooked.

He moved closer to Jack and lowered his voice. "I think Brother Mike may have got it wrong," he said. "Freddy has been at Delhi Station for almost six months and I've been to see him at least a dozen times. We've sort of become friends and he's changed. He's pleased to see me. Sometimes he makes jokes. We chat about lots of things – ordinary things like football and music. He uses his real name."

"If MI6 thought he wasn't dangerous any more, they'd have let him out," Jack said.

"That's true. He could just be pretending." Alex sighed. "Maybe all along he's been thinking he can fool us and somehow break out on his own. But I was with him in prison in Gibraltar and then in Crete, and I know him. He's done a lot of bad things, but I'm certain he's not the same person now."

"You think he'll help you?"

"No. But if I give him a gun, I don't think he'll go on a rampage."

"So how will you get him out?"

"I've been thinking about that. He doesn't have to kill anyone. He can use me as a hostage."

Jack stared. "Isn't one hostage enough?" She was thinking about Tom.

"He can hold the gun on me and use me to get him out of the compound."

"And what's to stop him shooting you the moment he gets in the car?"

"I don't think he'll do that."

"That's not good enough, Alex." Jack shook her head. "I feel sorry for Freddy. I know you've been trying to help him. But Nightshade turned him into a killer and you've just admitted it: there's every chance he still is. And I don't trust Brother Mike, or whatever he wants to call himself, one inch. You get into that car and I'll never see you again."

Alex took a deep breath. "I can't think of any other way, Jack. I only care about Tom. It's my fault he's in trouble. I have to try to help him."

The decision had been made, and Jack could see that Alex wasn't going to change his mind. The two of them walked back home in miserable silence and while Jack cleared the kitchen, Alex took the gun – still in pieces – along with the manual up to his room. Just as Brother Mike had said, it was made entirely of plastic apart from one small screw which acted as the firing pin, and he had no doubt he could smuggle it into the compound. It helped that the guards knew him. After so many visits, they wouldn't be looking for anything suspicious.

The first time he tried, it took him about five minutes to assemble, the pieces coming together with a satisfying click. He took it apart and did it again. This time it was the work of three minutes. Half an hour later, he had the whole thing down to just twenty seconds. The gun might look ridiculous, but he had to admit that it was brilliantly made.

He thought about what he had told Brother Mike. He had described the inside of Delhi Station quite accurately. The X-ray machine and walk-through metal detector. The CCTV. The electronic card reader on Freddy's door. The sophisticated lock on the way out. He had been sitting on his bed, but now he got up, went over to his desk and pulled open the bottom drawer, taking out an old metal box with a Simpsons cartoon on the lid. He hadn't watched *The Simpsons* for years, but that was how it had come when Smithers had given it to him. The box and its contents had been created by the gadget master at MI6, and although everything in it looked ordinary enough – a pencil sharpener, a pocket calculator, a ruler, several pencils and a library card – very little of it was what it seemed. There was also a red gel-ink pen at the bottom. He took that too.

Alex had often asked himself why he had hung on to it all. A souvenir of his adventure in Kenya? Or had he thought that one day he might need them? Well, that day had come. A plan was beginning to form in his mind, the different pieces slotting into place ... just like the gun.

He went over to the bed and checked the bullets. They were the one thing that worried him. Jack was absolutely right. There was no way he was going to swallow them and nor was he going to wear the brace. Could he risk going into Delhi Station without them? No. If Brother Mike heard that he had disobeyed his instructions, he would take it out on Tom. And anyway, the gun had to be loaded. He would have to prove that it really was a lethal weapon if they were ever going to make it out of the compound. Sitting on his own, Alex visualized the entrance to the prison: the X-ray machine on one side, two guards sitting behind it, the long table, the walk-through metal detector. The idea was taking shape. He wasn't going to swallow any of the Polos with whatever poison they contained, but they still might come in useful. He picked up one of the bullets and turned it in his fingers. Would it be possible to smuggle the ammunition through in plain sight?

Alex got up again and opened his wardrobe. He took out a coat and quickly examined it.

It might work.

He would have to hope that the weather wasn't too warm. And he would need a small pot of brown paint.

GETTING IN

Jack insisted on coming with him to Waterloo Station. She said she wanted to keep him company, but he knew that secretly she wanted one last chance to talk him out of it before he got on the train to Salisbury. They stood together at the ticket barrier.

"Alex..."

"This is going to work, Jack. I promise you."

It wasn't a particularly cold day, but Alex was wearing an old duffel coat he'd pulled out of the back of his wardrobe. He had a backpack over one shoulder. Jack examined him. He reminded her of someone, but it was only now that she realized who it was. As he was getting older, Alex was looking more and more like his uncle, Ian Rider. She shuddered, remembering what had happened to him. But she knew there was no point arguing.

"I still think this is a bad idea," she said. "And I'm going to be very cross with you if you get yourself shot."

"I'll take care," Alex promised her.

"Call me as soon as there's any news."

The two of them hugged. Alex didn't look back, but Jack was still there watching, worried, as he climbed onto the train.

And then it was the ninety-minute journey to Salisbury. Alex stared out of the window, going over and over what might lie ahead. He thought about Freddy Grey, an ordinary boy slowly coming to terms with what had happened to him. And Number Nine, a terrorist who had tried to kill two thousand people in St Paul's Cathedral. Which one was he about to meet? In a way, it was irrelevant. In his heart, he knew that Brother Mike had set him an impossible task and that Nightshade wouldn't really care if he succeeded or failed. This was their revenge and if he was shot dead trying to break out of Delhi Station, they would only smile.

But he wasn't going to let that happen. The Hampshire countryside was rushing past in a green blur, taking him ever further from London. Alex sat back in his seat, preparing himself. Somehow, he was going to get through this. Was Freddy Grey his friend or his enemy? Everything depended on that one simple question.

The train plunged into a tunnel and suddenly he was surrounded by darkness, the scream of the wheels and the smell of diesel fumes. Well, that was an answer of sorts.

An hour and a half later, he left the train at Salisbury and walked out to find the taxi that would be waiting for him in the car park. He spotted it at once, sitting slightly apart from the other vehicles, a grey Toyota Prius, registration NE11 ABC. The driver was a man in his fifties with a sullen face and drooping moustache, wearing an anorak. He was bald with a few strands of greasy brown hair trailing across his scalp. Looking at him, it was hard to believe that he could have anything to do with Nightshade, but that, of course, was the point.

"I think you're waiting for me," Alex said.

"Get in." The driver scowled.

Alex threw his backpack onto the seat and climbed in

beside it. Tidworth was sixteen miles away and Alex knew that the journey would only take about half an hour. As they came out of the station and joined the main road, he was aware of a strange sensation, as if there was something wrong with the car. Then he realized what it was. His heart was pounding. It was in overdrive. He knew that what he was doing was crazy and would almost certainly end in disaster. Jack had been right. He should have listened to her. But then he thought about Tom. He half-closed his eyes and forced himself to calm down.

They were driving north. Alex recognized the towns and the villages they passed. Through Amesbury, then turn left to Snoddington and Shipton Bellinger. He had done the journey many times and the odd names had once amused him, but not today. As he ticked off the landmarks – the pub, the converted barn, the electricity pylon – he knew he was getting closer and that if he was going to change his mind, he would have to do it soon. One thing was sure. He couldn't get the car to stop or turn round. The driver might look harmless, but he would almost certainly have a gun under that anorak and if Alex even seemed to hesitate, it would be a death sentence for him – and then for Tom.

The road was taking them through perfect English countryside. The sun was shining over the fields, hills and woodland, and the whole world seemed to be at peace. A row of modern houses appeared ahead of them and Alex knew they had reached the edge of Tidworth. They turned down a road with open countryside on one side and a long fence on the other. Behind the fence, Alex saw the first buildings of what might have been an enormous university campus. This was Tidworth Camp. The Toyota slowed down and turned into a narrow lane. A bright blue sign read: DELHI STATION.

After about a hundred metres, they found themselves approaching a square white building, two storeys high, with tall windows perfectly lined up, flower boxes and carefully trimmed shrubbery. Closer up, it looked less like a university, more like a private clinic or perhaps a retreat for wealthy people trying to lose weight. It was the fence surrounding it that gave the game away. This fence was much taller and more sophisticated than the one Alex had seen from the road, bristling with cameras that swivelled in different directions. A gravel drive led to the front door, but to get anywhere near it, you would have to pass through a barrier that rose and fell electronically, watched over by armed soldiers in a modern steel-and-glass control room. Delhi Station was a prison. There was no escaping it.

The Toyota driver pulled in a short distance away on the edge of a grass verge opposite the gate.

"This is as far as I go," he said. "I'll be here when you come out."

"Just so long as you're not expecting a tip," Alex muttered.

With his backpack hanging from his shoulder, Alex got out of the car and walked towards the barrier, which rose as he approached. The soldiers knew him by now and Alex hated what he was doing, betraying their trust. Ahead of him, the front door opened. Inside the building, his image would have been relayed to a dozen different TV screens and he would have been recognized as a regular visitor. It was only once he entered that things would start to get difficult.

The entrance hall was spacious with a black-and-white tiled floor, a wide staircase and corridors leading in different directions. Alex had been told that Delhi Station had originally been built as a hospital, and there was something about the building that felt calm and welcoming. But there were some less-welcoming additions. Alex was standing in front of an airport-style security check: an X-ray machine on one side, a walk-through metal detector on the other. Two soldiers in khaki were waiting for him. He would have remembered their names even if they hadn't been printed on ID badges, pinned to their chests. Harry and Samesh. Both in their twenties. Cadets. Not expecting any trouble and certainly not from him. That would help Alex with what he had to do.

He placed the backpack on the conveyor belt that would carry it through the scanning device. His watch and phone went into a tray, and then he stepped through the metal detector as if he didn't have a care in the world.

The metal detector alarm screamed out.

Samesh hurried round. "I'm sorry, Alex. I'm going to have to ask you to turn out your pockets."

"Sure." Alex looked annoyed with himself. He reached into the pocket of his duffel coat and took out a solid leather case with a pair of Aviator sunglasses inside. "I forgot these. Sorry." He pulled his pockets inside out to show he wasn't carrying anything else.

Samesh took the glasses, examined them briefly and

laid them on a table. "And I'm afraid I'm going to have to pat you down."

Alex undid the toggles so that his duffel coat came loose. "Go ahead."

Samesh searched him expertly from head to toe. Alex didn't seem to have anything else made of metal. He wasn't wearing a belt. Meanwhile, Harry was puzzled by something he had seen on the screen. He opened Alex's backpack and, fumbling around, took out a thick blue plastic cylinder with six holes running from one end to the other. "What's this?" he asked.

Alex felt a jolt of nervousness and forced himself not to show it. Harry was holding the barrel of the gun. "Someone gave it to me at school," he said. "It's a pencil holder."

Harry set it aside. It wasn't what he was looking for. He also ignored the two plastic springs, the packet of Polos and the unopened energy bar in its bright green wrapping. These were all completely innocent. His attention had been drawn to the metal box that Alex had taken from his desk – which was exactly what Alex had planned. Airport X-ray machines "see" plastic but not very well. Things like combs and biros will show up on the screen as faint ghosts of themselves. Anything metal, however, will block the electromagnetic waves and will be much more solid and distinctive. Machine operators are trained to give them special attention. After all, most dangerous weapons are made of metal.

It turned out though that the metal box was harmless. There was a picture of the Simpsons on the lid and when it was opened it contained nothing of interest, not even a pair of scissors. Harry turned over the library card in his fingers, perhaps wondering why Alex had brought it, then replaced it, snapped the box shut, and put the whole thing back in Alex's bag which he then handed across.

Alex was through! But even as he gathered his things, he knew that this had been the easy part.

A pair of milky-white glass doors protected the corridor ahead of him. As Alex waited, a third soldier approached, dressed in khaki like the others, with a throat mic looping around his ear and a pistol in his belt. Alex had no doubt that he would have other weapons concealed about him: a Taser, handcuffs, maybe a pepper spray. His name was Griffin and he was older than the others and much less friendly. Every time Alex had come to Delhi Station, he had made it clear that it was a waste of his time having to escort a teenager in and out.

"Come to see your little friend, have you?" he sneered.

"If you don't mind," Alex said.

"Actually, I've got better things to do than babysit the two of you, but since you're here, let's get this over with." He nodded at Harry, who pressed a button. The glass doors slid open.

Everything was white on the other side: the walls, the floors, the ceiling. The corridor seemed to stretch too far into the distance, as if it was longer than the building it was in. There was an antiseptic feeling about the place, a memory of its hospital days. The various doors could have led into private rooms. Or cells. Alex noticed the CCTV cameras twisting round to follow him and Griffin. It was impossible to forget that Delhi Station was now a maximum-security jail.

They stopped about halfway down at a door marked A7 and Griffin knocked, not to ask permission to come in but to tell the occupant that he was there. He took out a plastic card and ran it through the scanner above the door handle. There was a buzz and the door opened.

MI6 had done its best to make Freddy Grey comfortable while he was their prisoner. He was, after all, only sixteen, and no matter what he had done or how dangerous he was, his father was a distinguished army officer who had served in Iraq. Freddy had a suite of rooms. The largest of these was a living room with a sofa, a wall-mounted TV, a couple of shelves of books and a desk with a laptop computer. Freddy didn't have access to the Internet but he'd asked for some computer games and these had been supplied. There was a kitchen and an eating area on one side, and a bedroom and bathroom on the other.

Freddy had been sitting at the desk studying a history book, but he got up and smiled as Alex came in. He seemed pleased to see him. Was that because he enjoyed having company or had Nightshade somehow got a message to him? Did he know that Alex might be his ticket out? It was an unpleasant thought. Alex had told Jack that Freddy was slowly getting back to normal. He still wanted to believe it himself. But he couldn't get the thought out of his head: was he about to hand a loaded gun to a psychotic killer?

"Hey, Freddy!" he said, trying to sound casual.

"Hi, Alex."

As always, Griffin wasn't going to leave the two of them together. He pulled a chair over to the door and sat down with a scowl. "You've got forty minutes," he said.

"Thanks, Mr Griffin." Alex took out a tube of mints. He was about to help himself when he seemed to remember the guard. "Would you like one?" He held out the tube.

Griffin sniffed and took one of them. He threw it in his mouth, leaned back and sucked.

Alex had also taken a mint but he only pretended to eat it. So far, everything was going according to plan. He had been given the fake Polos by Brother Mike. They were supposed to make him sick so that he would throw up the bullets he had swallowed. But from the very start, Alex had decided he wasn't going to do things the way Nightshade wanted. He hadn't swallowed anything. He'd found another way to get the bullets into Delhi Station and, although Griffin was sitting there looking very pleased with himself, the complete professional, he was unaware that six of them were right in front of him, hiding in plain sight.

"So how are you?" Alex asked, focusing on Freddy. His voice didn't sound like his own. But it was never easy to talk when there was a guard in the room, so there was nothing unusual about that.

"I'm OK."

"Have they said when they're going to let you out of here?"

"They never tell me anything." Freddy was wearing the grey tracksuit that seemed to be his only clothes at Delhi Station. He had grown his hair longer and although he had the use of the garden and a gym, he had put on a bit of weight. "I've started school again," he said.

"How do you like it?"

"It's strange. Nightshade taught me seven martial arts,

parachuting, computer hacking, how to use an AK-47 automatic machine gun, and a whole load of other stuff, including French, Arabic and Mandarin Chinese. But they somehow forgot maths and history."

"I just did my maths GCSE," Alex said.

"How did it go?"

"It was only a mock exam but I think it was OK. Have you seen your parents?"

"Mum and Dad come in every week. Either together or apart. I'll be honest with you, Alex. I can't wait to get home. None of this was my fault and it doesn't seem fair keeping me locked up."

"Mum and Dad". The words had come easily to him. Freddy seemed to have an understanding of who they were.

"MI6 thinks you're dangerous," Alex said.

"I am dangerous. But not to them. One day, I'm going to find Nightshade and I'm going to make them pay for what they did to me. And all the others. Sometimes, when I'm stuck here and I'm feeling miserable, I think about what I'll do when I catch up with Brother Lamar and the rest of them. That's what keeps me sane."

There was a groan from the side of the room.

Griffin wasn't looking well. He had a hand over his stomach and he was hunched forward in his seat. His face had gone an unpleasant colour. He was clearly about to be sick.

"Mr Griffin? Are you all right?" Alex asked. He was amazed that the mint he'd given the guard had affected him so quickly.

"No. I feel bloody awful."

"You don't look too good," Freddy agreed.

"I need the toilet." Griffin pointed at Freddy. "Don't try anything stupid. I'll send someone else in. They'll be here in a minute."

He fumbled his security pass out of his pocket and swiped it through the door control. There was a second buzz. The door opened and Griffin almost fell into the corridor. He slammed it shut behind him.

From the very start, Alex had been worrying that Griffin would use Freddy's bathroom. If that had happened, everything would have gone wrong. He let out a sigh of relief – although he still had to move fast. Whatever happened, the two of them wouldn't be left alone together for long.

First of all, he upended the contents of his backpack. He transferred some of the contents of the pencil case to his pockets, then tore open the energy bar that he'd brought in. He'd carefully glued on the wrapper the night before. It actually concealed the handle of the gun, the only part that Alex feared the guards might recognize. He spread the different pieces out on the desk and began to assemble them, talking all the time.

"Freddy … you have to listen to me very carefully. I need your help. I've spoken to Nightshade…"

Freddy seemed genuinely horrified.

"They want you back and they've forced me to help them. They've kidnapped my best friend and they're going to kill him if I don't help you escape."

"But, Alex—"

"What happens after I get you out of here is up to you. I know you're not a Number any more. You probably don't even want to go back to them but if we don't do what they say, Tom is going to die. You have to help me. We have very little time but this is how we're going to do it. You're going to take me hostage."

"How?"

"With this." Alex had already assembled the gun. He felt ridiculous holding it, an oversized plastic toy. But he had to believe that it would do the job. Brother Mike wanted revenge. He wouldn't care if Alex was shot down. But he also wanted Freddy back with Nightshade. The gun had to work.

"I know what that is," Freddy said. "It's the Yoshee Six Shooter. We were trained how to use them. To carry them through airports. But it still uses metal bullets. And there's the firing pin too..."

A moment before, he had been talking about his GCSEs. Now Freddy had the smooth confidence of a professional gunman.

Alex reached for the case holding his sunglasses and tore open the lining. The metal firing pin for the pistol was concealed behind it. Samesh had assumed it was the frames that had set off the metal detector and it hadn't occurred to him that there might be anything else concealed in the case. Alex fitted it in place. It screwed in easily.

Now for the bullets.

"I managed to smuggle in six bullets," Alex said. "I'm going to load the gun now but you have to promise me, Freddy: nobody is to be killed. You can point it at me. Fire a bullet if you have to but don't hurt anyone."

Alex gazed at Freddy. The other boy nodded in agreement but all sorts of thoughts and emotions were reflected in his eyes as the two sides of his character came into conflict with one another. The boy he was now against the boy he had been programmed to be. Alex could see them both clearly. But which one had come out on top?

"Where are the bullets?" Freddy demanded.

"They're right in front of you."

"Give them to me."

Alex still hadn't taken off the duffel coat. It fastened with a series of toggles and as Freddy watched, he tore them free. Finally, understanding dawned. Each toggle was made of metal, not wood. In fact, each was a bullet, painted brown. All six of them had been in plain sight when Samesh did the search, but that was the reason he hadn't seen them. He had just assumed they were part of the coat.

Alex loaded the gun. He could imagine Griffin rushing for the toilet, made sick by the mints that he was supposed to have eaten himself. Would the guard have called for a replacement? It made no difference. They'd already crossed the line.

The moment of truth. Alex weighed the gun in his hands. He remembered the report from Rio de Janeiro, how Freddy had ruthlessly killed one police officer after another. Was he really going to hand him a lethal weapon and let him loose in Delhi Station?

"Freddy. Tell me I can trust you," he said. "Nobody can get hurt."

Freddy held out a hand. "Of course you can trust me," he said. His face showed no expression at all. He seemed completely calm.

Alex thought of Tom. He had no choice.

He handed Freddy the gun.

GETTING OUT

The moment Freddy Grey held the gun in his hand, he seemed to change. Over the past few weeks he had been quiet and thoughtful, unsure of himself. Now Alex saw his self-confidence come rushing back and suddenly the friendly, puzzled boy was gone and instead he was face to face with Number Nine, one of Nightshade's most successful killers. At that moment, he was almost certain that he'd made a terrible mistake – but it was too late to go back. One way or another, he had to see this through to the end.

"How do we get out of here?" Freddy demanded. He was in full control, already examining the scanner and the door. As Alex watched, he brought the gun round and aimed at the lock.

"Don't do that!" Alex warned him. "They'll hear!"

"You have a better idea?"

"As a matter of fact, I do..."

Alex was holding the metal box that Harry had examined after it had gone through the X-ray machine. It had been given to Alex by MI6 when he had been sent to infiltrate the eco complex run by Desmond McCain, and was one of the very few gadgets he'd been able to keep. Alex had never thought he'd need it again but he was glad now that he had hung on to it. Briefly, he wondered what had happened to Smithers, who had equipped him for so many adventures before he had decided to retire.

As Freddy watched, Alex took out the library card, swiped it through the door scanner and then slid it into a slot concealed underneath the metal case. Alex remembered Smithers explaining it all to him. There was a miniaturized flux reversal system concealed in the base. The machine read the code needed to unlock the door and automatically reprogrammed the card. He felt the whole thing vibrate as the tin box performed its tricks, and when he fed the card into the door a second time, the lock clicked and opened. They were out.

Alex glanced down the corridor. There was still no sign of Griffin and everything was silent but he knew that the moment they stepped out of the room, the cameras would pick them up and the entire base would go onto red alert. Freddy was behind him, holding the gun.

"Are you ready?" he asked.

Alex nodded.

A moment later, he felt his throat being grabbed from behind as Freddy put him in a vicious headlock, pointing the gun at the side of his neck. The two of them stepped out of the cell and, just as he had expected, alarms began to scream all around them, a light flashing red at the end of the corridor. Almost at once, Alex heard the stamp of military boots on the concrete floor and a few seconds later five men appeared, running towards them, all of them armed. He recognized Harry and Samesh. Griffin wasn't with them. The officer in charge of security was the oldest among them – stocky with greying hair and a scar under one eye. Alex had seen him several times but didn't know his name.

"Don't move!" he snapped. "If you take one more step, we will shoot." He had been cradling his weapon – an L22 compact assault rifle – across his chest, but as he spoke, he brought it round to aim at Freddy.

"He has a gun!" Alex shouted back.

Freddy jabbed the muzzle into Alex's neck. "If you come any closer, I'll kill him!"

The soldiers hesitated – but Alex knew that they didn't believe Freddy's threat. He was holding a blue plastic toy, like no gun they had ever seen before. As far as the soldiers were concerned, it could have been made out of Lego. The security officer smiled. Then Freddy moved. He swung the gun round and fired. There was a loud crack and Samesh cried out and reeled backwards, blood gushing from a wound in his shoulder. Alex felt sick. His worst fears had been realized. He had told Freddy that he didn't want anyone to be hurt but already the other boy had broken his word and now a soldier he thought of as a friend had been wounded. It was his fault! He should never have agreed to this.

But the single shot had an immediate effect on the group of soldiers. One of them was down. And no matter how peculiar Freddy's weapon looked, it was definitely no toy. Freddy had once again pressed it against Alex's throat. There was murder in his eyes. "I will kill Alex Rider if you don't get back," he shouted. "I want this corridor empty. I want the doors open. I will shoot anyone who comes close. Then I will shoot him and I will shoot myself. Do you hear me? Disappear! Now!"

The horrible thing was that Alex believed him. Freddy Grey had gone. Number Nine remained. He had made the worst mistake of his life. Without meaning to, he had unleashed a monster and already the first blood had been drawn. The soldiers had come to the same conclusion. The security officer had lowered his rifle and then made a gesture with his head. Retreat. Two of the men were supporting Samesh, one on each side. The whole group began to shuffle back, their eyes never leaving Freddy. They were furious and not just because they were surrendering. They had been beaten by a kid.

Suddenly, the corridor was empty. Alex could feel the plastic biting into his flesh. It hurt him as he turned his head to face Freddy. "I told you not to hurt anyone!" he shouted. He had to raise his voice over the din of the alarms.

Freddy didn't care. "I had to show them the gun worked," he replied. "They were going to rush us."

"You could have fired at the ceiling!"

"I could have fired right between his eyes. I didn't kill anyone. I just did what I had to do. If you want to get out of here and save your best friend, you'll stop arguing with me."

"If you shoot anyone else, I'll take you down."

"You can try, Alex. But I'm the one with the gun."

They began to edge forward, both of them looking in different directions, searching for any possible ambush. To the CCTV cameras, it would seem that Alex had no choice, that he was Freddy's prisoner. Nobody had yet asked how Freddy, who had been locked in a maximum-security prison, could have got hold of a weapon. If they had, they would have realized there was only one possibility:

that for reasons unknown, Alex must have smuggled it in. But things were happening too fast. A soldier had been wounded. The rest of them were trying to contain the situation, not explain it.

The alarms were still deafening, bouncing off the walls, somehow amplified by the flashing lights. Inch by inch, Alex and Freddy made their way down the corridor, heading towards the entrance hall. The white glass doors were closed and Alex felt a sick feeling in his stomach. What would happen if they refused to open? But as they approached, the doors slid apart and he saw the metal detector and X-ray machine on the other side, both of them abandoned. They entered the reception area. Freddy was becoming more nervous the further they moved from the cell. And with good reason. There were the stairs, different corridors, doors – lots of places to hide. Freedom lay ahead. The main exit from the complex was directly in front of them, unguarded. But a counter-attack could come from any angle.

"What happens when we get outside?" Freddy muttered.

"There's a car waiting for us."

"If we can reach it..."

Alex didn't say anything to that. He, too, had his doubts.

A whole battalion of soldiers – thirty or forty of them – were waiting, spread out on the lawns and the driveways on the other side of the door when they emerged into the fresh air. Alex had never seen so many guns pointing at him – rifles, machine guns, pistols. If someone gave the order, he wouldn't just be shot; he'd be cut to shreds. And there was no forgetting Freddy, who was still using one hand to hold a gun against his neck while the other hand curved around his throat, keeping him close. Inside the building, the alarms abruptly stopped and somehow the silence only made the entire situation more nightmarish. Alex could see the control room with two men behind the plate-glass window that took up one whole side of the guard house. They operated the gate and barrier he had come through – which were near by. The taxi with the Nightshade driver was in the distance, parked on the other side of the road, partly out of sight. Right now it seemed impossible that the two of them would reach it.

Another senior officer in combat uniform marched forward. The single star on his epaulette identified him as a brigadier. He alone was unarmed but he was clearly in charge. He halted about ten steps away from Freddy. There were dozens of people around them but none of them were moving. As they aimed their weapons at the two boys, they didn't even seem to be breathing.

The brigadier stopped. "Stay where you are and put down your weapon," he commanded in a voice that was used to being obeyed.

Freddy didn't blink. "Open the gate," he said.

"That's not going to happen. You're not leaving this compound. If you don't want to get hurt, do as I say."

Freddy pressed his gun so hard against Alex's neck that Alex almost cried out in pain. "I won't ask again," he snarled. "Do you know who this is? His name is Alex Rider and he works for MI6. He's a boy spy, their big star. You have five seconds. I want your people to move away. I want the barrier lifted. And if you try to stop me, you'll have his blood on your hands. In fact, you'll have it all over you."

"You can't fool us, Freddy. I don't know where you got that lump of plastic. But it's not a real gun."

Alex almost groaned out loud. Hadn't the officer heard what had happened outside the cell, that one of his men – Samesh – had already taken a bullet? If he wasn't careful, he was going to get someone killed.

And the next moment, Freddy acted. He suddenly spun Alex round, using him as a human shield, then fired a second shot over his shoulder. Alex wasn't sure if he was aiming at the brigadier or not, but there was a loud detonation behind him and the huge window of the control room shattered, the glass crashing down. The two soldiers behind it dived to one side and everyone else crouched down as if they were expecting to be the next target. Freddy stabbed the gun back into Alex's neck. He could feel the plastic, hot against his flesh. He was just relieved that nobody else had been hurt.

"You still think it isn't real?" Freddy crowed. "Just a lump of plastic?"

As his men straightened up, taking aim again, the brigadier tried to regain a bit of his authority. "It doesn't matter whether it's real or not," he insisted. "Even if you make it to the street, you won't get anywhere."

"Then you've got nothing to lose, letting me go." Freddy tightened his grip on the gun. "Five ... four ... three ... two..."

The brigadier's nerve broke. "All right!" he shouted. "Stand down! Open the gates!"

Alex allowed himself to be shoved forward, his neck contorted. Freddy had forgotten that this was meant to be make-believe, that Alex was the one who had actually supplied the gun and that he wasn't supposed to be a real hostage. Freddy was ferocious. All the soldiers had obeyed the brigadier's command and lowered their weapons. They watched helplessly as the barrier swung upwards, allowing the two boys to pass. They went through the gates. On the other side of the road, the car started up its engine – but Alex heard the same sound coming from behind him. Inside the army complex, a bunch of men were jumping into a number of different vehicles.

So it wasn't over yet. They weren't just going to be allowed to drive away.

They crossed the road and reached the Toyota. "Open it!" Freddy commanded.

Alex leaned down and opened the door.

"Get in!" Freddy gave Alex another push, propelling him onto the back seat, then climbed in beside him. The driver hit the accelerator and before the door was even closed they were speeding down the road with clouds of dust being thrown up by the wheels. Alex heard a series of sharp cracks and looked out the back window. The soldiers from the control room had run into the road and were firing at the wheels. But they had reacted too slowly. The car was already too far away. Alex saw the tarmac explode behind them but not a single bullet came close, and then they were away, back down the lane that led to the main road. They swung round the corner without slowing down, almost colliding with an army jeep that was turning towards them. Freddy fired twice more out of the window and, unlike the soldiers, he didn't miss. Two of the jeep's tyres exploded. The vehicle slewed round, blocking the lane. He had bought them time – but they still weren't in the clear.

"Welcome back, Number Nine," the driver said, glancing into the driving mirror without taking his eyes off the road.

"It's good to be back," Freddy replied and, once again, his voice was ice cold. "What do you want me to do with Alex Rider? I still have two bullets."

"We want him alive."

"Why?" Freddy sounded annoyed.

"You'll see."

Alex felt his heart sink. How could he have been so wrong about Freddy? All along, while he had been held captive at Delhi Station, the other boy had been pretending. That he wasn't a Number any more. That he remembered his parents. That he wanted to be normal again. All of that was lies. Now that Alex had managed to get him out, he had reverted back to his old self. Alex was furious with himself. He should have listened to Jack.

But then he remembered Tom. That was what this was all about. MI6 would find Freddy before he could leave the country. So far, nobody had been badly hurt. One soldier had been wounded, but surely that was in the line of duty. Everything would be all right if he could just find Tom and somehow get him away from Nightshade.

But first, they had to make it out of the Tidworth area. Alex heard the howl of sirens. The road behind him was empty but he knew that even though the lane that

led to Delhi Station was temporarily cut off by the jeep,
police cars and more army vehicles would be coming from
every direction and would catch up with them very soon.
He looked ahead and felt sick. The worst thing possible
had happened.

They were on the main road but it was narrow and the
way ahead was completely blocked by a motor home.
It was trundling along at about twenty miles per hour,
presumably on its way to some campsite somewhere. It
was pale blue, ungainly, with a sleeping section bulging
out above the driver's cabin and a bicycle strapped to the
back. It had doors and windows, none of which matched in
size, and although it might call itself a motor home, it was
actually neither: too slow for a motor, too small for a home.
There was no way to get past it. It was in the middle of the
road with only a few inches of space on either side. There
was a grass verge and trees on the left, a wall and a ditch
on the right. No room to squeeze past. Alex twisted round
in his seat and once again looked out of the back window.
There was no sign of any pursuers but he could still hear
the sirens and knew they could only be seconds away.

The strange thing was that the driver, with his tired
eyes and sagging cheeks, didn't seem at all worried. He
wasn't hooting. He wasn't even trying to accelerate.
And a moment later, with wide-eyed astonishment, Alex
understood why.

The back of the mobile home had clicked open. The
entire rear panel, with the bicycle firmly tied in place, was
being lifted by hydraulic arms. As the gap expanded, Alex
saw the inside of the vehicle. There were no seats, no beds,

no toilet, no kitchenette – just an empty space. At the same time, two narrow ramps were sliding out of the back and lowering onto the road, where they trailed behind the vehicle – which was carefully maintaining exactly the same speed. Finally, when the back was fully open, the taxi driver hit the accelerator pedal and the Toyota leaped forward. The man behind the wheel might have looked old and unprofessional but he knew exactly what he was doing. With expert skill, he edged closer, aligning the wheels of his car with the steel surface that he had to climb. The ramps were barely wider than the tyres, and one mistake could tip the car onto its side. Suddenly, twenty miles per hour looked a lot faster than it had a few minutes ago.

The driver must have practised this a hundred times before and with a touch of the accelerator, the Toyota leaped up, being swallowed by the motor home. They shot inside, almost crashing into the driver's cabin but stopping just in time. At once, the ramps were retracted and the back of the van swung shut again. Alex felt the camper van pick up speed. A moment later, he heard hooting behind him. The police and army vehicles had caught up. The van pulled over to one side and at least four jeeps sped past. Sitting in the back of the taxi next to Freddy, Alex couldn't see them.

There was one final surprise.

The driver had turned off the engine of the Toyota. And now he reached up and gripped the top of his bald head. He was wearing a mask. He pulled it off and suddenly it wasn't a fifty-year-old man who was sitting behind the wheel. It was a boy with fair hair cut short, freckles and a lazy eye.

Alex recognized Number Thirteen – he had always come first on the assault course in Crete. He was brave to the point of being reckless, throwing himself at the various obstacles. And he was a brilliant actor, easily taking on the voice and the body language of someone thirty years older than him.

The police cars had pulled ahead. Alex felt the van take a turning, following some country lane. "What happens now?" he demanded. "Where are you taking me? Where's Tom?"

"Do we have to listen to him?" Freddy asked.

"No. You can shut him up."

Before Alex could react, Freddy had lashed out, not with the gun but with his balled fist, driving it into the side of his head.

Alex was knocked unconscious and slumped into the seat.

The camper van drove on.

EXECUTION

Alex had no idea how long they had been driving. When he finally opened his eyes, he was still in the back of the car, inside the motor home. His neck was aching and there was an unpleasant taste in his mouth that told him he must have been drugged. A throbbing in his arm and a tiny puncture wound confirmed it. He'd been given an injection to keep him quiet. Freddy had moved into the front seat of the Toyota and was sitting next to Number Thirteen, who, of course, was no longer driving. Alex twisted his wrist round to look at his watch. Half past two. He had managed to lose three whole hours since they had broken out of Delhi Station.

"So you're awake." Freddy had noticed Alex moving. There was no emotion in his voice.

"Where are we?" Alex asked. The words were heavy in his mouth.

"Almost there. You'll find out soon."

With difficulty, Alex straightened himself in his seat, trying to get his muscles back into shape. It was a strange feeling to be hurtling down a motorway in a car that wasn't actually moving, and it unnerved him, having no view. Meanwhile, Freddy and the driver were sitting absolutely still, saying nothing. Nine and Thirteen. That's all they were. Numbers, not human beings.

About ten minutes later, the motor home slowed down and stopped. The driver pressed a button and with a hum of hidden machinery, the entire back wall rose up on its hydraulics, allowing bright sunlight to pour in. Alex looked out into the open. The first thing he saw was a windsock, blowing in the breeze, and – next to it – a large hangar. They were at an airport! Suddenly he was uneasy. He had visions of himself being spirited out of the country, flying off to the other side of the world. And what about Tom? Was he here? Why had he ever believed that Nightshade would keep their word?

Number Thirteen started the engine of the taxi and reversed back out down the ramps. The car hit the ground and stopped. As Alex got out, two figures moved forward, walking across the tarmac, one of them armed. Alex recognized another of the Numbers from the training camp in Crete: a Japanese girl, seventeen or eighteen, with bored, empty eyes. She was standing next to Brother Mike, who was dressed more casually now in a rollneck, cashmere jersey and cords. The man examined Alex with mild amusement, then turned his attention to Freddy, who had come from round the front.

"Hello, Number Nine."

"Brother Mike...!"

"How are you?"

"I'm angry with myself. I'm sorry. I allowed myself to be taken. And it makes me sick that I wasn't able to break free on my own."

"But you have broken free and I'm very pleased to see you. We have a new operation and we need your talents, Number Nine. But we'll talk about that later."

"Where's Tom?" Alex demanded.

Brother Mike turned to him, his eyes stone cold. "We're going to take you to him straight away. I'm sure you'd like a chance to say goodbye..."

"I did what you told me!" Alex protested. "You said you wouldn't hurt him."

"That's absolutely true and I intend to keep my word. On the other hand, I can't remember saying that I wouldn't hurt you, Alex – and that's exactly what I intend to do. You did a great deal of damage to my organization and I'm afraid it's time for you to pay the price." He snapped an order at the Numbers. "Thirteen! Twenty-Two! Take him to his friend. Tie him up and leave the two of them together but wait outside the door. I want to have a word with Number Nine and then we'll be with you shortly."

There was nothing Alex could do. The two Numbers led Alex across the airfield towards a smaller hangar, corrugated iron with no windows. Neither of them spoke to him. Apart from the fact that they were pointing guns at him, they seemed to have no interest in him at all.

As he went, Alex took stock of his surroundings.

His first impression was that he had travelled north. There was something about the light that was different from London. And this was not a major airport. Wherever it was located, it was being used for private jets as well as maintenance and servicing, rather than for commercial travel. There were some beaten-up planes sitting on the tarmac, and although he could see a terminal building with a sign reading DEPARTURES, there were no passengers in sight. He noticed a control tower in the far distance, shaped like a mushroom, with a circular observation room perched high up, and a few figures moving behind the windows. The motor home had deliberately parked as far away from these buildings as possible. If anybody did glance in their direction, they would be unable to see what was going on, and Alex knew that if he called for help or tried to run away, the Numbers would shoot him down before he had taken two steps. Anyway, his first priority was to find Tom.

He examined the first hangar he had noticed when they arrived. It was ten times larger than the one they were approaching – big enough to house the Airbus, a 300-seat commercial plane, that was inside. He could see its tail, the fins and the back wheel jutting out. Otherwise, he was surrounded by a great expanse of concrete, marked up with yellow-painted arrows, chevrons and double lines. A single runway seemed to stretch out an improbable distance, with a fence glittering at the far end. The whole place was surrounded by flat grassland and then a forest of oak and pine trees, with no other buildings in sight. Wherever it was located, this was a *very private* private airport indeed.

They continued round the side of the smaller hangar – and that was when Alex saw the jet plane, parked in its own docking area. There was a flight of steps leading up to an open cabin door and the plane was in the process of refuelling, clearly being made ready for departure. He could make out a woman with bleached hair behind the cockpit windows, a pilot in full uniform, checking the controls. So this was how Freddy would be leaving the country! But who would be going with him? Brother Mike and the two Numbers, obviously – but what about him and Tom? Would they be travelling too?

The plane was certainly big enough to carry them all. It was a Gulfstream G500, about twenty-five metres in length, with two high-thrust engines mounted at the rear. It could seat up to thirteen people, though it could be configured for fewer if they wanted to travel in luxury. Alex suspected it would have no trouble reaching America, Canada or anywhere on the other side of the Atlantic. A plane like that would have cost at least fifty million pounds. Did Nightshade own it, or had they rented it? He made a note of the alphabetical code, printed on the tail. N-GFYS. Things didn't look good for him right now but there was still a chance that the information might prove useful. If he ever got a chance to share it.

"Move!"

Alex felt the prod of a gun between the shoulders as Number Thirteen steered him towards a door leading into the hangar. They went into a wide, comfortless space that had been converted into an office complex with unattractive cubicles separated by cheap plasterboard walls. Each one was furnished with an identical desk, chair and filing cabinet. Nobody seemed to be working in this part of the airport, and Alex got the feeling the building had been abandoned some time ago. A narrow space ran between two corrugated-iron walls, leading them round a corner and along a passage that led to a door with a thick metal bolt drawn across it.

"Open it!" Number Thirteen commanded.

"Are you sure about this?" Alex asked. "I'm Number

Twenty-Six – don't you remember? I was with you in Crete..."

"Just do what you're told."

Alex had stopped on purpose. While he had been talking, he had been taking note of the exact location of the bolt. He would need to remember it later. He opened the door and walked into a square storage room, empty but for a line of shelves loaded up with engine components, ball-bearings, steel discs. There were three chairs and, with a huge sense of relief, he saw Tom sitting in one of them.

"Alex!" Tom's face lit up. He was dressed in the same clothes he'd been wearing at the skateboard park, although the Hawaiian shirt was hanging loose and crumpled. He was tied to the chair and trying not to look scared – but Alex had to remind himself that this was far beyond anything Tom had experienced. He'd been hurt once, wounded by a sniper. The two of them had been together in Italy when Alex was searching for Scorpia. And, more recently, Tom had helped Alex neutralize two men who'd followed him to Brookland School. But this was entirely different. Tom had been snatched in the middle of London, brought here on his own, tied up and left in this windowless room. What must he have been going through for the past twenty-four hours, unable to move, imagining the worst?

"Are you OK?" Alex asked. He wanted to run over to his friend, just to be close to him. He forced himself to stay calm.

Anyway, the Numbers had other plans for him. "Sit down!" Twenty-Two commanded, the first words she had spoken to Alex. "You can talk later."

Alex swore at her – as much to show Tom that he wasn't

afraid as to express the hatred he was feeling. But he did as he was told. Twenty-Two held a gun on him while Thirteen tied his hands behind his back. He felt the rope tightening around his wrists but it was done very quickly, the knots tied so tightly that his blood had to force its way into his fingers. The two Numbers took one quick look around the room, then went back to the door.

"We'll be right outside," Thirteen said.

The door closed. At last, Alex and Tom were alone.

"I thought you'd come to rescue me," Tom muttered sadly.

"I have," Alex lied.

"Forgive me for saying this, mate. But it doesn't look that way."

"I know. How are you, Tom?"

"They haven't hurt me. Those two clowns – they never told me their names – picked me up at the Undercroft. I was waiting for you and they just walked over to me, and the next thing I knew, there was a gun in my ribs. I had to go with them. I couldn't do anything else."

"You were right not to try," Alex said, trying not to think of all the things he might have done differently if he'd been in Tom's place. He began to twist his wrists, trying to loosen the rope that tied him.

"So what's this about?" Tom asked. "It's got nothing to do with me. It's you they want, isn't it?"

"Yeah. I'm sorry you got drawn into it, Tom."

"That's OK, Alex. Getting held at gunpoint, kidnapped and tied to a chair... What else are friends for?"

"You're going to get out of here."

"How exactly?"

"I did a deal with them. They're going to set you free."

Tom scowled. "So what did you have to do for them?"

"Don't worry. It was nothing."

But Alex was worried. The two of them were helpless and Brother Mike obviously had something extremely unpleasant in mind. There was just one flicker of hope. Despite all their planning, Nightshade were still making stupid mistakes. They might have knocked him out on the journey here but it seemed they'd forgotten to search him. Or if they had, they hadn't noticed two objects he'd brought with him from Chelsea. They were in the back pocket of his jeans, the one pocket he was able to reach. It wasn't easy but by stretching out his fingers and transferring his weight to one side, Alex was able to fish out the one he wanted.

"You all right?" Tom asked.

"Give me a minute..."

The pencil sharpener was silver and only three centimetres long. But holding it between his thumb and his index finger, Alex was able to slide the blade out, converting the whole thing into a miniature knife. The blade was incredibly sharp, just three nanometres thick at its cutting edge, and made not of steel but obsidian – volcanic glass. Smithers had told him it would slice through almost anything. He tried it now, turning one hand towards the other and holding the blade against the rope. He had been tied so tightly that he had almost no room for manoeuvre but very carefully he began to slide it back and forth. He felt it biting into the cord.

He had barely started before the door opened and Brother Mike came in. Alex was forced to stop. He couldn't risk giving himself away. He saw at once that the man was holding a gun with a long silencer, which somehow made the weapon look uglier and more lethal than it already was. Freddy was with him, half smiling. Alex wondered what the two of them had been talking about.

"Well, Alex," Brother Mike began. "We've come to the end of the road."

Struggling helplessly in his chair, Tom hurled a string of insults in his direction.

Brother Mike ignored him. His eyes were fixed on Alex. "You've done us a great favour," he continued. "We have been very much looking forward to welcoming Number Nine back into our family. We've missed him. But I want you to understand that wasn't the real reason we sent you to Delhi Station."

He took a step forward, relishing the moment.

"You have no idea how much we hate you, Alex. Operation Leap of Faith took years of preparation. Our reputation was on the line. And you destroyed it all! We spoke long and often about killing you. It was what we all wanted to do. But in the end, we decided it was too easy. So we decided to destroy your life instead."

He paused. It seemed to Alex that there was a mist clinging to his glasses. The heat of the moment? Or perhaps it was a fog of hatred in his eyes.

"This is what's going to happen," Brother Mike explained. "You're going to watch your friend die. We're going to do it right now, in front of you. We're going to leave you here, tied to that chair, and eventually Mrs Jones and her associates will find you and you'll have to live with the fact that you betrayed them and helped their enemies. They'll never want to see you again. MI6 will pretend you don't even exist. But that won't be the worst of it. What you're about to witness will stay with you for the rest of your life. You will spend your every waking minute wishing you had never heard of Nightshade. Tom is going to die – and it's your fault!"

Brother Mike aimed the gun at Tom. "Anything you want to say, either of you?" he sneered. "Any last words?"

"Stop him!" Alex shouted the words at Freddy, who had been listening to this with no expression on his face. "You know me. You know I never wanted to hurt you. I'm your friend."

"You're not my friend!" Freddy said. He walked over to Brother Mike and held out a hand. "Let me do it."

"What?" Alex couldn't believe what he had just heard.

"Alex Rider ruined everything," Freddy went on. "It was his fault I was taken prisoner to begin with and he kept coming to see me in that filthy place to taunt me, to gloat. I hate him. I want to be the one who kills his best friend. I want him to remember me, too."

Brother Mike thought for a moment, then smiled. "I don't see why not."

"Wait!" Alex was fighting in his chair, trying to saw at the rope – but his fingers were refusing to obey him. "Tom hasn't done anything. I'm the one you want. Shoot me if you have to, but leave him alone!"

Tom had gone white. But he was determined to have the

last word. He turned to Alex. "I love you, mate. You were always my best friend. Remember that – and don't ever let them get you down."

Freddy held up his hand for silence. "As the old saying goes, revenge is golden." He looked Alex directly in the eye. "Remember that."

He walked up to Tom, reached forward and patted him gently on the chest. "Don't worry," he said. "This won't hurt too much and it will all be over very quickly." He stepped back and took careful aim, standing with his back to Alex, pointing the gun directly at Tom's heart. Tom stared defiantly but at the last moment a look of puzzlement crossed his face, as if he couldn't believe this was going to happen. That was when Freddy fired.

The force of the bullet sent Tom recoiling backwards. The back of the chair crashed down to the floor. Alex had closed his eyes at the very end but when he opened them, Tom was silent and unmoving, still tied to the chair. His feet were raised in front of him, pointing into the air. There was blood coming out of his mouth.

"A bullet in the heart," Freddy said. "Maybe I made it too quick."

"Goodbye, Alex," Brother Mike said. "It's been a pleasure."

He went over to the door and opened it. The other Numbers were waiting on the other side. Freddy left without looking at Alex again. Brother Mike followed him. The door closed behind them and once again the bolt was drawn.

PUSHBACK

Fury, like molten lava, was coursing through him. He could hardly breathe. The blood was pulsing behind his eyes. It was as if his entire body was being crushed by an invisible hand. He wanted to scream.

Alex gripped the tiny knife behind him and, bending one hand at an unnatural angle, set about trying to saw through the rope that bound his wrists. His one thought was to go after Freddy and Brother Mike, to prevent them getting away and to make them pay for what they had done. He tried to ignore the voice that told him he should have listened to Jack and never gone along with this plan in the first place. He had tried to save Tom and he had failed. He couldn't bring himself to look at the still figure lying on its back at the edge of the room. He realized his hands were shaking, slowing him down. He could imagine the four members of Nightshade crossing the tarmac, chatting among themselves as they climbed into the private jet that he had seen outside.

Once they took off, they could disappear anywhere in the world. Alex would never be able to find them – and with every second that passed, his chances of stopping them were getting smaller. But the rope wouldn't give. He had to calm himself down. Forget what had happened. Concentrate on what he had to do.

The knife slipped in his fingers and nearly fell to the

ground. If he lost it, he would be doomed to sit on his own in this room until help arrived ... which was exactly what Brother Mike had planned, of course. Alex was a traitor. He had smuggled a gun into an army compound and he had helped Freddy break free. His career as a spy would be over. He didn't care about that. But he'd be lucky if he wasn't sent to jail.

And Tom. His best friend since Year Seven. Alex had come to his rescue the first time they'd met, when Tom was being bullied. Tom was the sort of kid who would cheerfully walk into trouble and only start worrying when he couldn't find the way out. He was always smiling, even when things didn't go his way. He...

Alex forced himself not to think back. He had to cut through the rope. That was all that mattered.

But however hard he sawed, the rope refused to give. The knife was sharp, but it was too small and it was impossible to see what he was doing with his hands behind him. Angrily, he tried again, and winced as the corner of the blade sliced into his own wrist. The trouble was that the faster he worked, the less progress he was actually making and he was painfully aware of the seconds ticking away.

One last cut and, with a sense of relief, he felt the ropes fall away. Already exhausted, Alex got to his feet, still avoiding looking at Tom. He would deal with all that later. Right now he was a prisoner, on the wrong side of a metal door that had been securely bolted from the outside.

But he had worked out how to get through the door. The pencil sharpener wasn't the only weapon he'd brought with him. He reached into his pocket and drew out the red gel-ink pen that Smithers had given him at the same time as the other gadgets. *The red one is much more powerful than the black one. Remember that.* It had been a while since Smithers had left MI6 but Alex could still hear his voice – his one true friend and ally. He twisted the cap and pulled the plunger upwards to activate the fifteen-second fuse, then pressed the pen against the door, confident that he had remembered the correct position of the bolt on the other side. The pen was magnetic and stayed in place. Hurriedly, he retreated to the other side of the room, crouching for protection behind the chair that had held him.

The explosion, in the confined space, was deafening. If the door and walls had been made of anything thicker or stronger than corrugated iron, the ricochet could have done Alex serious harm. As it was, the pen didn't just destroy the bolt. It blew the entire door out of the wall. Acrid smoke filled the air. With his eyes watering, Alex made for the gap he had created. He took one last look at Tom, still lying on his back with his feet in the air. Tom had always liked comedy. It was just like him to make his own death look slightly bizarre, like something out of a bad joke. There was no time to stop. Alex ducked through the hole and plunged into the corridor.

He hadn't taken more than a few steps before a figure appeared, turning the corner, running towards him. It was a man, dressed in overalls, obviously alerted by the sound of the explosion and hurrying to find out what had happened.

"What are you—?" he began.

Alex didn't give him time to complete the question. The man could have been an innocent airport worker, or he could have been part of the Nightshade team. Alex was in no mood to find out. Blind anger was still driving him, and without stopping to think, he struck out, driving one elbow into the side of the man's skull. The man crumpled. Alex caught him and lowered him gently to the floor. He would wake up with a bruise and a headache but otherwise he wouldn't be too badly hurt.

Stepping over the unconscious figure, Alex ran down the corridor, reaching the door that led out to the airfield. He kicked it open. The light had been dim inside the hangar and the full force of the sun slammed into his eyes, making him squint. Holding his hand up as a shield, he looked around him, searching for Freddy and Brother Mike. He saw at once that the private jet had moved. He was too late! The steps that had led up to the cabin door were still there, standing uselessly on the tarmac, but the plane itself was already twenty metres away, rolling towards the runway with its turbo jet engines roaring behind it. Alex almost cried out in frustration. What could he do? Part of him wished he'd kept hold of the gel-ink pen grenade – although if he had, he'd never have got out of the room. Anyway, he couldn't catch up with the plane now, not on foot. The runway was too long, stretching into the far distance. Once the plane reached the end, it would turn 180 degrees, go through final checks and then take off. It was unstoppable.

Desperately, he searched for anyone or anything that might help him. He would shut down the entire airport if he had to. He saw an oil drum marked with the word FUEL and briefly imagined flooding the runway with petrol and then starting a blazing fire. But the oil drum would be far too heavy to move and anyway he didn't have any matches. Could he get help from the control tower? Too far away. By the time he reached it, the plane would be in the air.

Something glinted in his eye and he twisted round, looking in the direction of the main hangar. What had just happened? Something was moving. A second later, he saw it. The commercial plane that he had noticed when he first arrived was reversing onto the tarmac. The sun had reflected off its metal skin. But that was impossible. Alex knew that planes can go backwards using reverse thrust, but this one's engines were silent, inactive. As it emerged, Alex saw that the plane was being carefully guided by a pushback tractor, a low vehicle with a yellow rod connected from nose to nose. There was a burly driver behind the wheel, wearing a hi-vis vest. He wasn't in a driving compartment but on a seat in the open air. As Alex watched, he parked the plane outside the hangar, then climbed down and went back inside. Meanwhile, the Gulfstream G500 was approaching the edge of the runway. In a few moments it would turn onto it and begin taxiing all the way to the far end.

Alex looked back at the Airbus. It was empty, its engines inactive, being wheeled out for repairs. Otherwise, the tractor driver would never have abandoned it. He examined the runway, working out the distances. Almost at once, an idea began to form in his mind, and before he'd even completed the full picture or worked out the consequences, he was sprinting forward.

It was crazy. Normally, he wouldn't even have considered

it. But what had happened to Tom was still blazing in his mind, wiping out any other thoughts. He was going to stop Brother Mike and Freddy leaving the country. He wasn't going to let them get away. That was all he cared about. With his heart pounding, one eye fixed on the Gulfstream as it continued to roll into the distance, Alex raced past the Airbus, which was so huge that it completely filled his vision, blanking out the sky. He ducked under the wing, and ran past the cockpit, finally reaching the tractor that was connected to it, the two of them face to face.

The pushback tractor was a white metal box, squatting on the ground on wheels that were almost as big as the vehicle itself. It was designed to be as heavy as possible, gripping the tarmac to help it move a plane that was twenty times bigger than itself. How difficult could it be to operate? Alex reached the driver's safety rail and leaped over it, catching his breath. Quickly, he examined the dashboard and the controls, glancing briefly back at the hangar in case the man in the hi-vis vest reappeared. He took in a steering wheel, two pedals (they had to be a brake and an accelerator), a gearstick and, behind it, a smaller lever which might be a handbrake. What else? Various displays, switches, a key in the ignition, a single black leather seat, no windscreen wipers because there was no window. Surely it couldn't be any more difficult to drive than an ordinary car.

Except it didn't look anything like an ordinary car.

The Gulfstream G500 had its back to him now as it began its journey down the runway to its take-off position at the end. Alex couldn't waste any time. He leaped into the driver's seat, rested one hand on the steering wheel, released the handbrake, then gripped the gearstick. He found a red button underneath his thumb and pressed it, then pushed the gearstick forward. There was a shudder as the tractor began to move backwards, in completely the wrong direction, straining against the giant bulk of the plane. Not a great start! Gritting his teeth, he pushed down with his thumb, pressing the button a second time. He jerked the gearstick back towards him, noticing the figure 1 come up on one of the display screens. First gear. More confident now, he pressed the accelerator with his foot. He heard the engine rev up and the whole tractor vibrated beneath him. It was working! Suddenly the tractor was inching forward, the Airbus facing Alex and rolling backwards with its entire weight propelled by the five metres of steel that made up the towbar.

Alex's plan was simple. He was going to push a commercial plane weighing one hundred and fifty thousand kilograms onto the runway, blocking the path of Brother Mike's jet. He was going to make it impossible for him to take off.

But did he have enough time?

The jet was already halfway down the runway, its turbines screaming, while Alex was trying to move the tractor across the same stretch of tarmac at about five miles per hour. At least the Gulfstream pilot wouldn't be able to see what was happening behind her – but that wasn't true for the rest of the airport. Any minute now, the tractor driver might return. The control tower would surely notice the illegal movement of one of its aircraft, crossing yellow and white lines as if they didn't exist. A handful of engineers and technicians had appeared outside the tower, chatting among themselves. So far they hadn't noticed what was happening, but that could change at any moment. Trouble could come from every direction. Alex thought about what he was doing. He realized now that this hadn't been one of his best ideas.

It was too late to stop. If anything, he was more determined to get it over with and pressed on the accelerator pedal, urging the plane towards the runway. He needed to bring it to a halt further along, closer to the far end – otherwise the pilot would simply fly over it. He eased the steering wheel to the left, swinging the plane in the opposite direction. It was the same principle as reversing a boat into a river. But he needed to be gentler. The plane reacted to the slightest movement and although he'd only turned the steering wheel a couple of inches, he felt the giant aircraft boomerang round. The entire tractor trembled violently and the towbar shuddered as if it was about to break in half. Suddenly, Alex was sweating. He brought the wheel back and slowed down, the engine hammering beneath him.

He had reached the edge of the runway. The rear wheels of the Airbus moved onto it. But the Gulfstream was almost at the far end. Would it turn immediately? Would there be last-minute checks before take-off? Alex assumed that the control tower would sound the alarm as soon as they saw what he was doing and they'd refuse to give the pilot clearance to proceed. Well, that wouldn't make any difference. There was no way Brother Mike was going to allow himself to be arrested. The jet would take off anyway.

Alex turned the steering wheel a fraction and pressed down with his foot, trying to persuade the pushback tractor to speed up. The engine shouted in protest and a warning light flashed on the dashboard. He had to change gear. He saw a switch with a plus and a minus sign on the gearstick and, with a silent prayer, thumbed the plus sign. The tractor coughed and rattled. For a moment, Alex was sure it was about to stall. But then, somehow, it righted itself. The dashboard display changed to the figure 2 – second gear – and the tractor continued forward more smoothly.

It was on the runway now. There was a straight run, perhaps a quarter of a mile long, ahead of him. Sitting in the open air with the wind streaking through his hair and the nose of the Airbus pointing at him as if trying to sniff him out, Alex felt a surge of excitement. So far, nobody had seen him. Maybe this was going to work after all.

Then the klaxons went off.

They were everywhere, mounted on poles and fenceposts all over the airport. There was no escaping the scream of the alarms that filled the air, bouncing across the tarmac. The private jet had turned, ready for take-off. Now the pilot had a perfect view of what must have seemed like an impossible development. When she had taxied to the far end of the runway, it had been clear. Now a broken-down Airbus had appeared out of nowhere, not just blocking the path but getting slowly closer. Alex looked back briefly and saw that the original driver of the tractor had come out of the hangar and was standing there staring at him, both hands on his head. At least he wasn't rushing over in pursuit. It can't have been every day that he had a commercial aircraft stolen from under his nose, but there must have been some sort of safety protocol in play at the airport. A lot of people must have worked out what was going on but they were forbidden to do anything. The situation was too dangerous. Alex turned back to the controls, relieved that, just for once, health and safety was on his side.

He concentrated on the Gulfstream G500 facing him, about one thousand five hundred metres away. For a brief moment, Alex was reminded of two fighters at a medieval joust, sizing each other up before the charge. Except that if the private jet was a knight on a horse, the Airbus was more like a huge metal dragon, its wings stretching across the entire runway, leaving no space either side. But there was still too much space between them. If Brother Mike ordered the pilot to move, there was every chance the Gulfstream would have enough of the runway to reach a hundred and fifty miles per hour, which, with enough headwind, would allow it to perform a short-field take-off. In other words, all Alex's work would have been for nothing. He'd simply watch them fly overhead.

On the other hand, the closer he moved towards them, the greater the chance of a horrible smash. It was the classic game of chicken. The jet might still try to pick up enough speed. If the pilot lost her nerve, she could take evasive action, swerving to one side at the last minute. But if she left it too late and crashed into the Airbus, they would all die. Already, Alex could see the ball of flame exploding all around him, the shattered metal, the flying debris.

Bad idea! Bad idea!

But it was too late to back out now.

He pressed on the accelerator one last time, only to find that the tractor would no longer respond. He had put too much strain on the gears. He pressed the button on the gearstick and changed down again. Very slowly, the plane slid further along the runway, still edging backwards as if being pushed unwillingly into battle. The Gulfstream was facing them, not moving. Alex could imagine the frantic arguments taking place between the pilot and the control tower. Brother Mike would have the final decision, and whoever was flying the plane would have to be very brave – suicidal even – to argue with one of the bosses of Nightshade. Were they going to risk it? With every second that passed, the Airbus was being pushed closer, swallowing up any room for manoeuvre. Alex urged the tractor forward. He just needed one more minute. Then they would be close enough. The runway would be blocked and it would all be over.

There was a howl of anger from the Gulfstream's engines and even as Alex watched in horror, the private jet jerked forward and began to thunder towards him.

The decision had been made. They were going for take-off even though the Airbus was already far too close, still swallowing the length of the runway between them. They had to stop! There wasn't enough distance left. A thousand metres. Nine hundred. Eight hundred... Alex sat, frozen in the seat, facing what looked like a gigantic silver bullet that had just been fired right at him. The sound of the twin engines was already deafening him as the bullet shot towards him, the Gulfstream G500 rapidly filling his vision. This was what death looked like. There was nothing he could do. Running away was out of the question. The devastation would be too huge and all he could do was sit here and wait for it to happen. At least Tom would have his revenge. And perhaps it was for the best. This was all Alex's fault. It was what he deserved.

Five hundred metres. Four hundred. The jet was still on the ground, the engines screaming, dust billowing upwards. And then, suddenly, it had disappeared from sight. It was behind the tail of the Airbus, concealed by the great bulk of the cabin and the outstretched wings. Alex refused to close his eyes. He knew that he was seconds away from the end. He could feel the air slamming into his face and tearing at his hair. He was half blinded by the dust. His ears, his entire head, were in agony, consumed by the hideous scream of the Gulfstream's engines as they hammered into him.

He couldn't stop himself. He brought his hands up as if he could protect himself from what was about to happen. He barely saw the shadow rise above him. But then, to his disbelief, he realized that the private jet had made it into the air. It was barely a metre above the Airbus, its wheels almost touching the roof of the cabin. For a moment, the whole world was blotted out. The very air was rippling, distorting his vision. The stench of aviation fuel suffocated him, rushing into his nose and mouth, burning his skin. With his eyes watering, gasping for air, Alex glimpsed the jet's underbelly, outstretched wings, the ridges in the rubber wheels – so near that he was sure they would knock his head off. He felt he was being crushed by the noise of the engines and pressed his hands against his ears.

Then, suddenly, it was over. The Gulfstream had gone and Alex knew with a sense of despair that he had failed, that Brother Mike had gambled everything and won, that the jet had got clear, with perhaps seconds to spare, and that despite all his efforts, they were on their way.

The pushback tractor was still moving forward. Alex stamped his foot on the brake and brought it to a final halt even as the jet disappeared into the sky over his shoulder. The tractor's engine cut out. At the same time, as he sucked in fresh air and tried to get the ringing out of his ears, Alex became aware of more movement. Half a dozen cars were speeding towards him from the hangars, the control tower, the building where Tom had been kept prisoner, from all directions. They stopped in a circle, surrounding him. One of the airport officials – a silver-haired man in overalls – got out of his car and shouted something at him but Alex couldn't hear a word he was saying. He knew he must stink of aviation fuel. He could feel it on his hands and all over his clothes. It was over. Sick at heart, Alex forced himself to climb down from the tractor, preparing himself for what he knew must come next: interrogation, humiliation, arrest. He had failed catastrophically.

Another car raced towards him. Clinging on to the protective rail of the tractor, Alex realized that everyone was waiting for it to arrive. It swerved to a stop and two people got out. Alex knew both of them.

Mrs Jones, the director of MI6 Special Operations,

stared at him. She was wearing a long, black raincoat, clearly angry, shaking her head slowly like a teacher having to deal with the world's worst schoolboy. John Crawley was standing next to her. He was her deputy and he was the one who had been driving the car.

And then the back door opened and a third figure emerged. Alex stared in disbelief. It couldn't be! He had to look again to make sure he wasn't imagining it or dreaming.

Alive, unharmed, not even wounded...

Tom Harris walked towards him and smiled.

EXPLANATIONS

There were a hundred questions Alex wanted to ask. Where was he? How had MI6 found him? Had Jack Starbright told them about Brother Mike's visit? Where was the Gulfstream G500 and was there any chance of intercepting it and bringing it down? How much trouble was he in? But he started with the one thing he wanted to know more than anything.

"Tom?" he asked. "How come you're not dead?"

Tom had been shot at close range in front of his eyes. Alex had seen it. The bullet had been aimed at his heart and Alex could even make out a hole in the fabric of his Hawaiian shirt. So what had happened? How was any of this possible?

The two boys were sitting in a club room inside the terminal building. This was where wealthy travellers might wait before their flights. There were leather sofas, a coffee machine, a fridge, pictures of foreign cities on the wall. Alex and Tom were facing each other across a table with Mrs Jones and John Crawley at either end. They'd been given drinks and biscuits but they hadn't touched them. Thirty minutes had passed since Brother Mike's escape but this was the first chance they'd had to talk.

"I really thought I was done for," Tom replied. "Brother Mike was a lunatic, and your mate, Freddy, seemed even worse. It's hard to believe he's the same age as us!"

"He's not my mate," Alex said.

"Wait a minute. I think you might be wrong there." Tom drew a breath. "You remember, just before he shot me, he came over and talked to me?"

"He said it wouldn't hurt."

"He was wrong about that. But while he was talking, he did something really strange. He sort of patted me on the chest. And at the same time, he slipped something into the top pocket of my shirt. I didn't know what it was but it was quite heavy. I was going to say something but while he was close to me, while nobody else could see, Freddy stared at me like he was scared and that was when I realized there was something weird going on." Tom reached into the pocket and took something out. "This is what he gave me."

Alex looked down. Tom was holding a highly polished steel disc that had been struck with force; it was bent out of shape with a crater in the centre. He remembered the engine components that had been stacked up on the shelves in the room where the two of them had been held prisoner.

"He was faking it all the time," Tom went on. "I could see he was trying to tell me something even as he was talking to me. And before he fired the gun, he winked at me. It was like he was telling me to go along with what was happening."

Alex remembered now. Tom had looked puzzled just before the shot was fired but Freddy had been standing with his back to Alex so he couldn't see what was going on.

"The bullet hit the disc!" Alex exclaimed.

"Exactly. It must be a fan disc or something. It protected me."

"But you fell backwards. And after that you didn't

move!" He thought back to that nightmare moment. "I saw blood!"

"Of course I fell over backwards," Tom replied. "You try having a bullet fired into you at close range. The disc stopped it killing me, but for what it's worth, it still hurts like hell." He pulled open his shirt to show an ugly bruise on his chest. "My head hit the floor and I must have knocked myself out. As for the blood, I bit my tongue. I have to say, Alex, being your friend isn't easy sometimes."

Despite himself, Alex couldn't help smiling. In the last twenty-four hours, his entire life had been turned upside down, but Tom was still Tom.

"I think, if you don't mind, Tom, I'd like to have a word with Alex alone," Mrs Jones said.

She had been listening silently all this while, sitting with her legs crossed. With her dark hair, her very pale skin and her sharp, expensively tailored suit, there was something dangerous about the head of Special Operations. Alex couldn't forget that the entire security of the UK rested on her slender shoulders. She had barely spoken so far and he still had no idea what she intended to do about what had happened at the airport. He had stolen a vehicle. He had knocked out an airport worker. He had almost caused a major incident.

Even so, he decided to stand up to her. "Actually, I'd prefer it if Tom stayed."

She looked at him with midnight eyes. "Why?"

"Because he's my friend. He took a bullet because of me. We don't have any secrets from each other."

"This is none of his business, Alex."

"If you want to talk to me, you talk to both of us. If not, we're walking out of here together." Alex wasn't budging. "Anyway, where are we?" he demanded.

"You're near Worcester." John Crawley answered the question. He was ten years younger than Mrs Jones, although in some ways he looked older than her with thinning hair, a sagging jawline and tired eyes. He worked as her deputy and he had a personal interest in what had happened at the airport. It had been Crawley who had helped capture Freddy Grey in Rio de Janeiro. He had almost been killed by him too.

"Worcester?" That was in the West Midlands, about a hundred and fifty miles from London. Alex was surprised. He was sure he'd travelled further.

"Very well. Your friend can stay." Mrs Jones nodded. For a moment, her eyes settled on Tom. "But I must warn you, if you repeat anything that is said in this room—"

"Yeah, yeah, yeah," Tom interrupted. "You know where I live."

"We know everything about you," Crawley muttered. "Including your probable GCSE results."

"Are they looking good?"

Crawley shook his head. "Not really."

Tom's face fell.

"How did you find me?" Alex asked.

"You're not going to like this, Alex. But we've been keeping an eye on you ever since that business in St Paul's Cathedral."

"You mean you've been spying on me?"

"Not spying," Crawley cut in. "Protecting you."

"It would be easier if you let me explain," Mrs Jones said. "I know you wanted to be left alone and we respected that, Alex. But we were afraid that after the trouble you had caused them, Nightshade might come gunning for you. After all, Scorpia nearly killed you right outside our office and we weren't going to let that happen again."

Alex nodded. He didn't like the idea of being watched but he understood what Mrs Jones was saying.

"You've been under discreet electronic surveillance. We haven't listened in on any of your phone calls – but we have made a note of everyone who has called you, looking out for numbers we don't recognize. We've done the same with your movements. We know when you leave for Brookland in the morning and when you come home, when you go out with your friends. But we'd be alerted the moment you headed off anywhere strange. If you were kidnapped, for example."

It took Alex a moment to work out what she meant. "You've bugged me!" he exclaimed.

Mrs Jones glanced at Crawley. "We're not listening in on you, Alex," he said. "But – yes. There are tracking devices in your trainers."

"How did you know which trainers I'd wear today?"

"We've put tracking devices in all of them."

Tom stared. "Mate, you've been, like, under a huge magnifying glass."

"Yes." Alex scowled.

"As soon as we'd heard that you'd helped Freddy Grey break out of Tidworth Camp, we started following you. The tracking signal brought us here."

"You took your time."

Mrs Jones shrugged. "We knew you were being held here, at Lower Wick Airfield, but we had to gather intel, and of course our first concern was to locate you before you were flown out. Who exactly was it in the Gulfstream G500 that you were just trying to destroy?"

"I wasn't trying to destroy it. I wanted to stop it taking off."

Quickly, Alex told Mrs Jones everything that had happened since Brother Mike had turned up at his home in Chelsea. Even as he spoke, he was grateful that Jack hadn't broken her word to him. She hadn't contacted MI6. But then, he wouldn't have expected otherwise.

"Can you find the plane?" he asked.

Again it was Crawley who answered. "We have the RAF out looking for them but I'm afraid they may have slipped through the net."

"So you've got no idea where they're going," Tom said.

"Actually, we have a very good idea where they're going but that's not information I intend to share."

"They're heading for the United States," Alex said.

Crawley stared at him. "They told you that?"

"Yes. Although they didn't mean to." Alex drank some of the apple juice he had been given. It seemed an age since Brother Mike had visited him and he hadn't had a mouthful of food or drink since then. "Brother Mike was angry when he came to see me," Alex explained. "He said I'd cost Nightshade millions of dollars. Not pounds or euros. Dollars."

"He could be on his way to Canada. Or to the Caribbean.

For that matter, there are countries all over the world with their own dollars," Crawley said.

"You didn't notice the registration code of the plane? N-GFYS. The first letter means that it came from America. And there's something else." Alex put down his glass. "It turns out I was wrong about him all along. Freddy Grey has turned against Nightshade. He understands what they did to him. As soon as we got out of Tidworth, he was pretending that he was still a Number, that the treatment hadn't worked. He even fooled me. But he was actually faking it. That's why he saved Tom. I bet it's the same with Sofia..."

Sofia was Mrs Jones's daughter. She had been captured at the same time as Freddy and, like Freddy, she was being helped by doctors and psychiatrists.

"Sofia is finding herself," Mrs Jones said. "It's taking time. But – yes – there has been some progress."

"Well, maybe Freddy can help us find the rest of Nightshade," Alex said. "Brother Mike doesn't know it – but Freddy's on our side. And just before he pretended to kill Tom, I think he left us a clue." Alex turned to Tom. "Do you remember what he said?"

"He said it wouldn't hurt." Tom rubbed his chest. "And it wasn't true."

"Before that. He also said: *As the old saying goes, revenge is golden. Remember that.*" Alex repeated the words carefully.

"How does that help us?"

"At the time I thought it sounded weird. When has revenge ever been golden? And why did he want me to remember it?" Alex paused. "I think it was a code. If he knew he was on his way to America, what's over there that's golden?"

"California," Crawley exclaimed. "It's known as the Golden State!"

Mrs Jones was suddenly excited. As ever, she barely showed any emotion but even she couldn't keep the gleam from her eye.

"You really are brilliant, Alex," she said. "You never fail to surprise me." She leaned towards him as if afraid of being overheard. "We have evidence that Nightshade is operating in the US. What you've told us fits in exactly with what we've already discovered."

"And what's that?" Alex asked.

Mrs Jones and Crawley exchanged the briefest of glances as if one was giving the other permission to continue. Neither of them needed it. The decision had already been made.

"I think you should look at this photograph," Mrs Jones said. "It was taken two months ago at the edge of Central Park in New York. It shows two girls. I think you may recognize them."

While Mrs Jones had been talking, Crawley had produced an iPad. He turned it round so that Alex and Tom could look at the screen. The picture had been taken by a CCTV camera, and the fuzzy image, in black and white, showed two girls dressed in coats and jeans. They were walking together, about to cross a road. Despite the poor image quality, Alex knew them instantly. They were Numbers Twenty and Twenty-Three: sweet little girls who spent their whole time together and liked to be sent out to commit murder together too. He had never learned their real names.

"The police circulated the picture following the unusual death of a private investigator who was found near by," Mrs Jones continued. "His name was Steven Chan. He was an ex-CIA agent working out of Santa Barbara. We ran the photograph through our facial-recognition software and it came up with this..."

Crawley showed them a second image of the two girls, this time dressed as Girl Guides. They had been photographed walking close to a river.

"These two girls have a connection with you, Alex," Mrs Jones said. "They were responsible for the death of the politician James Clifford."

Alex knew all about that. Clifford was the target chosen by Nightshade when they were planning their attack on London. The girls had given him a muffin – but it didn't just have chocolate pieces inside. There was an added ingredient ... potassium cyanide.

"How did they kill Steven Chan?" Alex asked.

"Actually, we still don't know." Crawley closed the iPad. "We've been in contact with the New York police but they have been unable to work out exactly how he died. That's to say, a piece of metal was fired into his head, between his eyes. But it wasn't a bullet. It was more like a miniature grenade. The police haven't identified the weapon."

"So what was Steven Chan investigating?" It was the obvious question.

"He was working for a private client. All we know is that

he had been hired to look into a major US company called Real Time. I imagine you may have heard of it."

Alex shrugged. The name meant nothing to him. But Tom leaned forward excitedly. "Yeah, I know who Real Time are," he exclaimed. "They're making these big computer games. Augmented Reality. You know, AR ... it's when you get, like, pictures projected into the real world. Their first game was *Trigger Happy*. It was a bit like *Pokémon GO*, except instead of capturing and training creatures, your job was to kill them. Basically, your phone turned into a sort of alien-splatter. And all the different creatures died in different ways. Pamola melted. Coyote got squashed. And Gluskab blew up. That was part of the fun, seeing what would happen when you pressed the button."

"A lot of people said the game was too violent." Crawley sniffed.

"It was just a cartoon," Tom replied. "You could tell it wasn't real blood. Loads of kids played it. The characters were based on folk heroes and there was a bit of trouble about that. But no one complained about the violence. Anyway, their next game was called *Eden Fall*, and it took AR to new levels."

"Who do you have to kill this time?" Alex asked.

"It's not just about killing, although you score points for taking out demons – and there are megademons too. With this new game, you can actually talk to the characters and they answer you back. The headsets have speakers concealed in the strap that goes over your ears. It sort of reimagines the world ... how it was created. So you've got all these freaky things living in your street. Flying pigs, demons, half-man-half-crocodiles. That sort of thing. You need to collect magic apples and fig leaves, and stuff like that, which allow you to ask them for clues. The aim is to find the secret laboratory where the world is made and meet the Inventor.

"It's always a big deal when they introduce new characters. Right now, everyone's waiting for the Blue Devil, who's the new bad guy, and the Blind Hedgehog called Shadrack. If you can find him, he's got some big secret that can help you win the game." Tom stopped himself, realizing that he'd been talking rather breathlessly. "I've never played it," he admitted. "But my brother's crazy for it and it's all over the world. Europe, America, Japan ... everywhere!"

"It seems that Nightshade is in some way involved with Real Time," Mrs Jones said. "For a start, the company is based outside San Francisco in California. The Golden State. That may be what Freddy Grey was trying to tell us. Then there's the link with this man, Steven Chan, who was investigating Real Time and who was killed by two of the so-called Numbers. I've spoken with the CIA but they've got a new director of their Covert Action Division and so far he hasn't been too co-operative. Maybe he's trying to protect Real Time. It's a huge corporation making billions of dollars and he doesn't want foreign intelligence services asking difficult questions."

She paused. When she spoke again, her voice was low, as if she was afraid of being overheard. "That's why I've decided to send out one of our own agents," she went on. "To be honest with you, I'm not interested in Real Time or their games. But if Nightshade are in California, I want to find them."

Alex understood why. Years ago, Mrs Jones had lost her two children – William and Sofia – and had always believed they were living somewhere in Russia. Alex had discovered the truth. They had both been kidnapped by Nightshade and – like Freddy and all the others – brainwashed into becoming spies and assassins. They'd even had miniature transmitters implanted in their skulls so that they could receive orders every minute of the day. Thanks to Alex, Sofia had been rescued. But her brother, William, was still out there. Alex knew that Mrs Jones would do anything to get him back.

"Who are you sending?" Alex asked.

"As a matter of fact, you know him. Ben Daniels was preparing to leave when this business with you began. He's flying to the South of France tomorrow."

Ben Daniels was someone Alex knew well. He had started his career with the Special Air Service – the famous SAS – but then he had been recruited by Mrs Jones. He and Alex had worked together many times.

"Why the South of France?" Alex asked.

"Steven Chan was working for a multi-millionaire called Wilbur White when he was killed. Mr White has a villa in Nice overlooking the Mediterranean and he's there now. We want to know why he needed a private detective and what he found out about Real Time."

"You know it's the school holidays," Alex said. "I could go too."

"That's a bad idea," Tom muttered.

"I have to say that I agree with Tom," Mrs Jones said. "I promised I wouldn't put you in any more danger, Alex. And we can handle this."

Alex shook his head. "I have to go," he said simply.

"Why?"

"First of all, I know what the Numbers look like. You've got a bad photograph of Numbers Twenty and Twenty-Three. But I spent time with them. I know all of them and I'm more likely to recognize them than Ben Daniels. Secondly, I owe it to Freddy Grey. He played his part brilliantly. He fooled everyone, me included. It's only a matter of time before they find out that he's not one of them and when that happens, they'll kill him. He saved Tom and he helped me, so I can't just leave him with them, wherever they are. I want to find him.

"But the main reason is this: Brother Mike came to my house and threatened me. He kidnapped my best friend and tried to kill him in front of my eyes. These people at Nightshade are disgusting. They're evil. They stole your daughter, Mrs Jones – and a lot of other little kids, too. I don't really care what they're doing with Real Time and these computer games, but I bet you it will mean lots more deaths – and I want to stop that. I want to bring them down. This time it's personal. I don't think you can stop me."

Alex glanced at Tom as if to ask him what he thought. Tom shrugged. The decision had been made.

"All right." Mrs Jones sighed. "It's your decision, Alex. But I hate to think what Jack is going to say."

OLD FRIENDS

Mrs Jones was right. Jack was far from happy when Alex came into the kitchen, carrying the backpack with his clothes for the trip abroad.

"I just don't understand you," she said. "You never wanted to be a spy and right now everything is going your way. You've caught up at school. You're coming up for sixth form. And after what happened in Wales, we've got tons of money in the bank. So why are you putting yourself in danger once again? Don't you think enough is enough?"

"You're right, Jack. And I'm sorry. But I didn't think I had any choice. If it wasn't for me, Freddy would be safe. Now he's back with Nightshade. I have to find him."

Jack sighed. "I should come with you," she said.

"You've got exams."

"So have you!"

"With a bit of luck, I'll be back in a week. And don't worry, Ben Daniels will look after me."

As if on cue, there was the sound of a car hooting outside the front door. Alex hoisted the backpack onto his shoulders. "I'll text you when I get there," he promised.

"And every day after that," Jack insisted.

The two of them hugged. Alex went over to the door and looked out. There was a black VW parked outside the house and he could see Ben Daniels sitting in the back seat. It was strange how often they had crossed paths since the time, right at the beginning, when Alex had been sent for training at the Brecon Beacons. "Fox" – as he was known – had been shocked to find a fourteen-year-old boy training with the elite SAS unit. But since then they'd become friends and Alex felt reassured to see the older man – Ben was in his late twenties – waiting for him. He was dressed in cargo pants with a tight-fitting T-shirt that showed off his muscles and a tattoo, the SAS dagger with wings, on his upper arm. With Ben, there was always a sense of violence just below the surface. He looked as if he was about to pull out a gun or get into a fistfight, but he was also thoughtful and kind. He had loved being in the army but he had made a smooth transition to intelligence. Mrs Jones obviously trusted him. She used him all the time.

"How are you, Alex?" Ben reached over and shook his hand. "I couldn't believe it when Mrs Jones told me you were coming along for the ride."

"Yeah. I'm not sure I believe it either."

Ben grinned. "You never can keep away from trouble, can you!"

The driver started the car. As they moved away, Alex took one last look back. Jack was watching him from the kitchen. Right then, Alex knew that he was on the dividing line between two worlds: safety behind him, danger ahead. Well, that was how it had been for almost as long as he could remember. He had made his choice.

They were on their way to Heathrow Airport, an ordinary commercial flight – although once they arrived there, they would be taken through a private channel to the plane.

Alex had no doubt that the contents of Ben's luggage would set off every alarm in the security area.

"I'm glad to see you again, Alex. It looks like you and I are becoming a team!" Ben settled back in his seat. He wanted to get straight down to business. "Here's what you need to know about Wilbur White, the man we're going to see. He's an American art dealer, very wealthy, married to a French wife. He divides his time between Nice and San Francisco."

"He hired Steven Chan."

"That's right."

"Do you know why?"

"Not exactly – and the CIA aren't helping. They've got a new director and he's a real hard-ass. But we think it may be connected with the death of White's son, Colin. He was seventeen years old and died in what you might call mysterious circumstances. He fell off the roof of a building in Mission Bay, on the east side of San Francisco. Or I suppose it's always possible he jumped."

"Did the police investigate?"

"They looked into it, of course. But only one crime had been committed and that was by Colin White. He was trespassing. The building was half finished and he'd broken in."

"Why?"

"Nobody has any idea." Ben fell silent for a moment. They had crossed the King's Road and were heading west out of London. "Or if they do, they're not saying," he added. "My job is to talk to his father and find out what he knows. Hopefully he has information that may lead us to Nightshade."

"And then?"

Ben shrugged. "Who knows? Nice today, maybe San Francisco tomorrow. We go wherever the trail leads." He fumbled in his pocket and drew out an envelope. "By the way, Mrs Jones asked me to give you this."

Alex took the envelope. He saw his name on the front, handwritten in green ink. He tore it open and pulled out a typewritten letter. He read:

Dear Alex,

It was not my choice to put you in danger again. You will remember that when we met at Tidworth, after St Paul's Cathedral, I urged you to put all this behind you and go back to school. That is still my hope for you. You've done enough.

That said, I would be lying if I tried to pretend that I'm not glad you've made this decision. It's thanks to you that I now have Sofia back after all these years and, although there is still a long way to go, I believe that one day she will be normal again and will be able to forget everything that Nightshade did to her. I will always be grateful to you for that.

But they still have my other child, William.

There isn't a day that I don't think about him and wonder if I will ever see him again. I have asked Sofia about him but there is very little she can tell me. She wasn't even aware that he was her brother. I long to see him. If he can be brought back to me,

I will finally be able to emerge from the dark place where I have been ever since I learned the truth, and will feel that my life belongs to me again. And if there is anyone who can do that, it is you. You know William. You have seen him and spoken to him. Maybe you will find him a second time.

If that happens, here's something that might help you. I'm enclosing a photograph of William that was taken on his first day at primary school, when he was five. This was just a few months before his father stole him from me. It's a day that every child remembers and if you show it to William, it's just possible that it will jog his memory and remind him who he really is. The school was called St Leonard's and he loved the elephant you can see in the picture. It always made him smile.

Perhaps you will be able to show it to him. I don't know. I would be happy if you got a chance to tell him about me and to say how much I miss him. I'm hoping you'll do more than that. But above all, look after yourself. In a way, you have been a bit like a son to me. Make sure you come home safely.

Best wishes,
Tulip Jones

It was the first time Alex had ever known Mrs Jones to call herself by her first name. He looked back in the envelope and found a photograph taken maybe ten or eleven years ago. It showed a small boy in a school uniform – short trousers and a jersey. He was holding hands with a woman Alex recognized at once. It was Mrs Jones, but younger, less hard-edged, dressed in brighter colours, smiling. The elephant that she had mentioned in her letter was a wooden construction in the middle of a playground. The children could climb up a ladder and crawl inside. Its trunk was actually a slide. Alex examined William. In the picture he looked both nervous and excited. His first day at school! Mrs Jones was right. It was something no child ever forgot.

Alex slid the photograph inside the letter and, without saying anything, put them both away.

Four hours later, Alex was sitting in a café on the Promenade des Anglais in Nice with a view of palm trees and the beach on the other side of a busy main road. That was what he most remembered about the South of France: the elegance and holiday atmosphere of the famous coast seemed to be at constant war with the traffic jams, overcrowding and noise of modern life. The flight from London had only taken two hours but Alex could have been a world away from London. It wasn't just the sunshine, the warm breeze. The very light was different and, despite the fumes of the traffic, he could still make out the scent of pine and cypress in the air.

He and Ben had been met at the airport by another driver and taken to a small hotel in the Old Town. They hadn't had time to unpack. Ben wanted to talk to Wilbur White as soon as possible and had left Alex on his own in a café while he drove up to the villa. There was a part of Alex that was annoyed. He had been sitting here for the best part of an hour and he hadn't come all the way to France just to be left on the sidelines like some unwanted kid brother. Ben had given him money for lunch but he had no appetite and had ordered nothing more than a glass of grenadine, still his favourite drink. He had texted Jack and Tom. Then he'd plugged in his AirPods and spent the remaining time listening to music while he browsed the Internet for anything he could find on Real Time and *Eden Fall*.

Eventually Ben arrived back. He wasn't in a good mood and ordered a beer even as he sat down opposite Alex. "He won't talk to me," he announced.

"Why not?"

"He's not talking to anyone. I was right about one thing. This is all about the death of his son – and after the police closed down their investigation, Wilbur White became very bitter. He's in touch with the CIA, but they're refusing to help us."

"So what's the plan?" Alex asked.

"White has a villa about half an hour from here," Ben said. "It's in Mont Boron, high up in the hills. It's a pretty swish neighbourhood. Elton John lives just down the road. We're talking ten bedrooms, indoor and outdoor pools, helipad and all the rest of it. You reach the house down a private lane and there are metal gates at the entrance, CCTV cameras, a five-metre brick wall, armed guards with Alsatian dogs..."

"You're planning to break in?"

"No, Alex. You are."

The beer arrived, carried by a surly waiter with an apron reaching down to his feet. Ben took a gulp, then set the glass down.

"I spoke to Crawley and he agrees. There's no chance that White will speak to me. I can climb the wall and get past the guards and the dogs, but the moment I walk into the room, he'll have me arrested."

"But me...?"

"You're about the same age as the boy he lost. You can tell him you were Colin's friend. That might make him open up."

Alex didn't like the sound of that. He doubted it would work – and if it did, wouldn't he be guilty of exploiting a father's grief? He was about to argue but then he remembered. This wasn't about him. His job was to find Freddy Grey – and, for that matter, William Jones. He had to put Nightshade out of business. He might not like what Ben was suggesting but there didn't seem to be any other way.

"So what do I have to do?" he asked. "Am I going to parachute in?"

Ben half smiled. "There's no need for that," he said. "As a matter of fact, we've got a special piece of kit that will do the job nicely. It's quite big and it's being put on a transport plane, care of the RAF. No expense spared. It won't be here for a few hours but that's OK because we've got a lot of work to do and, anyway, we need to wait until dark."

"And what exactly is it?" Alex asked.

"If you don't mind, I'm not going to tell you," Ben

replied. He picked up his glass and drained it. "I don't think you're going to like it."

They spent the rest of the day at the hotel. Alex had been to Nice before and would have liked to explore the city again with its old port, cobbled streets and markets – but Ben had other ideas. He had produced photographs and plans of the Castel Saint-Martin, which was the name of the luxurious villa where Wilbur White lived. The pictures showed a miniature castle, painted pink, with purple flowers cascading down the walls. Floor-to-ceiling windows led out onto terraces and balconies that must have provided glorious views of Nice and the Mediterranean far below. There was a ten-metre swimming pool a short distance away in the garden, partly concealed behind a grove of trees with a tennis court beyond. A flight of steps and a gravel path led down from the house.

"White paid twenty-five million euros for this house ten years ago," Ben told him. "He has an original Picasso in his bedroom which is probably worth the same again. There are expensive paintings in all the rooms, which is one of the reasons he has so much security but he's also thinking of his own protection. We've had at least one piece of luck. We've chosen the right time to break in. At the moment, he's at home on his own."

"Where's his wife?" Alex asked.

"She's still in America."

The London office had provided Ben with all the information he needed. He took out drawings that showed the security systems, the movement sensors, the cameras on the walls.

"You still haven't told me how I get past them," Alex complained.

"You'll find out soon enough. But you shouldn't have any difficulty reaching Mr White. He's a man of habit. He has dinner every evening at half past seven and when he finishes eating, he goes out onto the terrace to smoke a cigar." Ben slid one of the photographs in front of Alex and tapped it. "You'll find him here."

"And I just walk up to him and introduce myself?"

"Just make sure you start talking before he calls security."

"Are you sure it wouldn't be easier just to knock on the front door?"

"If we thought that, Alex, we wouldn't be going to all this trouble and expense." Ben went back to the plans. "These are the main gates. This building here is a sort of summer house next to the tennis court. The guards patrol the grounds every hour, moving in different directions. And it's important you stay out of the range of the cameras, which are located here and here..."

The briefing went on until the evening. Looking out of the window, Alex saw the sky turn mauve as the sun dipped down towards the sea. There were a few clouds but otherwise it was going to be a clear night with an almost full moon climbing into the sky. At half past six they went back outside and found another café, where Ben ordered soft drinks, salami, bread and cheese. Alex tried to eat but he wasn't hungry. He still didn't know how he was supposed to break into the Castel Saint-Martin and the fact that Ben refused to tell him unnerved him. He watched as Ben devoured most of the food and paid the waiter, speaking in fluent French. Suddenly it was time to go.

Ben had hired a car and they drove out of Nice, following roads that zigzagged up into the hills. Stone walls hemmed them in on both sides with houses and blocks of flats partly concealed behind them, just the upper storeys visible. But as they continued to climb, they left all the buildings and the parked cars behind them until they were surrounded by woodland, which seemed to stitch the darkness together with only the occasional streetlight and the beams of the car illuminating the road ahead. Fortunately, Ben knew where he was going. He spun the wheel, sending the car around a hairpin bend and, after a few minutes, turned down a narrow track that took them through the trees. Alex was beginning to wonder where they were heading. Then he saw a sign. PARKING MONT BORON. Ben slowed down. They had arrived.

The car park had been cut into the forest. At this time of night it was empty apart from a single vehicle, a delivery truck so big that it took up almost half the space. As Ben switched off the engine, the front passenger door opened and a man got out. Even though Alex couldn't see his face in the shadows, he recognized him at once and couldn't help smiling. There was only one man who was as fat as that, barely able to squeeze himself through the door, wheezing as he lowered himself to the ground.

Derek Smithers was back! He was the last person Alex had expected to see.

Of course, it was all fake. Alex knew that Smithers had created a "fat suit" for himself. In reality, he was a small and slender Irishman. Nor was he really bald. It was all a disguise that he had worn so often that it had become part of him. Smithers had been the head of the gadgets department at MI6 Special Operations and he and Alex were old friends. Recently, however, he had disappeared. So what was he doing back in action in a deserted car park in the middle of a French wood?

And what was in the truck? This was obviously the "special piece of kit" that Ben had mentioned. But what could it possibly be, taking up so much space? Had Smithers come all this way with a giant trampoline?

Alex went over to him. "I didn't expect to see you," he said.

"My dear Alex! How could I resist the opportunity to run into you once again?" Smithers was all smiles. "I hope you're keeping well. You've grown! What are you now ... sixteen? I must say, I have missed you since all that excitement in Cairo!"

Alex remembered the two of them being chased through the souk. "They told me you'd retired," he said.

"Not so much retired. I've moved into a new field." Smithers was wearing a three-piece suit, the waistcoat stretched across the great bulge of his stomach. He dug two stubby fingers into a pocket and pulled out a business card. He handed it to Alex. It read:

DEREK SMITHERS & COMPANY
PRIVATE DETECTIVES

"There's no email or address," Alex said.

"You don't need one. Just press the card against your mobile phone and it will connect you automatically. The card also dissolves in hot water. Slip it into a cup of tea and hold your breath. Ten seconds later, everyone in the room will be unconscious."

"Thanks, Mr Smithers." Alex was amused. It was so typical of Smithers that even his business card should contain two quite separate gadgets. He slipped it away. "So what exactly are you doing here?"

"Mrs Jones rang me. She said they were going to be using Big Bessie. It was something I was working on just before I left and it hasn't actually been tested yet. So when I heard it was you, I insisted on coming along. I wouldn't want to hear you'd broken both your legs or anything like that."

Alex grimaced. "What exactly is Big Bessie?" he demanded. "Why won't anybody tell me?"

Smithers rested a hand on his shoulder. "Come with me," he said. "I'll show you."

BIG BESSIE

Two more men had come out of the lorry. Alex watched as they threw open the back and pressed a button on a remote control. At once, a low platform began to slide out, carrying a metal cylinder, about eight metres long. It reminded Alex of the barrel of an enormous gun. As it emerged, the cylinder began to move upwards until it was pointing at the sky. There was a click of machinery and it locked into place, slanting at an angle of about seventy degrees. Feeling ever more nervous, Alex stepped towards it, noticing a ladder that would allow him to climb onto the top, where there were two handholds welded into place. Suddenly, he understood.

"I take it you've been to the circus," Smithers exclaimed. "That was what gave me the idea."

Ian Rider had taken Alex to the circus a long time ago, when he was eight or nine years old. In truth, he hadn't much enjoyed it. There had been performing elephants and lions in cages and he had felt nothing but pity for them. He had enjoyed the trapeze artists but the clowns had left him cold. In fact, he found them rather sinister. There had been one act, however, that he would never forget.

The human cannonball.

A man dressed in silver latex with goggles and a crash helmet had been loaded into an oversized cannon just like the one Alex was looking at now. The ringmaster had arrived with a flaming torch and had lit the fuse. After a countdown of ten seconds, the cannon had exploded with a great bang and a shower of sparks, and the man had been fired high into the air, almost touching the top of the tent before landing in a safety net strung across the ring. He had come bouncing to his feet to applause from the audience, who, like Alex, probably preferred humans to put themselves in danger without forcing animals to join in.

"You're not serious," he muttered.

"It's the easiest way to get you in." Ben Daniels had crept up behind them. He was examining the cannon. "Straight over the wall and you land in the swimming pool."

"I'm not going to be fired out of a cannon!"

"There's nothing to worry about," Smithers assured him. "There have only ever been thirty deaths among human cannonballs ... and maybe a dozen serious accidents."

"That's very reassuring!"

"Being fired is perfectly safe. It's landing that causes the problems. Most of the deaths occur when the performer misses the net. But this cannon is much more sophisticated than the circus variety. It's all computer-controlled. We've already programmed it with the air temperature, the wind speed and the distance to the pool. We'll also input your personal details. You'll land perfectly in the deep end. A quick splash and then you climb out and get on with the job."

Alex wasn't having any of it. "You said this thing was untested," he reminded Smithers. "You said I might break both my legs!"

"I was exaggerating, my dear chap."

"Anyway, if you set it off, the entire hillside will hear the bang," Alex went on. "Wilbur White will know something's happening before I get anywhere near his swimming pool."

"Actually, you're wrong there. Big Bessie won't make much more noise than a car backfiring. When human cannonballs perform in the circus, they add the explosion and the sparks to make it all more dramatic. In fact, the cannon uses a blast of compressed air. You might actually enjoy the experience."

"Really?"

Smithers considered. "Well, it'll be something to remember. You'll be travelling at about seventy miles per hour, reaching top speed in less than half a second. You'll experience 7 Gs as you leave – that's seven times the force of gravity – and about 10 Gs when you land. I've estimated you'll reach a height of about sixty metres so you should get an amazing view of Nice if you have time to look..."

"Sure. I'll tell you all about it when you visit me in hospital."

"It's not like you to be so pessimistic, old chap. I've come all the way out here to make certain nothing goes wrong. Surely after all our adventures together, you trust me by now!"

Alex let out a sigh. It was true that the gadgets invented by Smithers had saved his life on more than one occasion. "Are you sure you're going to aim it properly?" he asked. "I don't want to end up being splatted over the tennis court."

"We just need to key in your height and body weight." Smithers cast an expert eye over Alex as he stood in front of him. "I'd say about one metre seventy-five and sixty kilograms. You're certainly keeping yourself in shape. We'll program that into the computer, pop you into the cannon and then send you on your way."

Alex turned to Ben Daniels. "Just one question. Where's the Castel Saint-Martin?"

Ben pointed in the same direction as the cannon. For the first time, Alex noticed a wall running round the edge of the car park. "Why do you think we chose this place to stop?" Ben said. "This is the back end of the villa. The garden starts on the other side of the wall and the swimming pool is just fifty metres away. We'll get you ready now. Remember – keep away from the CCTV cameras. There's no need to worry about the dogs. A dip in the pool will make sure they don't pick up your scent."

"Have you checked it's actually got water in it?"

Ben nodded. "The trouble with you, Alex, is you worry too much. Yes – it's filled. It might be a bit nippy, though, which is why we'll supply you with a dry suit."

"It'll help with your posture too," Smithers added. "When you're inside the cannon, you have to stand as rigidly as possible. Think of yourself as a bullet. It'll all be over very quickly."

"Thanks, Mr Smithers." Alex sounded as gloomy as he felt.

While they had been talking, the two other men had been working on the cannon, locking it into place. Now one of them whistled and showed a thumbs up. The other was holding Alex's dry suit.

"Time to get going," Ben said. He took Alex's phone and

handed him a radio transmitter that was about the same size. "This is waterproof," he said. "You can call us if you get into any trouble. Or you can bring us in once you've spoken to Wilbur White. Good luck!"

Ten minutes later, Alex was draped from his neck to his ankles in black neoprene as if he was about to go scuba diving. Unlike the circus versions, the cannon had no decoration, no bright colours to make it look fun. It was just a cylinder of dull steel. With Ben Daniels standing underneath him, he climbed the ladder up to the top of the barrel and grabbed the handholds.

"We'll give you a countdown," Smithers called out to him. "Remember: stay rigid!"

Alex eased his legs into the mouth of the cannon and gently lowered himself into the tube. He could feel the smooth surface of the metal against the palms of his hands. It was like entering a circular coffin. It had been dark outside. Inside, it was pitch black. He felt his feet come to rest on a solid surface and knew that this was the platform that would propel him on this terrifying journey. There was only just enough space inside the cylinder to turn round. He positioned himself so that he was facing the edge of the car park and the wall. He rested his hands on his thighs, then tensed himself, trying to imagine himself as a bullet.

How had they managed to talk him into this? What would Jack say?

"Are you ready?" Smithers' voice sounded miles away.

There was no point trying to answer. Alex knew he wouldn't be heard. Anyway, his mouth was too dry.

"Starting countdown now. Five, four, three ..."

Alex took one last look at the mouth of the cannon, a circle of moonlight high above his head. He tried to lock down his body, his shoulders, his legs and his arms. He realized that he had stopped breathing.

"... two, one."

The pause seemed to last for ever.

Then he gasped as he was punched harder than he had ever been punched before. He felt his entire skeleton close in on itself, his stomach squeezed like a sponge. His eyes were sucked back into their sockets. His mouth stretched itself into a grin of sheer terror. He heard nothing and there was no sense of his leaving the cannon. The physical shock was so great that if he had been instantly crushed to death, it would have felt exactly the same. But the next thing he knew, he was high in the sky, rising further every second. He could feel the night air all around him. And there was the view of Nice that Smithers had promised: a scattering of tiny lights thrown across the black landscape. Alex couldn't breathe. It was as if he had been torn apart.

He was impossibly high, twisting in the night like a wounded bird. For a brief second, he saw the roof and the terraces of the Castel Saint-Martin bathed in amber light, far below. There was no sign of the swimming pool. Had Smithers overshot? Was he about to fall to his death, smashing into the ground? Somewhere in his mind, he was aware that he had reached maximum height and that he had continued over the curve, plunging back down. The city of Nice was no longer in his vision. Even the villa had disappeared. The night was swirling around him, the wind rushing past, and he had to grit his teeth to stop himself crying out as he fell through the sky.

Down, down, down. He couldn't bear to look at the ground rushing up towards him. His feet hit something and went through. It was water! Smithers had been true to his word. He had landed not just in the pool but in the deep end, perfectly targeted to the last centimetre. He felt himself pulled beneath the surface and suddenly he was completely blind, his arms flailing around him. He kicked out and forced himself to rise and, as his head and shoulders emerged from the water, he gulped in air, amazed that he was still in one piece. He had made it! He was alive. And it seemed that nobody had heard him arrive.

Still gasping, he swam to the edge of the pool and clung on to the side, allowing the tension of the last few seconds to slip away. Alex had been many things in his lifetime but a human cannonball was a new experience and it took him a minute to get over it. *Never again,* he promised himself. It was one ride he could do without.

And the worst of it was that his troubles were only beginning.

Alex pulled himself out of the water and crouched down, looking around him. There was a thin wall of pine trees in front of him, with a pathway cutting through the middle and the villa, all lit up, on the other side. The garden of the Castel Saint-Martin stretched out in every direction, soft and dark in the moonlight. Somehow, the surrounding walls seemed to have amplified the warmth of the evening as well as every sound and smell. The scent of the pine needles was intense and when one of the guard dogs let out a single bark, it felt so close that Alex was sure he was about to be attacked. But that was impossible. If anyone had seen him fly over the wall or heard the splash as he hit the pool, every alarm would already have been activated. He was on his own. For the moment, he was safe.

He stripped off the dry suit. He was wearing his own shirt and jeans underneath ... both of them perfectly dry, protected from the water by the synthetic fabric of his outer skin. His trainers had been pressed flat against his chest and although his feet were still soaking wet, he quickly slipped them on. According to the maps that Ben had shown him, Wilbur White would be sitting on a terrace on the other side of the trees, over to the left. All he had to do was cross the main lawn without being seen. Then he just had to hope that the art dealer wouldn't be alarmed by his sudden appearance and would tell him what he wanted to know. Perhaps he might even offer him a drink and a cigar.

He wanted to get this over with. He hurried between the trees, pausing only when he got to the edge of the lawn on the other side. The Castel Saint-Martin loomed up in front of him, a yellow glow pouring out of the windows and spilling onto the terraces. The building was even more magical than it had appeared in Ben's photographs: timeless, tucked away behind high walls that had been erected to keep the modern world at bay. Only the security cameras, glinting in the moonlight, reminded Alex that this was the twenty-first century and, worse still, that he was a trespasser. He still wasn't sure what sort of welcome he was going to receive.

He looked around him, but there was nobody in sight. Nor was there any sign of Wilbur White. What would he do if the art dealer had decided to go to bed early without his after-dinner cigar? Would he be able to break into the house? Alex drew a breath, then sprinted across the lawn, his trainers making no sound on the soft grass. Somewhere an owl hooted, but nobody else seemed to have noticed him. Alex reached a stone balustrade on the edge of the property and ducked down into the shadows. He counted to five. No alarms. No dogs. He had made it this far.

He straightened up and climbed a flight of wide stone steps that led to the terrace where White was supposed to be. He saw an ornate metal table and three chairs spread out in front of the open French windows – but there was no sign of the owner. Alex was about to go into the house, but just then he noticed a glow of red in the far corner of the terrace and made out the shape of a man, stretched out on a sun-lounger. It was Wilbur White. It had to be.

Moving more slowly now, Alex crept forward and stopped a few steps away. "Mr White?" he asked slowly.

Wilbur White lowered his cigar. As Alex's eyes got used to the darkness, he saw a bald head, a wrinkled, suntanned face, glasses, thin lips, scowling. Although he had surely eaten alone – Ben Daniels had told Alex that his wife was away – White was formally dressed in a velvet jacket and a white shirt with a loose, oversized collar. He was well into his sixties, maybe older. The sun had not been kind to his skin.

"Who are you?" he asked. He didn't sound particularly surprised. He was looking at Alex with distaste.

"Forgive me for interrupting you, sir," Alex said. "I wondered if I could talk to you."

"What about? You look too young to want to buy art."

"About what happened to your son. And what you know about a company called Real Time."

White's face changed. He had not been friendly to begin with but now he looked positively poisonous. "How did you get in here?" he demanded. "Who sent you here to ask me these questions?"

Alex never managed to answer.

He hadn't heard the person who had crept up behind him and he only became aware of them when it was too late. Suddenly there was a hand on his shoulder and a gun pressed against his head. A voice spoke, very close to his ear. An American accent. A woman.

"Don't make a move. If you try anything, I will put a bullet in you. Nod if you understand me."

Alex nodded slowly.

"We've got this, Mr White." The second person who had spoken was a man. He was also behind Alex, out of his vision.

"Put your hands out in front of you. Very slowly."

Alex did what he was told. He was furious with himself. When had he been spotted? Had he been careful enough crossing the lawn? Or had they seen him crashing into the swimming pool? So much for Smithers and his ingenious gadgets! The woman had produced a pair of handcuffs. There was nothing Alex could do as the cold steel snapped shut around his wrists.

"How the hell did he get in here?" Wilbur White growled.

"We don't know, sir," the woman said. "But we'll find out."

"Maybe you'd better go back into the house, sir," her partner suggested. "He may not have come alone."

"I'm going in now." White rose to his feet. He gazed at Alex with hatred. "First you take my son. Then you come for me!"

"That's not true..." Alex began.

But the art dealer had already walked away. Alex felt the hands grab hold of him and he was dragged backwards into the night.

TEN SECONDS

Alex had no idea who had taken him prisoner. The man and the woman seemed to be working for Wilbur White. Perhaps they were private security, hired to protect him. But what had White meant when he had made those accusations moments ago? *First you take my son. Then you come for me.* And where was he being taken? Alex had assumed he would be bundled into a car and driven away from the villa, but instead he was being taken back across the garden, the same way he had come. The three of them passed the swimming pool where he had landed and continued towards a building next to the tennis court.

Alex remembered it from the photographs he had been shown. Ben Daniels had described it as a summer house, but it was much more than that: a two-storey pavilion with ornate pillars and a roof that curled round at the edges like an old Japanese temple. The front entrance led into a well-equipped gymnasium, with sliding doors opening onto showers and changing facilities on one side and a small kitchen on the other. Alex had to ask himself: why had they brought him here? He rather doubted they were going to invite him to join in a workout.

Once they were inside, with the lights on, Alex was able to examine the two people who had taken him. For a moment, he got the sense that they had turned into a whole army. They were being reflected again and again in the floor-to-ceiling mirrors that lined the walls, queuing up to interrogate him. The woman was dressed in a loose-fitting jacket and trousers, with a thin gold necklace around her neck. She had short fair hair, and a square, expressionless face. Her partner was a few inches shorter than her but with well-developed muscles and a thick neck. He was wearing a leather jacket and T-shirt that could have been deliberately chosen to make him look even tougher than he was. From his appearance and his accent, Alex guessed he might have come from somewhere in Central America.

The woman still had her gun and kept it trained on Alex while the man patted him down.

"He's clean," the man said.

Satisfied, he pushed Alex into a wicker chair between a set of weights and a treadmill, holding him down for a moment before stepping away. Whoever they were, they were both being extremely careful. Alex was a teenager. He was handcuffed. There were two of them and only one of him. But they were still nervous.

"What's your name?" the woman began. She seemed to be the one in charge.

"It's Alex," Alex said. "What's yours?"

"We'll ask the questions. OK?" The man was examining Alex as if he was trying to work out which bit of him to hit first.

"What are you doing here?" the woman asked.

"I came to talk to Mr White."

"What about?"

"Why don't you let me speak to him? Then you'll find out."

The woman considered this for a moment. "How did you get into the grounds?" she asked.

They hadn't heard the cannon and they hadn't seen him fall out of the sky. That was interesting. It told Alex that they probably weren't quite as smart as they were pretending to be. "I'm not going to say anything until you tell me who you are," he said.

"You're going to tell us everything we want to know, or you'll be leaving here on a stretcher," the man replied. "Where are your friends?"

Alex refused to answer. He kept his lips sealed.

The woman sighed. "All right, Alex. We'll play it your way. My name is Klara Zak. And this is Joe Mendoza. OK? Now we all know each other. So why not answer our questions?"

"We need to find your friends," Mendoza said.

"I don't have any friends," Alex replied. He had to be careful. He couldn't tell these people anything about himself until he knew exactly who they were and what they were doing at the Castel Saint-Martin. It was quite possible they were private security guards, hired by Wilbur White, but there was something about them that made Alex think otherwise. Maybe it was their attitude. They might have called the art dealer "sir", but they hadn't behaved as if they were taking instructions from him. It could almost have been the other way round.

Mendoza took a step forward. He looked much more dangerous than Klara Zak, even though she was the one with the gun. He was acting like a gangster who wouldn't care about getting his hands dirty. "You were sent to kill Mr White," he muttered.

"What?" Alex's head spun. How could they have got that idea?

"We know who you work for," Mendoza added.

"And who is that?" Alex countered.

"Nightshade." Mendoza smiled, pleased with himself. "They employ kids – right? And you're a kid. What are you? Fifteen?"

"You've got it completely wrong," Alex growled. "It looks like we're on the same side. I'm looking for Nightshade too."

"Why?"

"I'm working for British intelligence." He took a breath. He didn't like giving them this information, but he seemed to have no other choice. "My name is Alex Rider. I'm with MI6 Special Operations. You can check me out."

Mendoza stared at him. "Oh, really? So what are you, then? James Bond's kid brother?" He laughed unpleasantly. "Nice try, Alex, but we happen to know that Nightshade are the ones with the boy soldiers."

He glanced at Klara, who nodded, giving him permission. At once, he lashed out, grabbing hold of Alex's collar and twisting the fabric in his hand so that the fabric tightened like a noose around his throat. "We know exactly who you are. We were expecting you. And you might like to know that the whole lawn was wired for sound. Your goose was cooked the moment you took your first step on the grass."

So that was how they had known he was there. For all his maps and diagrams, it was something Ben Daniels had never suspected.

"You've got it all wrong!" Alex writhed in the chair, trying to break free. "You can call the people I work for. I've got a radio..."

"You've got nothing!" Mendoza replied. He twisted the shirt a second time, cutting off Alex's air supply. "Where are Nightshade?"

"I have no idea!"

"Oh – sure you kids are tough. But we're tougher. And I'm warning you now: if you don't tell us what we want to know, this is going to be a night you won't forget."

"OK – that's enough, Joe," Klara said.

Mendoza released him and walked away. Alex made sure he wasn't being watched, then felt inside his trouser pockets, moving both hands at the same time. They were empty. He thought back to the moment when the man had frisked him, after they had brought him to the pavilion. He hadn't found anything. So the transmitter Ben Daniels had given him must have fallen out of his pocket. He was unarmed and on his own.

Or was he?

"You know what we have to do," Mendoza said.

He was standing next to Klara. She didn't look happy. "Really?"

"You go outside if you want. I'll see to it."

Mendoza went over to a shelf and picked something up. When he turned round, Alex saw that he was holding a pair of pliers. "You want him to lead us to Nightshade?"

he asked Klara. "Two or three toenails and he'll sing like a canary."

"I don't know, Joe. Are we really gonna do that?" Klara looked sickened. "He's just a kid. My sister's boy is the same age as him."

"Maybe you're forgetting, Klara. It was two kids that killed Steven Chan in New York. This is Nightshade we're talking about. Trained killers. Take his shoes off!"

Klara hesitated. "There's got to be a better way."

"Like what?"

"Well..." She thought for a moment, then nodded in the direction of the pool on the other side of the pavilion. "Suppose we duck his head under water. In the pool!"

"You mean ... like, waterboard him?"

"Why not?"

"Toenails is faster."

Alex could hardly believe what he was hearing. This was him they were arguing about – whether to half drown him or pull off his toenails. But he already knew what he had to do. "Please!" he exclaimed. "Don't hurt me. I'll tell you everything you want to know." He jerked his head in the direction of the kitchen. "Can I just have something hot to drink? I'm so cold. A cup of coffee or tea. If you do that, I'll tell you where you can find Nightshade."

"He's lying!" Mendoza snarled.

"Let's give him a chance," Klara muttered. "You keep a gun on him. Don't go near him. If he moves, shoot him."

She went into the kitchen and Alex heard her click on the kettle. Meanwhile, Mendoza had taken out his own gun and stood a carefully measured distance away, his face cold and unsmiling. "So how did you get into the villa?" he demanded.

"I climbed the wall," Alex said.

"That's impossible. There's a sensor all the way round."

"Not where I came in." Alex pointed, his two hands still chained together. "Just over there, next to the tree." Mendoza turned round and looked out of the open door of the pavilion. He didn't notice Alex dip his left hand into his shirt pocket and draw something out. By the time Mendoza turned back again, the object was concealed in Alex's palm.

"Are you really going to hurt me?" Alex asked.

"It's the job," Mendoza replied. "You should have thought of that before you got messed up in all this."

He fell silent and the two of them waited until Klara Zak returned with a single steaming mug, which she set down on a table next to Alex, all the time making sure she kept a safe distance. Alex briefly cupped his hands over the lip as if feeling the warmth. At the same time, he took a deep breath ... and held it.

Nobody noticed him drop a small square of white card into the mug. It was the business card that Smithers had given him and which had been in his shirt pocket, protected by the dry suit he had worn when he was fired into the pool. Smithers had been absolutely clear. *The card dissolves in hot water. Slip it into a cup of tea ... ten seconds later, everyone in the room will be unconscious.* Was he being serious? As he sat facing Zak and Mendoza, Alex very much hoped so. He glanced between his fingers. At least there was no sign of the card, which did indeed seem to have dissolved. He would have felt ridiculous if it had simply been floating in the hot coffee.

Klara was already becoming suspicious. "What are you doing?" she demanded.

Mendoza brought his gun round. "I told you..." he began.

Both of them rolled their eyes, staggered briefly, then collapsed.

They hadn't even hit the floor before Alex was on his feet, running for the door. Only when he had pulled it open and stepped outside did he draw a breath. Looking round, he saw the two bodies lying sideways, unconscious. Good old Smithers! Alex was glad to have him back.

But what next? Alex had no doubt that Klara Zak and Joe Mendoza weren't the only ones protecting Wilbur White. They wouldn't have sent him into the villa if they weren't confident he was safe and, quite apart from their own people, the villa was patrolled by armed men with dogs. The alarms would go off the moment he stepped on the lawn. The gates were closed and guarded. He couldn't climb the wall.

There was only one thing he could do. He needed back-up and that meant finding the radio transmitter that Ben Daniels had given him. There was only one place it could be. It must have fallen out on the terrace where he had met Wilbur White. It could have happened when Klara Zak and her partner grabbed him from behind.

Alex moved quickly. He didn't know how long Zak and Mendoza would remain unconscious and he was horribly aware that, at the Castel Saint-Martin, a single footstep could give him away. He just had to hope the transmitter would be lying somewhere he could see it.

He ran back through the trees, once again crossing the centre of the lawn. This time, the effect was instant. The whole villa must have been on a state of high alert because instead of a secret signal, huge floodlights burst into life, an alarm bell began to sound and, from somewhere round the back of the villa, a ferocious howling cut through the night air. Alex ignored it all. He was heading back to the terrace as fast as his legs would carry him. There was nobody in front of him. He had perhaps thirty seconds to act.

Where was the transmitter?

Alex tried to think. When was the last time he'd had it in his hand? He remembered slipping it into his trouser pocket, but he hadn't touched it since then. It could easily have dropped out when he took off the dry suit next to the swimming pool. Still running, he scanned the grass in front of him, hoping against hope that it would reveal itself. He became aware of figures moving through the brilliant light, heading in his direction. He heard a vicious snarling and saw two dogs leaping over the grass like monsters out of a burglar's nightmare. A line of armed men, dark shadows stretched out behind them. They had seen him of course. In the artificial daylight created by the floodlights it would have been impossible to miss him.

Where was it?

He reached the terrace and stared at the empty paving stones. It wasn't there and Alex was about to give up when, quite by chance, his eye fell on a small rectangle of grey plastic, lying to one side, partly concealed by a plant. The dogs were one leap away. Alex dived forward, snatched the transmitter, pressed the single button and held it to his lips.

"Ben!" he shouted. "This is Mayday! Mayday. I'm in big trouble. Get me out of here!"

Still clasping the transmitter, he turned round and stared into the white light.

Two Alsatian dogs, their eyes blazing, had come to a halt in front of him, snapping and growling, the fur around their necks sticking out as if it had been electrified. They were awaiting the final instructions from the men who had caught up with them ... armed security guards. If Alex so much as moved, they would tear him apart.

"Where are Joe and Klara?" one of the guards demanded.

"He's killed them!" another said.

"Goddamn punk!"

Alex was quite certain he was finished. It just needed someone to either pull the trigger or give the command to the dogs. He opened his mouth to speak, but the words wouldn't come. What could he possibly say that would persuade them he was on their side?

Then he heard the revving of an engine. The guards heard it too and turned, wondering what was happening. A large vehicle was rapidly approaching the property and although it was getting ever closer to the gates, it wasn't slowing down. The next moment there was an explosion of wood and metal, and the gates seemed to blow themselves off their hinges. A shaft of light blazed out of the darkness and Alex realized that someone had driven the huge truck that had brought Big Bessie to the Mont Boron car park straight through the gates without bothering to open them first. As everyone stared, frozen in their places, the truck roared along the drive and then onto the lawn, the wheels tearing up great chunks of grass. Finally, it slewed to a halt just a few metres away.

The doors flew open and Ben Daniels leaped out, an automatic pistol in his hand. Smithers was right behind him. Two more men appeared around the side.

"Nobody move!" Ben shouted. He repeated the words in French. *"Ne bougez pas!"*

Smithers was holding up an umbrella. "I should warn you that this contains an Active Denial System," he called out. "It's an extremely efficient high-energy weapon and if anyone takes so much as one step towards Alex, it will send out a microwave ray that will fry them faster than a Turkey Twizzler, so I really do suggest you do as my friend says."

Alex got unsteadily to his feet. The Alsatians slunk away as if they had somehow guessed that they were no longer needed.

"Alex, are you OK?" Ben moved between Alex and the guards who were facing him.

"Yeah. I'm fine."

"Where's Wilbur White?"

"I think he's gone to bed."

There was a movement and Klara Zak and Joe Mendoza appeared, arm in arm, supporting each other. They were walking with difficulty and didn't look well. "What's happening here?" Zak demanded.

"Klara Zak!" It was Smithers who had spoken. He

lowered his umbrella. "What on earth are you doing here?"

"Smithers!"

"You know each other?" Alex could hardly believe what he was seeing.

"It's been a while since we met," Smithers replied. "But you could say we're friends."

"Well, your friends were threatening to pull my toenails out!" Alex exclaimed. "Who is she?"

"The last time I saw her, she was a special agent working with the Covert Action Division of the CIA," Smithers replied.

"I still am!" Zak said. "For heaven's sake, what are you doing here, Smithers? Are you telling me this kid really works for you?"

Smithers looked around him at the smashed gates, the parked truck, the dogs, the men with guns, the garden and the villa all bathed in white light.

He smiled. "Why don't we all go inside and have a nice cup of tea?"

THE TIGER

They met inside the villa, sitting round a long marble table in the main kitchen. Joe Mendoza had indeed made tea, but the atmosphere in the room was far from friendly. In fact, the two CIA agents hadn't spoken a word to Alex since Smithers and Ben Daniels had come smashing through the gates. It was always possible that they felt guilty about the way they had treated him, but Alex suspected it was more to do with the fact that they had allowed themselves to be fooled. They were both looking unwell – much to the amusement of Derek Smithers.

"I see you used my business card!" he exclaimed.

"What was in it?" Alex asked.

"Oh – it was quite simple really. It isn't made of paper. It's a compound of citric acid and baking soda. The same as a dissolvable aspirin. Put it in hot water and it releases carbon dioxide."

"But how did that knock them out?"

"The ink on the card was a chemical derived from etorphine. Etorphine is a drug used by vets to knock out large animals and the carbon dioxide carried it into the air. It's very fast-acting." He beamed. "Don't worry, Klara, old thing! You'll be fine in the morning."

"You deserved it for what you were going to do to Alex," Ben growled.

"All right. I'm sorry." Klara looked across the table at

Alex. Mendoza sat down next to her. "We were sent to the Castel Saint-Martin because we believed that Nightshade might have Wilbur White as their next target," she said. "We know they use teenage killers ... and then Alex showed up, appearing out of nowhere and sneaking around in the dark. What were we meant to think?"

"Why would Mr White be a target?" Ben asked. "What has he got to do with Real Time?"

Klara shook her head apologetically. "We can't tell you that," she said.

"Why not?"

"Because we've got a new boss."

"Dwain Garfield." Smithers turned to Ben. "As hard as nails. He lost both his legs in Afghanistan, but he didn't go to the doctor. He bandaged the wounds and took care of himself and he didn't even mention what had happened. He doesn't trust anyone. When he took over at the CIA, he made it clear that there was only one way to do things and that was his way. He wants to make American security great again and he won't work with other intelligence agencies. He won't even take calls from the US president!"

"That's about it," Klara agreed. "Dwain would fire us both if he knew we were talking to you."

There was a long silence. Then Ben Daniels spoke. "Why does he have to find out?" He sighed. "Look, we're all on the same side here. We all want to find Nightshade. And after what you nearly did to Alex, I'd say you owe us."

"Perhaps an exchange of information?" Smithers suggested.

"Do you have any information?" Mendoza asked suspiciously.

"We might..."

Ben nodded. "Why don't you let me start?" He looked at Klara. "We know that Wilbur White hired a private investigator called Steven Chan to investigate a company called Real Time. Chan was killed in New York by two agents working for Nightshade."

"I knew Steve," Klara said. "He spent three years with the CIA and we worked together in Santa Barbara."

"I'm sorry to hear that. But that's not the reason we're here. To be honest, we have no interest in Real Time."

He paused.

"Six months ago, Nightshade launched an attack on London and just last week they kidnapped Alex and nearly killed his best friend. We want to find them and finish them for good. We came to the Castel Saint-Martin because we thought Mr White might be able to give us information. We couldn't get through to him, so we sent Alex in to try to persuade him. We didn't know the CIA were here and we don't want to get in your way. Help us if you can and you won't see us again."

It took Klara a few moments to come to a decision.

"All right. I'll tell you as much as I can. I guess I owe it to you after what happened – and I'm really sorry about that." She smiled at Alex. "We weren't really going to hurt you," she said. "We were just saying all that stuff to make you scared."

"Of course." Alex wasn't sure if he believed her or not, but this wasn't the time to argue.

"If Garfield hears I've spoken to you, I'm toast. OK?"

"Just tell us what we need to know," Ben said.

"OK." She drew a breath. "You may not be interested in them, but we need to start with Real Time because that's what this is really all about.

"Real Time is a major American success story. It's one of the most powerful companies in the world. Five years from now it could be bigger than Microsoft and Apple combined. They already employ a thousand programmers and technicians and they're investing ten billion dollars a year, developing technology that could change the lives of everyone on the planet. You probably know them for their games, but that's just the tip of the iceberg.

"The Pentagon has already ordered twelve thousand Real Time headsets for soldiers in the field. Our military personnel are able to look at maps, enemy positions, approaching aircraft, even weather conditions, at the same time as they're aiming their weapons. In hospitals, American doctors don't just see their patients any more. They see *inside* them. Broken bones, cancers, blood disorders. You just slip on the Real Time goggles and there they are – in front of your eyes. And American police are using Real Time products connected to facial-recognition software and artificial intelligence, which allow them to know everything about everyone they see in the street. Can you imagine that? They can spot the criminals before the crimes are committed!

"The CEO of Real Time, Rudolf Klein, is fifty-three, which is a lot older than most people in the industry, but he was the first man to see and exploit the full potential of augmented reality. There's absolutely no question that he's a genius. Last year, he was awarded the Presidential Medal of Freedom in recognition of his contribution to business. He's been Person of the Year in *Time* magazine for two years running. He's given millions of dollars to charity. He's a very private person, unmarried, with no family that we know of. But nobody has a bad word to say about him. He was born in Germany, by the way, and came to America when he was five. But he's still an all-American hero.

"At least, that's what we always thought...

"Steven Chan was investigating Real Time and Steven Chan was murdered. That's what's at the heart of all this. What had he found out? What did he know? Is Rudolf Klein developing some sort of new technology we haven't heard about? Has he done a deal with the Russians or the Chinese? Is he planning something that makes him our enemy? The only reason the CIA is interested in Nightshade is because they may provide us with the answer to those questions."

"So what are you doing here?" Ben asked.

"We were sent to protect Wilbur White. If Nightshade killed Steven Chan, there's a good chance they'll come after Mr White too. Our orders are to keep him safe – but at the same time, if we can get our hands on one of their agents ..."

"... you can find out why Nightshade is working with Real Time and why Steven Chan had to die." Smithers completed the sentence for her.

It was all beginning to make sense. Alex understood now why he had been taken prisoner and why the two CIA agents were so keen to make him talk.

"I've got just one more question," Ben said. "Why did Wilbur White hire Steven Chan in the first place? Why was he investigating Real Time?"

"Because Real Time killed my son."

The voice came from the doorway. Everyone looked round to see Wilbur White standing there, still wearing his velvet jacket and holding the cigar, which had now gone out. The art dealer had crept in unseen, drawn to the sound of voices that he must have heard from upstairs. Now, as everyone got to their feet, he came slowly into the room, moving like an old man. He lowered himself into a seat opposite Alex and examined him, his grey eyes staring out behind the thick lenses of his spectacles. "You're the boy from the terrace," he rasped.

"Yes, sir," Alex said.

"You wanted to ask me about my son."

"That's right." Alex sat back down. "I never got the chance."

Everyone else took their places.

"It turns out that Alex is working with the secret service in Britain," Klara explained. "They want to know why you hired Steven Chan."

"Then why don't you tell them?" White's voice rattled in his throat. He rested a hand on the table. "Damn CIA! You people don't know what you're doing. All right! I'll tell them! They deliberately killed Colin, my only son. The police don't believe it. The CIA won't listen to me. But I know the truth and I'm going to prove it, no matter how long it takes."

He reached out with a trembling hand and Joe Mendoza passed him a glass of water. He drank then set it down.

"Colin was a bright, happy kid. He was doing fine at high school. Good grades. His teachers had nothing but praise for him. He had plenty of friends. And then he started playing these goddamn games. I don't know when it started. Every kid these days is stuck in their laptop or their cell phone, eyes glued to the screen. Nothing you can do about it. Nobody reads any more.

"His mother and me, we didn't notice he was drifting away from us. He had nothing to say at the dinner table. He lost his appetite. He fell behind with his schoolwork. Maybe it was our fault for not noticing earlier but it was as if the life was being sucked out of him. And always it was games ... games! *Gotham Knights. Total War.* But the one that really hooked him – the one that devoured him – was created by Real Time."

"*Eden Fall,*" Alex said.

"*Eden Fall.* Colin wore these goggles that connected him to a different world. Every minute he had free, he went out looking for all these weird creatures, trying to find secret doors and stairways. The company said the game was tested. It didn't take you anywhere you weren't allowed. Places that weren't safe: railroad tracks, rivers ... that sort of thing. They were all off-limits. That was what they said, but it was all lies. Colin had played hooky the day he died and why do you think he broke into that building in Mission Bay? Why would he do a thing like that? Because he was playing the game. That's why. The game led him up to the roof and to his death.

"Of course Real Time denied liability. They investigated the software and they were able to prove, one hundred per cent, that there was no reason the game would have taken my boy anywhere near the building where he died. The police believed them. They said Colin might have broken in for a dare. I even got a letter from Mr Rudolf Klein. *We send you every sympathy for your untimely loss*. It was all lies and cover-up. Real Time killed Colin as sure as if they'd put a bullet in his head, and maybe he won't be the last. That game needs to come off the market and Real Time needs to be shut down."

Wilbur White had almost finished speaking. His whole body was shaking and he was breathing hard.

"I am never going to let up," he announced. "They killed Steven Chan. That's fine. I'm a wealthy man. I can hire another fifty private detectives. I'm gonna find out the truth about Rudolf Klein and his company if it takes me the rest of my life. I've told them! I won't rest until I've discovered the truth."

He fell silent. Alex couldn't help feeling sorry for him. He had lost his parents before he was old enough to know them properly but it was even worse the other way round. For a father to lose a son like this must have been unbearable.

The CIA agents were looking uncomfortable too.

"I think we're done here," Klara muttered.

"You go back up to bed, Mr White," Joe Mendoza said. "We'll leave agents down here in the kitchen and the hallway. The main gates need repairing, but we'll have a car out there all night and we'll get them fixed tomorrow, first thing."

"You think they're going to come after me? Let them try! I'm not scared of them. I'm not scared of anybody."

Wilbur White got up and stumbled out of the room. As soon as he had gone, Klara led the others back out into the garden. The truck with the cannon had already gone and, just as Mendoza had promised, there was a car parked in the space between the shattered gates.

"What are you two planning to do next?" Klara asked.

"You want to tell your new boss?" Ben Daniels sounded bleak. "Maybe we shouldn't tell you."

"I thought you said we were on the same side."

"Yeah, but we do things different ways." Ben was still angry that Alex had been taken prisoner and threatened.

"We won't talk to Garfield. We don't want to get in your way..."

Alex wasn't sure when he first heard the helicopter. Later on, he would think that the sound of the rotors must have been audible even before they left the villa and began to walk towards the broken gates. At first, they might not have noticed it. After all, it wasn't so unusual in this part of the South of France, where millionaires were constantly flying in and out of their homes. But as they left the Castel Saint-Martin behind them, he was suddenly aware that the noise had risen in intensity and with every moment it was getting closer.

Smithers was the first to react. "That's a Eurocopter Tiger," he said. "The EC665 battlefield helicopter. Manufactured in France."

Somehow Alex wasn't surprised that Smithers could identify the make of a helicopter simply from its sound. Before he could say anything, he felt the wind stirring up around him, the dust whipping into his eyes. The engine had become a deafening roar and suddenly there was a blaze of light, slicing through the trees, turning the branches into nightmarish skeleton bones. Even as he watched, the huge black bulk of the machine rose up in front of them, the glass cockpit with its tandem seats illuminated by a soft green glow. Alex could just make out the dark shape of the pilot in the front seat, with a gunner sitting above and behind. He already knew that the helicopter had nothing to do with the CIA or with the French air force. There could only be one reason why it was here.

"Get down!" Ben Daniels shouted, the words torn out of his mouth and sent spinning into the night.

Nobody needed to be told twice. Alex, Smithers and the two CIA agents threw themselves onto the grass as the helicopter fired four missiles, two from each side of the fuselage. Even as he hit the ground, Alex saw the brilliant sparks and the burst of orange light as they flashed past, far too close to their heads. He twisted round as the villa exploded, the entire top floor disappearing in a massive ball of flame.

Alex knew that the gunner had been aiming at Wilbur White's bedroom, but the damage was huge and horrific. Flames travelled sideways in two directions, blowing out the windows and smashing the brickwork throughout the villa. Alex felt the intense heat on his arms and the back of his neck. Debris, much of it on fire, showered down. If they hadn't already been a good distance from the building, close to the gates, they would quite probably have been killed. As it was, something about the size and weight of a cannonball slammed into the lawn just a metre from where Alex was lying. For a horrible moment, he thought it was somebody's head. And in a way, it was. A sculpture had been blown out of the top floor, part of Wilbur White's art collection. It lay on its side in the grass, the flames reflecting in its bronze cheeks.

The Tiger had done what it had been designed for. It rotated as if on an invisible spike and now Alex saw the crimson glow blasting out of its Rolls-Royce turboshaft engines. He was still being battered by the backdraught and there was no way he could get to his feet. Even when the helicopter flew away, rising diagonally over the treetops, he stayed where he was, his ears ringing, his whole body feeling battered.

"Alex!" Ben Daniels, lying a few paces away, reached out to him.

"I'm OK! I'm not hurt!"

Alex's throat was dry and there was a foul taste in his mouth. He propped himself up and examined what was left of the villa, the flames still roaring, smoke pouring out of the smashed windows. When he had first been shown pictures of the Castel Saint-Martin, it had looked like something out of a fairy tale. Now it had become a horror story. So Nightshade had decided to attack after all. One thing was certain. It would be a miracle if anybody in the building had survived.

Klara Zak and Joe Mendoza were covered in dust. They both looked beaten down; not just by the violence of what had just happened, but by the knowledge that they had failed.

"We'd better see if anyone else is hurt. We had other people inside. They..." Klara didn't finish the sentence.

She and Mendoza began to move towards the ruined villa, leaving Alex and Ben Daniels behind.

"What now?" Alex asked.

Ben took one last look at the desolation. "You need to get some sleep," he said. His forehead was streaked with dirt. He wiped it away with the back of his hand. "Tomorrow we leave for San Francisco."

MISSION BAY

After fourteen hours in the air, Alex was feeling tired, grubby and a very long way from home. Because of the nine-hour time difference, he had flown through a day that had stretched on and on, so that although the plane had left Nice at seven in the morning, they'd still managed to arrive in San Francisco in time for lunch.

Not that a restaurant stop was part of the plan. Ben Daniels was in a hurry to find the answers to his questions and they drove out of San Francisco International Airport in a rental car – a silver Chevrolet – heading straight for Mission Bay and the building where Colin White had died. Wilbur White had hired a private detective to find out what had happened to his son. As a result, he had been killed in a highly organized – and expensive – helicopter strike. A CIA agent had also died and several more had been injured. Nightshade had to be behind the attack and Ben was now certain that Colin's death was the key to everything that was happening.

They picked up the 101 freeway outside the airport and headed north. For a while, the eight-lane motorway led them through an uninteresting landscape of old houses and industrial buildings separated by patches of wasteland, with no sign of the city itself. Then they came to the ocean's edge and Alex saw the huge sky and seemingly endless stretch of water that briefly reminded him of the happy times he'd spent in California. He had actually lived here for a few months, staying with one of his closest friends – Sabina Pleasure – and her family. He had already called them and arranged to see them later that day.

The road took them inland and the sea disappeared, replaced by a suburban sprawl, until suddenly, ahead of them, a wall of skyscrapers sprang up and, seeing them, Alex felt a surge of excitement. The Transamerica Pyramid, the Millennium Tower, the Avery... They stretched across the horizon, glinting in the sun. For Alex, San Francisco had always been one of the most beautiful cities in the world, glittering and modern, yet full of old-world charm. They followed a ramp down into the city itself and made their way through a series of intersections. The sky was a perfect blue, but this was the first week of April and the people they saw on the pavements were still wearing light jackets or jerseys.

"Mission Bay is in front of us," Ben explained. "It used to be an industrial zone, but it's being redeveloped. That's why there are so many new buildings going up."

"So what was Colin White doing there?"

"That's a good question, Alex. Maybe he was looking for hedgehogs and demons."

They came to a harbour. The water was concealed behind a line of low-rise buildings, but Alex could see the masts of sailing boats on the other side and there were occasional glimpses of blue in the gaps. Ben pulled into a parking space opposite a huge sports arena, advertising itself as the home of the Golden State Warriors. They were a basketball team. Sabina's father had often watched them on TV and Alex had been with him when they beat the Boston Celtics in the finals. That could have been a century ago, another life. Alex opened the car door and got out.

"It's just down there," Ben said.

They walked back the way they'd come, following the edge of the sea, where dozens of cranes were waiting for the cargo ships that would moor here. A few seagulls wheeled overhead. It was early afternoon and there was a sense of emptiness about the area. Cars were parked all the way along the main boulevard and there were a few more passing by – but there was no sign of any pedestrians, no shops, no activity of any sort. It was as if the entire area was somewhere to pass through rather than visit. Maybe it would be busier first thing in the morning or at night, especially when there was a game on. Right now, it was a ghost town.

They came to a junction – and there it was in front of them. Alex took a breath. He knew he was jet-lagged, but there was still a sense of unreality about everything he was seeing: the silent sports arena, the docks, the empty sky ... and now this.

The building was unfinished. One day it would be an office, a block of flats or a hotel, but for now it was like an enormous 3D game of noughts and crosses: white concrete lines crossing each other horizontally and vertically with shadowy rectangles in between. There were no windows, no lights or fittings, just this bleached-out skeleton, sitting on its own, surrounded by barely used expressways.

Alex wondered if they had shut down construction

following Colin's death. There was no sign of any workers on the site. Nor did there seem to be any security. A makeshift fence surrounded the new building, but it was hanging loose, open at the front. Alex could see rubble, bits of scaffolding, bags of cement – but even after the recent death of a teenage boy, there was nothing to stop anyone walking in.

"What do you think?" he asked.

"I want to go up to the roof," Ben said.

Alex nodded. He could understand the need to follow in Colin White's footsteps, to examine the place where he had died, but he didn't know what Ben hoped to find. Wilbur White had been certain that his son was playing the game – *Eden Fall* – and that was what had brought him here. He had climbed up to the top floor and he had fallen. What was there to see?

They crossed the road and entered the building, leaving the sunlight behind. The interior was damp and neglected. It didn't feel as if any construction had happened for some time. Could it be that the workers had refused to come back after what had happened? Alex followed Ben over the uneven ground, stepping round oil drums, wheelbarrows, metal girders, more bags of cement. Wires hung down from the ceiling but there was no illumination, and the further they went, the darker it became. Ben reached into his pocket and took out a miniature torch. A narrow strip of light leaped ahead of them, penetrating the dust and the gloom and showing a concrete flight of stairs leading up. The stairs had no safety rail. They were half finished, going nowhere.

"Who owns this place?" Alex asked. He was almost whispering, although he didn't feel he was in any danger.

"Developers," Ben said. "They're turning it into an apartment block. Retail on the ground floor."

"So where is everyone?"

"Good question. Maybe they're having a long lunch."

They kept climbing. The ceilings were lower on the upper floors, but otherwise every level was the same, seemingly abandoned by any builders or security staff. Looking behind him, Alex could see the marina on the other side of the boulevard with the sea beyond. If the building was ever finished, the residents would have a great view. Ben was quickening his pace, anxious to get to the top, and Alex followed. Finally, after nine flights, they emerged into the sunlight. This was where Colin had come. The steps they had just taken had been his last.

"So, this game ... *Eden Fall*." Ben looked around him. The roof was a flat area with nothing very much to see. "How would it have worked exactly?"

"Well, if he was playing the game, Colin would have been wearing his goggles and he'd have seen one of these creatures on the roof, where we are now. He'd have had to approach it if he wanted to talk to it. So he'd have come into the building and climbed up, just like we did."

"And what happened then? Did it push him off?"

"It couldn't do that."

"So he just slipped?"

Alex walked to the edge and glanced down into the street, at the grey concrete and the parked cars, which looked very small from this height. It was a long way to fall. There was no chance Colin could have survived. Suddenly, Alex felt sick. Still worn out from the long flight, he wanted to be anywhere but here.

"Hold it! Don't move!"

The voice came from behind him. Alex turned to see a woman standing with both hands gripping a gun, high up in front of her face. She was African American, dressed in a dark blue uniform: short-sleeved shirt, trousers and baseball cap. There was a radio clipped to her belt.

"Who are you and what are you doing here?" she demanded.

So the building was being protected after all. The woman had her name – KATE MOSES – on a badge pinned to her chest and when she half-turned to check on Ben, Alex glimpsed the single word SECURITY stitched across the back of her shirt. She was in her late thirties. She looked nervous.

"It's all right, Kate," Ben said. "We're with the security services, investigating the death of Colin White."

"Nobody told me nothing about no security services coming today." She examined Ben suspiciously. "You're not even American. What's that accent of yours?"

"I'm from London."

"You've come all the way from London? That doesn't make any sense at all." She turned to Alex, the gun swivelling between the two of them. "And who's he? You're not telling me he's with the security services, are you? He's just a kid! He should be at school."

Her words reminded Alex of Brookland. How many days had he been away? Kate Moses knew nothing about him, but she was right. He wanted to get back before the end of the holiday.

"I sort of knew Colin," he said. He wasn't exactly lying. He did feel a strange closeness to the boy who had died. "We're trying to find out what happened."

"The police have already been here. You should talk to them."

"Where is everyone?" Ben asked.

"The company building this place – they went bust. Now there are lawyers arguing over who gets to take it over. I don't know! I'm just paid to keep people out." She waved the gun, although it seemed to Alex that she was a little calmer. "And that includes you."

"We won't stay here long," Ben assured her. "Can you just show us exactly where Colin fell?"

The security guard thought for a moment, then lowered her gun. "You're on the wrong side," she said. "It was at the back."

Alex and Ben walked across the roof, away from the sea. Kate followed them. There was another new-build right in front of them, only a few metres away, with a narrow gap between. Looking down, Alex saw an alleyway with a row of dustbins. It wasn't wide enough to park a car.

"He didn't fall. He just walked right off," Kate said.

"How do you know?" Ben asked.

"One of the builders saw him. He just stepped off the edge, and that was that." She shook her head. "Poor kid. I have a daughter the same age. It doesn't bear thinking about."

Meanwhile, Alex was thinking. The death of Colin White

was reminding him of something that was in some way connected to him. The trouble was, he was still exhausted after the flight. He couldn't remember what it was.

"Do you know if he was wearing special glasses?" Ben asked.

"Oh yes. We had a private detective come up here and he asked me the same thing. He was wearing them, all right. It seems he was playing some sort of game up here on the roof and he didn't look where he was going. What a way to end your life! Doesn't that just make you sad?"

But Ben had picked up on the first thing she had said. "You met Steven Chan?" he asked.

"That's right. That was his name. He was investigating what had happened. Just like you."

Ben and Alex exchanged a quick glance. It seemed that the security guard hadn't heard that Steven Chan was also dead and they weren't going to tell her. The news would only spook her.

"Did he tell you anything about his investigation. Had he found anything out?"

"No. He was a nice man, though. Very friendly. We chatted quite a bit while he took a few photographs. He asked me about the building. And then he left." She paused. "There was one funny thing, though."

"What was that?" Ben asked.

"Well, I mentioned that my daughter, Martha, loved playing that game, *Eden Fall*. The same as Colin. There are times I can't get her off her screen. She'd never go breaking into other people's property though."

"So what did he say?"

"Well, just before he left, he took hold of my arm and he came up to me real close. 'Don't let Martha play *Eden Fall*,' he said. 'They're introducing new characters … in April. The whole world's going to be playing. But you keep her away.' For a moment, I thought he was joking with me. But he was deadly serious."

"Did you ask him what he meant?" Ben asked.

"Well, I assumed he was thinking about what had happened here. But, like I said, my girl wouldn't go anywhere she wasn't allowed – she's not like that. So I just thanked Mr Chan and sent him on his way." She frowned. "Actually, I did have a word with Martha. There were plenty of other games she could play, so I told her to stay off *Eden Fall* for a while. And that's what she's done."

Alex took one last look at the edge of the building. Something was screaming at him inside his head, trying to get his attention. He knew he had the answer. There was something here that he had seen before. No. Not here…

Suddenly it hit him.

Point Blanc. That was it!

The mission that had led Alex to the mysterious Point Blanc Academy high up in the French Alps had begun with the murder of a billionaire in New York. Michael J. Roscoe had stepped into a lift in his penthouse office – except that the lift hadn't been there. It had been a projection, a hologram, and Roscoe had fallen sixty floors to his death.

"Ben…" he said.

"What?" Ben turned to him.

"I think I know what happened here. Let's go back down."

Ben Daniels shook hands with the security guard and

he and Alex made their way back down the concrete steps. As they went, Alex explained what he had worked out.

"You're saying that Colin White walked across a bridge that didn't exist?" Ben didn't sound convinced.

"With Michael Roscoe, it was a hologram. He thought he was stepping into a lift, but it wasn't there and he died. With Colin, it could have been the same. There was another building opposite. It would have been a crazy thing to do, but if Colin really wanted to explore the next roof, he could have jumped across. He didn't do that. The builder who saw him said he took a step. It was as if he thought there was something under his foot."

"Are you saying there's some sort of glitch in the game? That it shows things that aren't there?"

"Maybe it's not a glitch. Maybe it's deliberate."

"But that doesn't make any sense, Alex. You're saying that Colin White was killed deliberately. Why would anyone want to do that?"

"Wilbur White believed his son was murdered. He must have known it wasn't an accident."

Ben took a breath. "Well, one thing's for sure. We're going to have to take a closer look at Real Time."

They had reached the ground floor and emerged into the sunlight. Ben Daniels had been completely relaxed, but Alex saw the moment when he changed, his dark eyes narrowing, his whole body tense. He looked at the street and saw a black vehicle parked in front of them, an SUV with a sliding door that allowed wheelchair access. Four men in dark suits were facing them, one of them indeed in a wheelchair. Alex knew at once who he was looking at. This must be Dwain Garfield, the new chief of the CIA – Covert Action. How had he found them and what was he doing here?

He didn't look pleased to see them.

"Don't tell them anything," Ben muttered. He began to walk forward.

"I wasn't planning to," Alex said, and followed.

They stopped in front of the group of CIA agents.

"You must be Ben Daniels," Garfield growled. He spoke as if he had broken glass in his throat. "And you're Alex Rider? I've heard a lot about you, although I never expected we'd meet."

"My pleasure," Alex said.

"Not mine. What do you think you're doing here in San Francisco?"

"We're visiting friends," Ben said.

"Let me tell you something, son. You don't have friends here. Only enemies. And I'm one of them."

Dwain Garfield looked like a man in pain. His whole body was twisted, slumped in the wheelchair as if it had been forced into it. He had steel-grey hair, a long neck and thin glasses that sat awkwardly over his eyes. It was hard to tell his age. With his grey skin and stooping shoulders, he could have been anything from forty to sixty. His hands were resting on his knees. He was wearing black leather gloves.

"How did you know we were here?" Ben asked.

"I know everything that happens in this city," Garfield replied. "I heard you were on the flight from France and I had you followed from the airport. I almost had you picked up at passport control, but I wanted to see where you were going. I guessed right. I've spoken to Klara Zak. She told me you were at the Castel Saint-Martin. It seems to me that you're sticking your nose in business that has nothing to do with you."

"I'd have thought finding Nightshade would matter to all of us," Ben said.

"Nightshade are a bunch of terrorists who need to be wiped off the face of the Earth," Garfield agreed. "And if I ever come across them, I'm going to do just that. But you've got no evidence that they're here in America, and right now, Mr Daniels, you're just making things worse."

Ben raised an eyebrow. "How do you work that one out, Mr Garfield?"

"I've spoken to Klara Zak and Joe Mendoza in Nice, and from what I understand, the two of you bust in there and that distracted them. While they were dealing with you, Nightshade was able to launch a helicopter attack, and that's the reason Wilbur White was killed. I also lost one agent and have two more in hospital – all thanks to you!"

"That's not true!" Alex couldn't stop himself. It was a completely fake version of what had happened at the Castel Saint-Martin.

Garfield ignored him. "I think the two of you should get on the next plane and head back to England," he suggested. "You understand what I'm saying? I want you out of here!"

"Is that an order?" Ben asked.

"It's a polite suggestion. But if you're still here by the weekend, you may find out what I'm like when I'm not being polite." He reached down with both hands and wheeled himself round. "Leave Nightshade to us!" he called out with his back to them.

The other CIA agents closed in, to help their boss back into the SUV. Alex and Ben waited until the doors had closed and they had driven off.

"What's his problem?" Alex asked.

Ben watched the two vehicles disappear around the corner. "We are," he said.

INSIDE INFORMATION

Later that afternoon, Ben dropped Alex off in Presidio Heights, one of the most attractive parts of San Francisco. It was a proper neighbourhood, full of old-fashioned houses, tree-lined streets and a sense that everything was right with the world. The Presidio itself was a huge park with woodland so thick you could easily get lost in it. It was located on a hillside with superb views of the Golden Gate Bridge, San Francisco Bay and the ocean itself. This was where Sabina lived with her parents, Edward and Liz. They had been in America for almost two years now, renting a slightly chaotic house near the park. Edward was still working as a journalist and had become a bestselling author. Liz had also written a book about the world of fashion and some of its most famous designers. Apart from Jack, they were the closest thing Alex had to a family. He wondered what it would be like seeing them again.

He had stayed with Sabina and her parents for a couple of months after his encounter with Scorpia in Egypt, when he had been captured and taken to Siwa, in the Western Desert of Egypt. He had been tricked into believing that Jack Starbright had been killed and he still didn't know what would have happened if Edward and Liz Pleasure hadn't taken him into their home. They had looked after him, showing him nothing but kindness, while he recovered and tried to adapt to life in California.

And how had he repaid them? Alex still felt guilty. He had slipped away without warning them, returning to Egypt, following a clue that told him that Jack might – just possibly – be alive.

"I'll see you soon," Ben said, as the two of them sat in the Chevrolet with the engine turning over.

"What are you going to do?"

"Dig a little more into Real Time. It might be interesting to find out if there are any other kids who have died playing *Eden Fall*."

"You think they're covering it up?"

"Why do you think the CIA want us out of town? You heard what Klara Zak told us. Real Time is massive! How do you think we'd feel if the Americans came to London to investigate the royal family? It's the same thing." Ben smiled. "Anyway, you deserve a rest. Have a nice time with your girlfriend."

"She's not my girlfriend."

"Why are you blushing?"

Alex got out of the car, slamming the door behind him. He knew that Ben was teasing him, but he wasn't quite sure how to think of Sabina. When he had been staying with the family, they had been a sort of brother and sister. Before that they had been friends. Now they were both sixteen. They'd texted a few times, but they hadn't spoken for months. So what exactly was their relationship? Was Sabina still going out with the boy she'd met at the Elmer E. Robinson High School where she was studying? Alex didn't know the answers to these questions and he wasn't entirely sure he wanted to find out.

He waited until Ben had driven off, then crossed the road and rang the doorbell. Almost at once, the door was opened by Liz Pleasure, wearing a striped apron and holding a wooden spoon in one hand, a huge smile on her face. Rocky, the family's Labrador, was right behind her, barking in excitement.

"Alex! I can't believe it's you. Look at you! You're so much taller and bigger."

She threw her arms around him and held him close.

"It's so wonderful to have you back again. Come in! Come in! Edward is here. Sabina's on her way back from art class."

"Alex!" Edward Pleasure had appeared in the corridor. He had never completely recovered from the bomb blast that had nearly killed him two years ago in the South of France. He walked slowly, leaning against the walking stick with the duck's head handle that he always carried, and there was more grey in his beard. But he was as happy as Liz to see Alex, reaching out to embrace him. "Welcome back to San Francisco," he said. "Sabina tells me this isn't a vacation..."

Alex noted the use of the Americanism. "Vacation" not "holiday". "Not exactly," he admitted.

"I was hoping you'd have left all that behind you."

"Don't go on at him!" Liz scolded. "He's only just arrived – and we don't want him vanishing on us a second time. Come into the kitchen, Alex. I've got cake and lemonade. Sabina will be here any minute."

In fact, Alex had barely sat down at the pine table in the cheerful, cluttered room before the front door opened again and suddenly Sabina was there, standing in the doorway, a little hesitant. For his part, Alex felt a rush of emotions. It was incredible how much Sabina had changed since he had last seen her. The very dark hair, the bright blue eyes and the freckles were the same, but nothing else was. She seemed to have aged five years and he had to remind himself that she was only a few months older than him. He got up and went over to her, aware that her parents were watching them both.

"You look great," he said.

"You too."

"It's good to see you..."

"Yeah."

"Oh, sit down, both of you!" Liz exclaimed. "You come over next to me, Alex, and have some lemonade. I'd offer you a beer – I bet you're drinking by now – but this is America and we'd all get arrested. How was school, Sabina? Actually, don't tell me. We want to hear about Alex."

They gathered around the table and suddenly the moment of awkwardness was over, exactly as Sabina's mother had intended. There was so much news to exchange, so much to catch up on. Alex didn't like talking about himself. He had never chosen to be a spy, but he knew that was what he had become and he had a duty to stay silent. Worse than that, he had grown used to lying – to his teachers, to his friends, or to anyone who asked him about his latest injury or wondered where he had been for the past few weeks. It was part of his life.

But Sabina's family was different. They had looked after him when he was at his lowest ebb and he knew he had no secrets from them. So he answered all their questions, telling them about his first encounter with Nightshade and the attack on St Paul's Cathedral, then going on to describe everything that had happened to bring him back to San Francisco.

"You know what amazes me?" Liz said, when he had finished. "How do you ever get any schoolwork done?"

"Mum!" Sabina looked amazed. "Alex has been shot at, blown up, blackmailed and fired out of a circus cannon – and all the rest of it – and that's all you can think about?"

"School's important." Her mother sniffed.

Meanwhile, Edward Pleasure had been thinking.

"You believe that Colin White may have been killed deliberately," he said. "He went up to that building and crossed a bridge that was actually part of the computer game, and that was how he fell to his death."

"It could have been an accident," Alex said. "A fault in the game's software. But Steven Chan warned the security guard that something was wrong. He knew something bad was going to happen."

"The whole thing sounds daft to me," Liz muttered. "Have you ever played it, Sabina?"

"No," Sabina admitted. "But lots of people in my school do."

"Do you think it's possible that Rudolf Klein is up to something?" Edward asked. "Could he be another Damian Cray?"

It was true. The possibility had been running through Alex's head. Damian Cray had also been developing computer games. But the launch of his new product, an Aztec-themed shooter called *Feathered Serpent*, had actually concealed a much deadlier plan that might have led to a nuclear holocaust.

"I don't know," Alex said. "MI6 are looking into Real Time, but nobody seems to know anything very much about Rudolf Klein except that he's super rich and he's some sort of genius."

"Well, maybe I can help you." Edward took out his phone and scrolled through his contacts. "I've never met Rudolf Klein, but earlier this year I interviewed someone who used to work for him." He found the name he was looking for. "I've still got his number. Jon Lucas."

"Who's Jon Lucas?" Sabina asked.

"He's an interesting man. He's young – a health freak. Last year, he came ninth in the San Francisco Marathon, which is quite an achievement considering about six thousand people entered. A strict vegan. Real Time may be number one when it comes to augmented reality systems, but he runs a company that's not too far behind. He used to work for Real Time and he probably knows Klein better than anyone."

"Can we talk to him?" Alex asked.

"He has a ranch down in the Redwoods State Park, about fifty miles south of San Francisco. El Dorado is an extraordinary place in some of the most beautiful countryside I've ever seen. That's where I met him. But he also has offices here in the city. I can give him a call and ask if he'll see us. He's a nice enough guy and he liked the piece I wrote about him. Maybe he can give us some inside information."

"We need to see him tomorrow." Alex was thinking of Dwain Garfield. The head of the CIA had only given him until the weekend to get out of San Francisco.

"Don't you think that's rather short notice?"

"We may not have much time."

"I'll see what I can do."

"Why don't you and Sabina go and chat outside while I start cooking the supper." Liz Pleasure put an arm round Alex's shoulder. "And I hope you're going to stay with us tonight, Alex. I've made up your old room."

"Thanks. I'd like that," Alex said. Ben had booked twin rooms in a grim business hotel near the airport. "It's good to see you again," he added.

"It's wonderful to have you here. And this time, no slipping away, if you don't mind. At least not before you've eaten!"

There was a terrace with a swing chair at the front of the house and this was where Alex and Sabina sat as the sky grew dark over San Francisco Bay. Rocky, the dog, was stretched out on the wooden decking beside them. There were terracotta pots full of flowers all around them. Liz had planted lavender and California poppies, which had already blossomed, filling the air with their scent. A few cars drove past, commuters on their way home, but otherwise the street was quiet, the lights coming on in the windows of the neighbouring houses.

Neither of them had spoken for a while. Alex broke the silence. "Are you angry with me, Sab?" he asked.

"Why would you think that?"

"Because I walked out on you and your family."

"You thought Jack was alive and you found her. No, I'm not angry with you. I'm just sorry you're still mixed up with Mrs Jones and all the rest of it. Why can't you just be ordinary?"

"I didn't think I had any choice."

"You never do."

"I promise you, this is the last time."

"You've said that before."

"This time I mean it!"

There was another long pause.

"Are you still seeing Blake?" Alex asked.

"Blake?" It took Sabina a moment to realize who he meant. Blake was the senior basketball captain at Sabina's school. "I was never seeing him," she said. "Not in that way, anyway. He was just a friend." She turned to Alex. "There's something we haven't told you. We're coming back to London."

Alex couldn't stop himself smiling. "When?"

"Quite soon. Dad hasn't been very well recently and he's worried about health insurance. And Mum's missing her friends. We'll be home by July."

"That's great news. I mean, I'm sorry about your dad but..." Alex was already thinking ahead. "Will you go back to your old house?"

"Yes. We never sold it. I'm going to sixth form college in Wimbledon."

That was where Alex and Sabina had first met, at the famous tennis tournament. And it reminded Alex how much she had been a part of his life. Wimbledon was only a few miles from Chelsea, where he lived.

"Anyway, maybe it means we can see a bit more of each other," she said casually.

"I'd like that."

"Really?"

"Yeah. Really."

Sabina reached out and took his hand and the two of them sat peacefully, talking together, watching the moon rise.

The next morning, Edward Pleasure and Alex took a taxi to Jon Lucas's office in the Financial District of San Francisco. The Transamerica Pyramid was no longer the tallest skyscraper in the city but it was definitely the most famous, with its white quartz exterior and its extraordinary design, like something between an enormous church steeple and a space rocket. Vision-X, the company owned by Lucas, had offices on the top five floors.

Vision-X had its own dedicated lift that whisked them up to a spacious reception area, all white marble and glass, with such high ceilings that entire trees were able to sprout out of trenches that had been cut into the floor. There were half a dozen receptionists, male and female, talking into headsets. One of them greeted Edward and Alex, took their names and handed them passes which already contained their photographs. Looking at his own picture, Alex realized there must have been a camera in the lift. The passes had been prepared even as they were travelling up.

A smiling assistant, young and enthusiastic, appeared a moment later.

"Mr Lucas is waiting to see you," she said. "Please come this way. And would you like some water or coffee?"

"No, thank you," Edward said.

If they'd asked for a drink, Alex was fairly sure it would have been waiting for them when they arrived.

They went along a corridor, then up a private escalator which took them to the next floor. Alex glanced down. Astonishingly, the escalator was carpeted.

The assistant saw the look on his face. "Mr Lucas designed the escalator himself," she said. "It's the only one like it in the whole world. He wanted it to be more homely."

They came to a hallway with silver doors that slid open as they approached. The office on the other side had floor-to-ceiling windows looking out over the ocean and the bridge. A huge aquarium, full of exotic, multicoloured fish, stretched across an entire wall, almost a second ocean in itself. But the desk, the sofas and chairs arranged around a low coffee table, the bookshelves, the sideboard with a few glasses and bottles of water were all quite ordinary. At the end of the day, this was just an office.

The man who had been sitting behind the desk looked nothing like a business executive. He was young, bearded, quite scrawny with tangled hair and glasses, dressed in a UCLA hoodie and faded jeans. As he came round to greet them, Alex noticed he wasn't wearing any shoes or socks.

"Hey – Ed!" He was all smiles as he greeted Edward Pleasure, reaching out with both hands. "Good to see you again. That was a terrific piece you wrote about me in the *Chronicle*." He seemed to notice Alex for the first time and his smile broadened. "You didn't tell me you were going to bring your son."

"Actually, he's not my son."

"I'm Alex." Alex introduced himself.

"And you're here because—?"

"Alex knew Colin White," Edward cut in. He was choosing his words carefully. He didn't want to lie to Jon Lucas, but nor could he tell the whole truth. "As I told you on the phone, Mr Lucas—"

"Jon, please."

"We believe there may be a problem with *Eden Fall*. We're trying to find out more about Rudolf Klein to know if he's involved."

Lucas considered for a moment. "Come and sit down," he said. "I don't know if I can help you, but I'll do anything I can. Have you been offered tea? Or perhaps you'd like a ginger shot?"

"No, thanks." Edward answered for both of them.

They moved over to the sofa. Lucas sat first, crossing one leg over the other and exposing his bare foot. He glanced at Alex. "I hate wearing shoes," he said. "I hope it doesn't bother you. It just reminds me of the beach." He gestured at the aquarium. "It's the same reason I keep the fish."

"It doesn't bother me at all," Alex said.

"I like your accent. You're from the UK, right?"

"Yes."

"It's been a while since I was in London, but it's a great city." There was a bowl of sugar-free apple crisps on the table. Lucas helped himself to a handful and leaned forward. "Anyway, you haven't come here to chat. You want to know about Rudolf!" He sighed. "We were really close. I worked with him for ten years, as I'm sure you know. The two of us developed *Trigger Happy* and I helped him design the Arena. Do you know what that is?"

Alex had read something about the Real Time E-Sports Arena when he was researching *Eden Fall* in Nice. "It's like a games zone," he said.

"It's much more than that. Real Time is based just outside Orinda, fifteen miles from here. We're not talking about an office. What Klein has built is more like a community. It's a fantastic place with a whole load of buildings, including offices, apartment blocks, restaurants... There's even a movie theatre and a sports complex. The Arena sits in the middle of it all and I'm not sure there's anything like it on Earth.

"The Arena is a huge, multi-purpose workspace dedicated to showcasing the best that augmented reality has to offer. It can seat an audience of two thousand people on four tiers overlooking the main stage. The play area is only a little smaller than a soccer pitch. You have to see it to believe it, and believing it isn't easy because, I'm telling you, the technology is far out, man." Lucas could hardly contain his excitement. "We had concerts there with bands and orchestras from all over the world – only they didn't even have to leave home. They were simply projected into the Arena. We did Shakespeare with actors who were brought together from twenty-six different places, but none of them were actually there. Penn and Teller came in and did a magic show, except this time it was real magic ... with a little help from augmented reality. They produced an elephant out of a top hat. I saw it with my own eyes.

"The army are regular visitors. You can fight a war inside the Arena with no chance of getting hurt. Press a button and you're in Afghanistan or Vietnam or the Arctic Circle. We can even throw in the smell of the jungle or the chill of the ice. And we can track every man or woman who participates ... how accurate they are with their weapons, their fitness levels, how scared they are.

"And yes, Alex. Rudolf Klein has regular game evenings. There's one tomorrow. Forty contestants playing the next level of *Eden Fall* on multiple levels with platforms, staircases, hidden doors, secret rooms. You should try it! I tell you, Alex, it's intense!"

"You said you were close," Edward muttered. "What happened?"

"Rudolf fired me."

"Why?"

Lucas smiled ruefully. He looked in the palm of his hand, picked out two pieces of dried apple and ate them.

"Look, I'm not going to bad-mouth Rudolf Klein. In a way, leaving Real Time was the best thing that ever happened to me. That was when I went into business for myself and set up Vision-X." He waved a hand. "As you can see, I haven't done too badly. We may not be as big as Real Time and we don't have quite so many government contracts, but there's a huge market for augmented reality systems and there's plenty of room for us both."

He paused.

"Rudolf was never an easy man to work with. I've never met anyone so driven, so determined to succeed. Maybe it goes back to his childhood. His parents were pretty harsh. He once told me that his father used to take a belt to him if he ever got anything less than top grades in his studies. His mother was very religious. If he used bad language or forgot to say his prayers before bedtime, she'd lock him in the cellar. Even in the middle of winter. I don't think he enjoyed a single day of his childhood."

"Did you ever meet the parents?" Edward asked.

"No. They both died when he was sixteen. There was a gas explosion at their home and they were killed instantly. Rudolf was away at a summer camp so he knew nothing about it. Anyway, from that moment on, he was determined to succeed. Most of his staff were terrified of him. He demanded one hundred per cent loyalty and commitment – and that wasn't the worst of it."

Lucas leaned closer towards Edward as if he was afraid of anyone else overhearing.

"I know you're a journalist, Ed. But you must promise me you won't write about this."

"That's not why I'm here."

"Well, Rudolf cut corners. That was why we fell out. In my original design, there were all sorts of safety features built into the Arena but he ignored half of them."

"Why?" Alex asked.

"To save money. To save time. The first week it opened, someone fell off one of the ramps and broke their leg. We had an incident when a soldier was almost blinded by a laser beam and at one stage the government was threatening to cancel their contract with Real Time. That was when he fired me. He needed someone to blame for the accidents, so he blamed me. He said it was all my fault, even though I'd done everything in my power to make him see sense." Lucas drew a breath. "I was lucky I didn't end up in jail! And there's something else..."

Another long pause. It was clear that Jon Lucas was unwilling to continue.

"You told me on the phone last night that this kid – Colin White – had died playing *Eden Fall*," he said at length.

"It looks that way." Edward nodded.

"Well, he may not be the only one."

"Other kids have died?"

"I can't say for sure." Lucas sighed. "But there have been lots of rumours on the net. You know ... gossip exchanged on gaming forums and stuff like that. Two names have come up time and again. Kiana Reade and Brendan Connor. I've asked my people to find out more, but we haven't been able to come up with anything. Maybe you should check them out."

Alex couldn't believe what he was hearing. "You think *Eden Fall* is dangerous?" he asked.

"I hope not. I really hope not." Suddenly, Lucas was looking scared. "The accidents at the Arena happened a while ago and I heard that Rudolf has added a lot of extra safety features since then. I hope he's learned his lesson. There are millions of kids all over the world playing *Eden Fall* and if there's something wrong with it – if there's something dangerous – well, it doesn't bear thinking about."

"This is a huge story!" Edward exclaimed.

"And you promised me you wouldn't write it. I don't want to do Rudolf any harm. I learned so much from him. He may have treated me badly in the end, but the truth is that he was my friend for a long while and I couldn't have created Vision-X without him."

"You mentioned there was a game at the Arena tomorrow night," Alex said. "Could you get me in? I'd like to see the Arena for myself. And maybe I could even get to meet Rudolf Klein."

"Alex..." Edward looked uncomfortable. "Are you sure that's a good idea?"

Jon Lucas thought about what Alex had asked. "As a matter of fact, I could get you in," he said. "Because I helped design the Arena, I still have access to the ticketing and entry systems. They forgot to cancel it when I left. The only reason I'm telling you this is that I don't want any other kids to get hurt. But if you get stopped or questioned, you must promise me you won't mention my name."

"Sure," Alex said. "That seems fair enough."

"All right then. Are you staying with Ed?"

"That's right. We're still in Lyon Street," Edward said.

"I'll have a security pass sent over to you." Lucas looked Alex straight in the eye. "But take care of yourself, Alex. Rudolf Klein is a genius, but he's also a fanatic – and that makes him dangerous. There may already have been three deaths connected with *Eden Fall*. Just make sure there isn't a fourth."

THE CHURCH

Freddy Grey – Number Nine as he now called himself – lay stretched out in the long grass, aiming at a figure a thousand metres away. The weapon he was cradling was a Barrett M82, made in the United States. It was remarkably powerful – a semi-automatic anti-materiel gun, meaning that an enemy soldier could be hiding behind a wall but it would do them no good. The bullet would simply smash through the bricks and cement and blow them away. Carefully, he settled the crosshairs on the target. His eye focused on a man in his twenties, wearing a white coat, with a stethoscope around his neck.

Freddy checked the wind conditions one last time, making a minute adjustment to allow for wind velocity, then fired. The gun, with its built-in recoil reduction technology, barely shuddered in his hands. The .50 calibre bullet made its fast, lethal journey. It hit the man exactly between the eyes, drilling a perfectly round hole in his forehead.

Freddy lowered the gun and got to his feet.

"That's a kill, Number Nine. Well done."

The voice came from one of the speakers at the edge of the firing range which had been erected on a stretch of grassland surrounded by hills. Freddy examined the life-sized photograph that had been staked out in front of him. It was typical of Nightshade that they had used a picture of a doctor. They weren't just testing his accuracy. They wanted to know that he was psychologically ready to kill anyone. The other targets set out in front of him included images of a woman, a child, a charity worker, a man in a wheelchair, even a puppy dog. Each one of them had been chosen quite deliberately. If Freddy or any of the other Numbers had hesitated or shown disgust, they would have failed before they had squeezed the trigger.

But Freddy never failed. He had always been Nightshade's best shot. He wondered if that was why Brother Mike had arranged for him to escape from Tidworth Camp. Was there somebody he was meant to kill? One of the worst things about his current situation was that he still had no idea what he was doing here. Nightshade was clearly involved in some operation, but no one had told him what it was or what part he had to play.

As soon as he had been driven here from the airport, Freddy had understood that he would be under constant surveillance. He knew he was being taken to Nightshade's new headquarters, and here he was. On the first day, he had spent six hours being interrogated by the Teachers – non-stop, with no food or water and with every word recorded. They wanted to know what had happened to him while he was in captivity. They needed to be certain that nothing had changed and he hoped he had managed to fool them, answering their questions in a way that was cold and matter-of-fact, showing no emotion. They had to believe him! After all, he had shot Tom Harris in cold blood. Brother Mike had seen it with his own eyes. At that moment, Freddy had surely proved that he was still a Number with no conscience at all.

It seemed to have worked. At the end of a long day, he had been reintroduced to the other Numbers with almost no explanation as to where he had been and they had known better than to ask. He had immediately returned to training: hand-to-hand knife fights, assault courses, martial arts and the shooting range. The Numbers had been neither happy nor sad to see him. He had disappeared for a while and now he was back. That was all there was to it.

But Freddy was not the same. He had met Christopher and Susan Grey – his parents. Army psychiatrists had carefully explained what had happened to him. He knew now that the Teachers were not priests as they pretended. They were criminals who had snatched him from his parents when he was just five years old and turned him into a machine. His entire life had been stolen from him and it was hard to conceal the hatred he felt for them, the desire for revenge.

He had been thinking a lot about Alex Rider.

Alex had visited him regularly when he was at Tidworth Camp – the first real friend Freddy had ever had. He had come to trust Alex, which was why, in the hangar at Lower Wick Airfield, he had tried to tell him where he was being taken in America. He'd had to be careful. Brother Mike had been listening. Freddy still had no idea if Alex had understood the clue concealed in his words. Could he rely on Alex to find him? If not, how was he ever going to get back to freedom?

"Numbers Nine and Seven to remain behind to clear targets. Other Numbers to return to the classroom."

The voice barked out the instructions. A group of half a dozen Numbers had been practising on the rifle range and now the rest of them peeled away, leaving Freddy with Number Seven, a slim, dark-haired boy with intense eyes. Ever since he had been flown out of England, four days ago, Freddy had been hoping that the two of them would get a chance to speak.

The Numbers had always been told they had no real names but he knew exactly who Seven was. His name was William Jones. Six, who had been taken prisoner in London, was Sofia Jones, his sister. Mrs Jones, the head of MI6 Special Operations, was their mother. Freddy had met her, too. The question was: could he talk to William? And if he did, would he be sentencing himself to a fast death? He took a look around him. Armed guards were employed all over the complex. At the moment, there were none of them in sight. He and William Jones were alone on the range. He realized that this was the only chance he might get.

He had to talk to him now.

As they walked forward to collect the targets, he fell into step with the other boy. "I was hoping to have a word with you," he said, speaking in a low voice. He didn't think there were any microphones hidden on the shooting range but he couldn't be sure.

"What about?" William was surprised. Conversation between the Numbers was usually limited to mealtimes and focused on the work they were about to do.

"It's difficult," Freddy said. "I could get into a lot of trouble – but it's important. Will you promise me you won't tell anyone what I'm about to say to you?"

William stared at him. "The Teachers know everything we say. We have no secrets from them."

"But there's something you have to know, Seven. I was outside, in the real world."

"You got caught. You ended up in prison." Seven didn't try to hide his contempt.

Freddy ignored him. "I met my parents," he went on.

Seven's eyes narrowed. "That's impossible. We have no parents."

"That's what they told us. But it's not true. My name is Freddy. I have a mother and a father. They were told I was dead, but that was just another lie. My mother cried when she saw me. I was taken away from her all those years ago. She thought I'd drowned..."

He paused. This was the moment of truth.

"I met your mother, too."

That stopped him. Seven froze mid-step and turned to him. "What the hell are you talking about? That's not possible..."

"Your real name is William Jones. Your mother is the head of a department in the British secret service. Number Six is your sister – don't try to deny it; you were always close. She's still being held in England. Her real name is Sofia. You were both kidnapped by the Teachers when you were very young. Just like me. Your mother thought you'd been taken to Russia but it wasn't true. All of us have been turned into killers. We've been trained and made to do everything we're told. But the Teachers have been lying to us all our lives. This is not who we are. This isn't what we're meant to be."

A whole range of emotions had crossed William's face. Shock, disbelief, sorrow and fear. Freddy wondered if

William would run straight to the Teachers and tell them what he had just said. If so, he was finished. But when William finally spoke, he was angry. "Why are you telling me all this?" he demanded.

"Because I have to. A lot more people are going to die unless we break out of this place and find ourselves. Our true selves, I mean. I need you to help me persuade the others. If they learn the truth, they can help us escape. There are lots more of us than there are of them. We don't need to kill anyone. We just need to leave."

William stared at him. "What happened to you in England?" he whispered.

"Nothing happened to me. They were very kind. Nobody hurt me. You remember Julius Grief, the boy who joined us when we were at Kavos Bay? You would have been killed if it hadn't been for him!" This was true. Alex had saved William's life during a horrific parachute jump that had gone wrong. But William showed no emotion now. "His real name is Alex Rider," Freddy went on. "He's my friend. I think he's looking for me. He can help us."

They had reached the targets. Freddy looked at the picture of the doctor with the neat hole drilled into his head. He had made that hole and he had shown no emotion. In fact, it disgusted him. "We have the hike tomorrow," he said. It was true. The Teachers had told them they would be in full combat gear, carrying heavy backpacks as they marched twenty-four miles over the hills. "That means we'll be away from here. If you could help me persuade the others, we could just take off. Think about it, William. Forget what the Teachers have told you. Look into your heart. Don't you feel ashamed when you hurt people? Can you really say that you do it because you want to? And what makes you believe that the Teachers are on your side? What have they ever done for you?"

William turned on Freddy, raising his fists, threatening a fight. "I don't want to hear this!"

"But you have to listen. Eventually, the CIA or the army are going to find us and they're going to kill all of us. The Teachers don't care. They'll escape – but we'll be left behind. I've put my life on the line, talking to you like this. But that's because I met your mother. You even look like her – and there must be something of her inside you. Believe me! We don't need to be like this. We can be ourselves. We just have to break free."

There was a long silence. William let out a deep breath and lowered his fists. He grabbed the target showing the doctor that Freddy had hit. "We need to take these in," he said.

"William...!"

"Don't call me that! I'm Number Seven! That's all I am!" He began to walk away, then turned one last time. "I'll think about what you've told me. All right? But don't talk to me about it again."

"We don't have time to think. Brother Mike is planning a lot of deaths. He boasted about it on the plane. And it's going to happen soon. Is this what you want to be for the rest of your life? Doing what you're told? Never thinking for yourself?"

"I said – that's enough!"

"If you tell the Teachers what I've said, they'll kill

me. But we've been close all our lives. We can talk more tonight, after dinner. We're both on the washing-up rota. We can meet in the kitchen..."

"I don't want to talk."

"We won't just be saving ourselves. We can save other people, too."

"Leave me alone, Freddy!" William walked over to the next target and pulled it out of the ground.

He didn't want to hear any more. But he had called him Freddy.

Perhaps it had worked. Perhaps William Jones was on his side.

The order came later that day, just as the sun was dipping down.

Freddy was in the gym, finishing a workout, when he became aware that he was no longer alone. The two girls, Numbers Twenty and Twenty-Three, had crept up while he was doing the last of his bench presses. They were standing close to each other as if they were twins, joined at the hip.

"You're wanted," Twenty said.

"In the church," Twenty-Three added.

"When?" Freddy asked.

"Now."

"All right. I'll go straight after my shower."

The girls turned their backs on him and walked away.

Standing in the shower with ice-cold water gushing down his back, Freddy wondered what the summons meant. Could the Teachers have overheard his conversation with William? No. That was impossible. Had William repeated what Freddy had said to him? That was more likely and if it was true, he was dead. What were his options? He realized he didn't have any. He must be miles from the nearest town. If he tried to run away, he would be shot down before he had managed a hundred metres. He had no choice but to obey. Perhaps the Teachers had some task for him. This could work out to his advantage.

He stepped out of the shower, dried himself and got dressed. All the Numbers wore the same clothes. In Greece, the uniform had been grey trousers and dark blue jackets, but here in America they wore checked shirts and jeans so that they looked almost like young cowboys. He dried his hair, checked himself in the mirror and left the gym. Two guards with rifles watched him go past. He ignored them.

The church was a ten-minute walk away. It stood at the end of an extraordinary town, the sort of place that had sprung up more than a hundred and fifty years ago, when the American gold rush had led prospectors further and further into what had become known as the Wild West. Two lines of buildings stood opposite one another, separated by a long narrow street. There was a bank, a saloon with swing doors, a hotel and a guesthouse, a general store, a post office, a funeral parlour, a courthouse where trials would take place and, next to it, a jail. Most of them were made of wood but the bank, the courthouse and the jail boasted solid red-brick walls, clearly designed to stop people breaking in ... or out. The street itself was covered in sand, edged by a series of wooden railings that had been constructed for horses – although there were none in sight. Every cowboy film ever made could have been shot here. The town had been renovated: the shopfronts painted, the brass work polished, the sidewalks swept. But it was still a hundred and fifty years out of date. As he walked down the road with the sun casting long shadows across the fields, Freddy could almost imagine the crack of the whip, the jangling piano and the rattle of carriages that would have brought it all to life.

Right now, he was alone.

The church was ahead of him. Like the town, it was almost too perfect – a compact wooden structure that might have been mistaken for a storage barn or perhaps a school but for the narrow, pointed windows on each side and the tower with a single, iron bell hanging in an archway directly over the entrance. There was a porch at the front with three steps leading down. A tiny cemetery stood next to it with just half a dozen graves grouped together, as if whoever was buried there needed each other's company even after death. A couple of the guards – grim-looking men in dirty jeans – were bending over the dry earth with spades, digging a new grave.

Freddy realized he was nervous. It was a strange sensation, one he had never felt before, but there could be no mistaking it. His mouth was dry. There was a hollow in his stomach. He forced himself to calm down. He couldn't show that he was afraid. He took a deep breath and went in.

The four Teachers were waiting for him in front of the simple table that was used as an altar. They looked up as Freddy made his way between the two rows of wooden pews. The evening light, streaming in through the windows, lit his way.

He stopped in front of them.

They were dressed in their long, flowing robes and sandals with golden discs around their necks. Brother Lamar, their leader, was bald and overweight, with a face that could have been made out of Plasticine. He was sitting with his hand resting on an iPad. Brother Mike was next to him, his round spectacles flashing red in the reflected sunlight. The two Sisters – Jeanne and Krysten – were on either side. Jeanne was the oldest of them but had tried to disguise her age with chestnut hair dye and make-up. Krysten, though younger, had perfectly white hair cut short, and pale skin. Her long fingers and dangling jewellery made her look vaguely witchlike.

Brother Lamar spoke first. "Good evening, Number Nine."

"Good evening, Brother Lamar."

"I imagine you're wondering why we wanted you to come to the church." Brother Lamar's lips folded into something resembling a smile. He seemed to be in a good mood.

But Freddy wasn't falling into the trap. Numbers never wondered about the orders they were given. They never questioned them. "No, Brother Lamar," he replied. "You asked me to come, so I'm here."

Brother Lamar nodded, pleased with the response.

"Are you aware that Alex Rider is in America?" Sister Krysten asked. She had once been a highly respected scientist before Nightshade had recruited her. She had created the tiny radio transmitters that the Numbers carried inside their heads and which had whispered instructions to them day and night when they were in Greece.

Freddy showed no emotion. "I didn't know that," he replied.

"Do you think Alex Rider is looking for us or for you?" Sister Jeanne asked.

"Why would he be looking for me?" Freddy replied.

"Well, he might not be too happy with you," Brother Mike said. "After all, you killed his best friend."

"I don't know." Freddy shrugged. "I killed Tom Harris because you told me to."

"Actually, that's not quite true," Brother Mike said. "I was about to shoot him but then you volunteered."

Freddy hesitated. "I hated Alex Rider," he said. "I wanted to hurt him."

"*Hated*, Number Nine?" Brother Lamar raised an eyebrow. "You were always trained to feel no emotion. And there's something else that's puzzling us." He paused. "It seems that Tom Harris is still alive."

"I'm sorry?" Freddy sounded innocent but his blood had turned ice cold.

"You're surprised? So are we. But take a look at this picture. It may interest you."

Brother Lamar opened his iPad and showed Freddy a photograph. It had been taken outside Alex's home in Chelsea. There were two figures standing in the doorway, embracing each other. One was Jack Starbright. The other was Tom. "We've had Alex Rider's house under surveillance," he said. "We thought it sensible to keep an eye on what was happening. This was taken yesterday."

"You shot Tom Harris at close range," Brother Mike recalled. "Even if by some miracle the bullet had missed his heart, he would still be in intensive care. But here he is, smiling, and in perfect health. How do you explain that?"

Desperately, Freddy searched for an explanation. "The gun can't have been working," he tried.

"It was my gun. It was in perfect condition. I loaded it myself."

The four Teachers waited. Freddy said nothing.

"To be honest, I did wonder about what you said to Rider in those last moments," Brother Mike continued. *"Revenge is golden.* Those were your exact words. Could it be, Number Nine, that you were giving him a clue as to where to find us?"

"Why would I do that?" Freddy stammered.

"That's exactly what we're asking you," Brother Lamar said.

The Teachers knew the truth. Freddy realized that he was trapped. He had to make an instant decision. He could run or he could fight. There were four of them and they were almost certainly armed. But he had been superbly trained. When he was being held in Rio de Janeiro, he had single-handedly brought down five members of the toughest police unit in the world. If he moved fast enough, Freddy was confident that he could do the same now. Neutralize the Teachers. Make a break for freedom. It was his only chance.

He leaped forward. But he hadn't taken a single step before what felt like two fishhooks hit him in the back, cutting through his shirt. A second later, he was literally blown off his feet as an electric pulse carrying fifty thousand volts coursed into his body. At that moment, all conscious thought left him. He was aware only of terrible pain and of the world spinning around him.

Freddy had been hit with a Taser gun, a weapon used by police forces all over the world. It was supposed to be a non-lethal weapon, although it had been responsible for many deaths. The idea was that criminals would be brought down by what was called "neuromuscular incapacitation", which was what Freddy was feeling now. He no longer had control over his own muscles. He couldn't stand. He couldn't move.

He opened his eyes to see four or five of the Numbers standing over him and he was furious with himself for not having heard them creep up on him. It was Number Thirteen who had fired the Taser. He had been there when Alex was taken prisoner at Lower Wick Airfield in the UK. Number Seven was with him, watching what was happening with something in his eyes that might have been fear – or shame. Even now, Freddy was certain that William Jones hadn't betrayed him. He didn't look happy about what had just happened. He was just doing what he was told.

Then Brother Mike walked forward, looming over him. He was not angry. His eyes were filled with sadness.

"We are a family," he exclaimed. "We live for each other and we fight together. That is what Nightshade is all about – and there is nothing worse in the world than when one of the Numbers allows evil to find a way into their heart and that evil takes them from us. Number Nine was the best of us until he allowed himself to be captured by the enemy, and now he has turned against us. We all know the price he must pay."

"Amen," all the Numbers muttered.

"Take him to the town jail. He is to be guarded night and day. Nobody is to speak to him until the time of his execution, which will take place very soon. That is all." He leaned towards Freddy. "We will pray for you, Number Nine."

Still unable to walk on his own, Freddy was dragged out of the church. As he went, he remembered the two men he had seen, digging the grave. It was only now that he realized what he should have known all along.

The grave was meant for him.

THE ARENA

A courier delivered Alex's security pass the following morning. He was having breakfast with Sabina and her parents when the doorbell rang. He and Sabina went out to the hall. A uniformed driver was standing on the other side of the door, holding a padded envelope addressed to Edward. Inside was an identity badge with a picture of Alex – it was the same one that had been taken in the lift at Vision-X – with his name, ALEX RIDER, in bright red letters at the bottom. The right-hand corner of the pass was taken up by a QR code which would be scanned when they arrived at Real Time.

There was a handwritten note from Jon Lucas.

Hi guys,
Well, I hacked into the system and this should get Alex into Real Time. The Arena opens at 4 p.m. and he should join the other contestants before the game starts at five. Real Time HQ is signposted from Orinda but you can't miss it. The satnav system in your car will actually tune in automatically when you're five miles away. It's like … the only place you'd want to go.

With a bit of luck, you might get to meet Rudolf Klein as he often likes to greet new players personally. Just don't mention my name!

Good luck, Alex – and take care of yourself.
Best,
Jon

Alex took the pass, which was on a long cord, and put it around his neck. There was something final about the action. It was almost as if he was afraid Sabina would take it from him.

"Are you really going?" Sabina asked.

Alex nodded.

"Rudolf Klein sounds like a monster – just like all the other monsters you've met. He's rich. He's powerful. It could be that three kids are dead because of him. Everything we've been told about him is scary."

"That's why I have to meet him."

Sabina sighed. "Sometimes I don't understand you, Alex. You told me you never wanted to be a spy, that you had no choice. But whenever I see you, you're always getting yourself into trouble. I'm beginning to think you enjoy it."

Alex considered what she had just said. "I don't enjoy getting hurt," he said. "When I thought Tom had been shot dead, that was one of the worst moments of my life because it happened right in front of me. It was the same thing with your dad. I don't know why the world is so full of horrible people: Scorpia, Nightshade, Damian Cray, Sarov, Julia Rothman and all the rest of them. I don't want to spend the rest of my life fighting them. I promise you. I don't want any of this."

"Then why?"

"Because it's what I am. It's what my uncle made me. I don't think Ian Rider thought he was doing any harm but he turned me into something I never wanted to be. And now I'm stuck with it. Sometimes, when I think about the Numbers, all those kids who are around my age, working for Nightshade, I wonder if I'm not the same as them."

"You're nothing like them!"

"You really think so? They never had any choice either." Alex sighed. "I am going to stop. I told you that the other night. Once this is over, it's the last time."

"Do you really think they'll let you leave?"

It was something Alex had often thought about himself.

"I think even Mrs Jones realizes it's over," he said. "I'm sixteen now. MI6 only ever wanted me because I was so young. I didn't look like a spy. That was the whole point. Another year or two and I won't be any use to them."

"Sabina!" Liz's voice called out from the breakfast room. "You're going to be late for school."

Sabina looked at Alex.

"I'll be gone by the time you get back," Alex said. "And I'm hoping to be back in the UK by the end of the week. So I suppose I'll see you there."

"Just promise me you'll take care."

"Promise me you won't go off with Blake."

"As if!"

Sabina turned her back on him and went to get her books. She let herself out the back way.

Alex heard the door close. That was when he knew how much he wanted to see her again. He was missing her already.

* * *

Ben Daniels arrived at the house later that day. Edward and Liz Pleasure greeted him politely enough but Alex was aware of a certain coolness – and he could understand why. Ben was wearing a cut-off T-shirt, once again exposing his muscles and SAS tattoo. With his military haircut and hard eyes, he looked like a mercenary soldier, the very worst company for someone like Alex, and Liz watched with alarm as they walked together to the car. Ben had refused an offer of coffee. He was anxious to get on the road.

They drove out of San Francisco, crossing the Oakland Bay Bridge. As they approached Oakland itself, the motorway rose up on concrete pillars, taking them not so much through the city as above it, the traffic roaring along between the rooftops. Alex couldn't help wondering what it must be like to live with hundreds of cars and lorries rushing endlessly above your head. Neither of them talked. Ben was concentrating on the road and Alex was thinking about Sabina and having her back in London. What with sixth form and Tom leaving school, he had the feeling that his whole life was about to change.

After about twenty minutes, they reached Orinda and pulled in for a break. It was one of those typically California towns with wide, empty streets, trees planted every few metres, tinkling fountains and flowers in tubs. The shopping malls were neatly tucked away and there was enough parking space to ensure that nobody would ever have to walk. The buildings were low-rise and felt old-fashioned – they had been deliberately built that way. Ben pulled in opposite a cinema that could have come straight out of a film itself. There was a coffee shop near by with tables on a terrace and they sat outside.

Alex found himself examining an advertising board on the other side of the road. It showed a mother and two children drinking orange juice around a kitchen table. The line at the bottom of the picture was in Spanish. *Cada gota es dorada*.

"Every drop is golden," Ben translated.

An ordinary family in an ordinary kitchen. It was something Alex had never experienced.

A smiling waitress appeared at once and they ordered coffee and sandwiches. Ben waited until she had gone, then spoke in a low voice. "I think you need to be very careful when you go into the Arena," he said.

"I'm always careful," Alex said.

"I know that – but I checked out those two names Jon Lucas gave you. I thought it might be important, so I rang London last night and they connected with Interpol to get the information. Kiana Reade was seventeen years old, living with her parents in Amsterdam. She stepped in front of a tram. She wasn't killed but she was badly injured. Brendan Connor was twenty-two. He lived in London. He stepped onto the live rail at King's Cross tube station."

"Were they both playing *Eden Fall*?"

Ben shook his head. "That's exactly the point. Both families are trying to pretend that they were just random accidents. But we've looked into their finances and it turns out they've banked very substantial sums of money. And where do you think that came from? It looks as if Real Time has paid them to keep their mouths shut – and you can understand why. If it got out that the game wasn't safe, they could lose a fortune."

"Is that what Steven Chan discovered? Would that have been enough to get him killed?" Despite everything, Alex didn't believe it. And he still couldn't see how Nightshade fitted into it all.

"What other reason could there have been?" Ben replied. "And there's something else that might interest you. The New York police have taken witness statements. Several people saw Steven Chan before he went into Central Park – which is where he died. He was wearing a set of Real Time goggles. They saw the logo on the side. And he had them on when he was killed."

"How do you know that?"

"They found pieces of black silicone inside the wound. But the headset had disappeared by the time the police found the body. They may have been stolen by a homeless person. That's their theory, anyway."

Alex thought about all this. "I still think we're missing something," he said.

"You may be right." Ben paused as the coffee arrived. "As far as I can see, it all comes down to the boss of Real Time, Rudolf Klein. What sort of man is he? What's he doing?"

"That's why I'm going in," Alex muttered.

"And that's why you have to be careful," Ben said.

REAL TIME 1 MILE. A road sign led them off the motorway, taking them down a purpose-built road that skirted the edge of Briones Regional Park, twisting through sand and brushland. It finally brought Alex and Ben to a solid white-brick gateway consisting of six archways with manned security booths and CCTV. It was like the entrance to a movie studio. All traffic had to stop here and nobody could enter or leave without showing ID and the necessary permits. Four of the entrances were for staff, the other two for visitors. It was the only way into the compound and, as they both realized immediately, the only way out.

Alex showed the pass that Jon Lucas had given him and watched as it was scanned by an unsmiling security man in a black parka jacket. He breathed a sigh of relief as it was accepted. So he was in!

"You can drop him off here," the security man said, speaking to Ben.

"Can't I come in with him?" Ben asked.

"I'm sorry, sir. You don't have a pass. Orinda's just a few miles down the freeway or you could head up to Lafayette. Alex will be able to call you when he's done."

"Are you OK with that?" Ben asked Alex.

"Sure. I'll see you soon."

Alex got out of the car and, without looking back, walked through the archway and into the world of Real Time.

An electric, open-top car that looked a bit like a futuristic golf buggy was waiting for him on the other side of the entrance and Alex climbed in, feeling a little self-conscious as he waited for the driver. It was only when the vehicle jerked forward and set off that he realized there *was* no driver. The car had been programmed to take him wherever he was going and guided him through the middle of what could almost have been a small town with a whole collection of different buildings – pale pink, blue and yellow – connected by quiet, clean roads, bridges and walkways with more driverless vehicles gliding from location to location and a sleek AirTrain whispering along metal tracks above. Alex saw various offices, a convenience store, what might have been a museum or a conference centre, a park with climbing equipment for children, several tennis courts. Everywhere he looked there were lawns with sprinklers, lines of trees perfectly trimmed, colourful flower beds.

The car turned a corner and went under a bridge. And there it was, suddenly, in front of him.

The Arena was astonishing, years ahead of the other buildings, a glass-and-steel construction with a network of silver rods supporting it on every side. It was almost the size of a football stadium, floating above the ground like an enormous shiny egg. Alex remembered Jon Lucas saying that it could hold two thousand people and he could easily believe it. The Arena was surrounded by spotlights and he could imagine it at night, lit up, with crowds pouring in. It would be as if they were entering a spaceship.

The car stopped in front of the main doors. A smartly dressed woman carrying a clipboard came towards him and checked his ID a second time.

"Welcome to the Arena, Alex," she said. "Did you have a good journey?"

"Fine, thank you. Although the driver wasn't very talkative."

She smiled at that. "Please come this way."

She led him inside; looking back, Alex noticed other electric vehicles arriving with gamers, some about the same age as him, some in their twenties. He went through the doors and found himself in a wide entrance hall that must have curved all the way round the building, an unbroken circle with open staircases that looked like slanting ladders leading up to the different levels. There were giant TV screens everywhere, flashing up different images of the Arena, demons and weird animals from *Eden Fall*, characters from *Trigger Happy* being killed in different ways, advertisements for other games, videos promoting the company. Neon tubes threw garish-coloured lights across the walls and ceilings, and pop music was pounding out of hidden speakers.

"This way!" The woman with the clipboard was gesturing at a sliding door that had been opened to reveal a private room on the other side. "Mr Klein is waiting for you."

So Alex was going to meet Rudolf Klein after all. He quickened his pace and went in.

He found himself in an executive lounge, carpeted and with steel-panelled walls that blocked out most of the music. There were rugs, expensive leather seats, a well-equipped bar, no windows. About forty or so gamers had already arrived, gathered together with paper cups of coffee or soft drinks. A small group of white-coated technicians had formed in a line facing them, some of them with laptops and notepads. And in the middle, on his own, stood a man who was shorter and older than any of them but who somehow dominated the room.

Rudolf Klein was in his fifties but had spent a lot of money and time trying to make himself look younger. His black hair was obviously dyed. The colour was unnatural, like spilled oil. He'd had some sort of work done on his face but without great success. His skin might not have any wrinkles but it was lifeless, frozen in place, and his lips were somehow too big for his mouth. He was wearing the wrong clothes, too. The green velvet jacket and mauve T-shirt clashed and his trousers were struggling to contain his bulging stomach. Even his teeth were wrong. They had been whitened until they shone, making him look quite freakish every time he smiled.

He was smiling a lot now, delighted to see the gamers who had arrived to experience *Eden Fall*. More and more people were entering the room and when the door was finally closed, he began to speak.

"Good afternoon, everyone!" Even though Alex knew he had been in America since he was five, he still spoke with a German accent. "Welcome to Real Time and to the Arena. I want to thank you for coming tonight. There are many of you that I recognize, and I think, also, I see some new faces.

"So let me explain. You are very lucky young people because you will be meeting two new characters that we are adding to *Eden Fall*. The rest of the world must wait until tomorrow, but while you are in the Arena, if you look carefully, you may find my new friends.

"First, there is the Blue Devil. His name is Orobas – and he is not a very pleasant fellow. In fact, you will receive a reward of five magic apples if you manage to shoot him. Remember that once you have ten magic apples, you have the power to enter a new level. So kill Orobas and you will be halfway there!

"However, the winner of this evening's session will be the first person to find our other new character. He is the Blind Hedgehog and his name is Shadrack. He is very timid and I can promise you that he will have chosen a clever hiding place somewhere inside the world you are about to visit. He will be doing everything he can to stay out of sight. But there are plenty of clues to help you locate him. Look out for signs. Listen to what the other creatures tell you. If you meet him, you must give him your name and you will go home with the very latest model of the Real Time AR Headset, which is worth six hundred dollars!"

There was an excited muttering in the room when the gamers heard this. Klein held up a hand for silence.

"When I have finished speaking, you will be taken to the changing rooms and you will be given a two-piece full-body motion-capture suit, which – I must warn you – will be impossible to remove until you quit the game. The suit is like a second skin and while you are wearing it, you will feel heat and cold. If you walk into a river, you will sense the water around you even though the river does not really exist! Many of the demons in *Eden Fall* carry weapons and if they decide to attack you, you will feel that also. You cannot get hurt. The sixty-eight haptic points built into your suit are kept at very low, safe settings. But we want the experience to feel as real as possible. You may have noticed, that is part of our name!

"If you wish to quit because you are tired or have had enough, simply press the button that is built into the side of your belt. This will neutralize the haptic suit you are wearing and will immediately summon one of my staff to take you out of the Arena. I hope, though, that we have no quitters here!

"Finally, you will also be given wireless AR handguns – but remember: these will not work on other players! You are not here to shoot each other. That's the Blue Devil's job! If he sees you before you see him, he will send a fireball your way and, thanks to your haptic suit, you will definitely feel it. Don't say you haven't been warned!"

He laughed at his own joke, the white teeth briefly glinting.

"Anyway, enough talking from me. We are about to start. But first, are there any questions?"

A tall, good-looking guy with reddish hair put his hand up. Like Alex, he was wearing a security pass with his name – JAMES REID – clearly printed. "How much did this place cost?" he asked.

Klein laughed. "That is an impossible question to answer. More than a billion dollars, for sure. A billion is one thousand million – I'm sure you know that. The Arena has been in development for more than ten years. I have hundreds of people working for me." He spread his hands. "This is my life's work!"

"How many people can fit in here?" someone else asked.

"There is no audience today. You don't need to worry. But when we play proper competitive games, we will have two thousand people watching here, and maybe another ten million watching on television. Make no mistake, my friend, e-sports are the future and the future is here."

He paused.

"Is there anybody else?"

Alex hadn't intended to draw attention to himself but he realized that this might be the only chance to interrogate Rudolf Klein. He raised his hand.

Klein saw him. "I don't think I have seen you here before," he said.

"It's my first time," Alex admitted.

"What is your name?"

"Alex Rider."

"You have an English accent. I would be interested to know who invited you here. But that can wait. What is your question?"

This was the moment of truth.

"Has anyone ever died playing *Eden Fall*?" Alex asked.

There was a sudden hush in the room, a sense of discomfort. It was as if Alex had sworn or said something very rude. The technicians turned to one another, wondering what to do. Klein took a step forward. "What a very strange question," he remarked. All his good humour had left him. His whole face seemed to have darkened. "Why would you ask something like that?"

Alex played innocent. "Well, you were talking about guns and bullets and pain. I just wondered..."

"The guns and the bullets are not real. This is not the real world. It is impossible to get hurt. Nobody has ever died."

Alex shrugged. "It's just that I used to have a friend called Colin White..."

"And what happened to your friend, Colin White?"

"He fell off a building."

Rudolf Klein knew the name. He knew what had

happened. He couldn't disguise the fear in his eyes. "I am very sorry to hear it," he said. "But he could not have been playing *Eden Fall*."

"Why not?"

"Because the software would not allow him to put himself in danger." Klein moved forward until suddenly he was very close to Alex. "I think you're too scared to play the game," he said. "Maybe it would be better if you left."

"I'm not scared at all," Alex said.

The two of them locked eyes. Right then, Alex wondered if he had gone too far. Was Klein about to throw him out?

The chairman of Real Time made his decision. His eyes never left Alex but he clapped his hands together. "It's time to get killed out!" he exclaimed. "Everyone to the changing rooms!"

The other gamers began to stream out, passing on either side of Alex and Rudolf Klein. Klein seemed to be examining Alex, as if trying to see inside him. "You're sure you want to play?" he asked.

"Absolutely," Alex said.

"Then I wish you luck." Klein took one last look at Alex. "I'm sure it's an experience you won't forget."

He turned, and surrounded by his technicians, walked briskly out of the room.

THE BLUE DEVIL

Alex stood in front of a full-length mirror, examining himself in his haptic suit. It was as if he had been dipped into a tank of liquid plastic that had dried all over him so that every contour of his body, every muscle, stood out. The zip that sealed it ran down his spine, locked into the collar so that he couldn't undo it on his own. There were two white discs on each arm, two on each leg, three on his back and two more on his chest. Targets. Klein had said he couldn't get hurt but he still felt uneasy having them there.

He was holding the headset that he had been given. It was made of some sort of grey silicone, with a strap that went all the way round his head and miniature speakers that fitted neatly over his ears. Sight, sound and feeling were all going to be part of the augmented reality experience. He also had a gun – although it didn't look like a weapon at all. It was more like the sort of thing a doctor might use to take your temperature electronically – flat and lightweight, with a trigger and a glass screen at the front, ready to fire a pinprick of light rather than a bullet.

Alex might have felt a little ridiculous but he wasn't alone. There were forty gamers, who were all dressed and equipped identically, standing in the narrow changing room with lockers and benches on each side. It had taken half an hour for everyone to get changed, and now Alex was waiting for the doors to the Arena to open and the game to begin. He still had no real idea what to expect. The technology was brand new. All of this was outside his experience.

"Your first time?" James Reid – the young guy who had asked the first question – was standing next to him.

"Yeah."

"Me too. I've taken the day off work."

"What do you do?"

"I'm a lawyer." He thought for a moment. "At least, I used to be. I'll probably get fired. But it'll be worth it. I think *Eden Fall* rocks."

There was a stir among the gamers as the technicians finished their final checks. One of them came over to Alex. "Alex Rider?" He was a Black guy, friendly, maybe in his thirties.

Again Alex wondered if he was going to be thrown out.

But the technician was smiling, matter-of-fact. "The control room can't get a signal from your headset," he said. "We may have a technical issue. Can you use this instead?"

He handed Alex a second headset. It was a different colour to everyone else's: black not grey. Alex took it, swapping it for the one he had first been given.

"Have a great game," the technician said and walked away.

The lights dimmed. At the far end of the changing area, the doors slid open with a soft hydraulic hiss. The crowd of young people had been chatting excitedly but now they fell silent and moved forward. Alex went with them. He remembered being taken on rides at theme parks when he was very young. He was feeling the same nervous excitement.

He entered the Arena.

His first impression was that it was an enormous space. In the half-light, the play area seemed to stretch as far as the eye could see, an oval shape surrounded by thousands of empty seats that rose up in four tiers. People sitting at the very top would look a centimetre high. Dozens of screens were suspended on cables from the ceiling, the screens facing down; there were so many that they almost formed a second ceiling of their own. Spotlights were mounted all over the Arena, a few of them already turned on but with the beams dimmed, swinging lazily back and forth. Alex noticed a control box on the first tier with shadowy figures moving behind the darkened glass observation window. Was this where Rudolf Klein was sitting? Was Alex being observed even now?

After the long build-up, Alex's first impression was that the play area itself was disappointing. Ahead of him, he saw a series of constructions that could have belonged to a poorly designed children's playground. There were slopes and slides, ladders leading to platforms and gantries, deep trenches snaking along the ground, elevated walkways, walls of different sizes, some of them studded with hooks and bolts for climbing, irregularly shaped arches and doors – all jumbled together with no seeming thought. None of them had any colour. They were covered in some sort of drab grey cloth. The overall effect was of an alien graveyard that had been forgotten and abandoned on some distant planet. Four hundred people could easily have fitted into it but there were just forty of them playing. Were they really going to spend the next hour dodging and ducking behind these dull, random shapes?

There was a click and a faint hum that came from hidden speakers and travelled in all directions. A moment later, a female voice boomed out. "Please choose a position. The game will begin in two minutes."

Alex watched as the other players spread out across the floor, some of them disappearing behind the different pieces of the huge jigsaw. He climbed a short ladder and tucked himself away on a platform from which he could see the whole Arena without, hopefully, being seen himself.

Nobody was making any sound. From his vantage point, Alex saw the other players moving quickly, separating, finding places to hide. Time seemed to have slowed down. He was waiting for something to happen. Nothing did.

"Please put on your headsets." Once again, the voice echoed through the Arena.

Alex did as he was asked. There was a small part of him that was bothered. Why had his headset been replaced at the last minute? And his alone was black. Everyone else's was grey. He wished now that he hadn't been so quick to challenge Rudolf Klein. He had exposed himself as an intruder, uninvited and perhaps dangerous.

"Ten ... nine ... eight ... seven ..."

The voice managed to make even the countdown sound unexciting. Alex drew a breath, waiting to see what would happen.

"... three ... two ... one ... action!"

There was an explosion of light and colour as the

spotlights burst into full life and all the screens came on at the same moment. For the first time in his life, Alex – quite literally – could not believe his eyes. At the flick of a switch, the Arena had transformed itself into a different world, a reimagined Garden of Eden, with fields and woodland, grass bending in a breeze that he could feel blowing across his arms, and huge exotic flowers that almost overpowered him with their scent. The sun was blazing down and, again, he could feel the heat of it on his neck and shoulders. He had to remind himself that everything he was seeing, feeling and even smelling was being created by the haptic suit working with the AR headset; that none of it was real.

The platform he had been standing on had become a grassy hill and he was no longer alone. One after another, animals, birds and insects had begun to appear – but they were like nothing Alex had ever seen before. The birds were brilliantly coloured, and some were shaped like tennis balls with wings; others were feathered insects. The saddest bird was a ready-prepared supermarket chicken wrapped in plastic, which walked past awkwardly on two legs that were poking out of the bottom. The birds weren't whistling. They seemed to be singing a hymn; it was hard to be sure as there was an electronic humming, a sort of tuneless music, which was enveloping the entire scene. A herd of half-sized zebras were moving across the hillside – except instead of being black and white, they were orange and green. A rabbit with a pocket watch across its chest scurried down a hole. A butterfly hovered briefly in front of him and, to his horror, Alex saw a tiny, bald human head peering at him between the beating wings.

"Hello," it said.

Alex didn't reply.

"Well, be like that!" The man-butterfly scowled and flew away.

Alex was struggling to absorb what he was seeing. The world of *Eden Fall* was beautiful and yet somehow threatening. He could have been inside the head of a child having a bad dream – a mash-up of their life and all their worst fears. But he couldn't help wondering at the extraordinary detail of it all: every blade of grass, every feather had been perfectly realized. He had never been particularly interested in computer games but this was something else. He could understand gamers like Colin White losing themselves here. Put on a pair of Real Time goggles and you might never want to take them off again.

He looked up. Above him, screens were showing a blue sky with a few cotton-wool clouds. An angel flew by underneath, playing "We Are the Champions" on its harp. The trenches that he had noticed were now rivers fed by a waterfall at the far end, tumbling down a rocky cliff-face. He saw a silver fish leap up and somersault in the air and heard its squeal of excitement. The creature didn't make it back into the water. A miniature dragon swooped out of the sky and barbecued it in mid-flight with a single puff of flame, then snatched it away in its beak. He spotted some of the other gamers in their light blue haptic suits. Like him, they were exploring their surroundings. Some of them were already deep in conversation with the strange animals they had encountered.

None of it was real. All the images were being overlaid on top of the reality of the Arena. He reached up and snatched off the goggles; at once everything disappeared and the stadium was exactly as it had been when he arrived – a collection of grey structures of different shapes and sizes spread out across an indoor football pitch. The sight reassured him. He had nothing to fear here. The headsets might show him a monster or a giant but all the players would be seeing the same thing and nothing could touch them. They could search for clues or secret doors or whatever. But there was no way any of them were going to get hurt.

He put the headset on again. At once, the man-butterfly was back, hovering right in front of his face.

"Are you just going to stand there?" it demanded in a sulky voice.

This time, Alex decided to respond – just to see what would happen. "What am I meant to do?" he asked.

"You really don't know? Haven't you ever played this game before? Weren't you listening?" Now the creature sounded like an angry schoolteacher. It settled on a nearby leaf, folding its wings. "The aim is to find the Blind Hedgehog. There are clues all around you!"

As if on cue, a series of neon letters appeared over the landscape, floating in mid-air. Each one spelled out the same word – **CLUE, CLUE, CLUE** – with arrows pointing in different directions.

"Or you can ask me questions," the man-butterfly continued.

"All right." Alex took a breath. "Where is the Blind Hedgehog?"

"I'm not allowed to tell you ... obviously! It would spoil the whole point of the game. Ask me something else!"

"Who killed Colin White?"

The man-butterfly looked at Alex in shock. It opened its mouth to speak. Then something leaped out of the grass. It was some sort of cat, but one with six legs. With a vicious snarl, it caught the insect in its mouth, its white teeth biting down. And then it was gone, leaving nothing but a few drops of blood on the grass.

Alex was unnerved. Had someone been listening in on the conversation? Had the man-butterfly been about to tell him something? What had just happened was horrible, and it was hard to believe that such violence could be part of the landscape created by *Eden Fall*. Was it a warning? Could it be that he was in danger after all?

And then something struck him in the arm with incredible force. A blast of pain shuddered through him. It felt as if he had been hit with a club and electrocuted at the same time. He clamped a hand to the wound, expecting to see blood, but when he looked down there was no sign of any injury; no tear in the haptic suit, nothing. He turned round and saw one of the gamers pointing his gun at him. About ten different thoughts arrived in Alex's head at the same time. The first was that shooting at other players wasn't allowed. There was no reason for it. Rudolf Klein had said that the guns wouldn't work if they were fired at other players. Also, Alex knew his attacker. It was James Reid, the boy who had spoken to him in the changing room. At the time he had seemed pleasant enough, but now he looked possessed.

Worse still, he was preparing to fire a second time.

This last thought decided Alex. He threw himself down the hillside, turning into a ball and rolling through the long grass. When he got to the bottom, he hurled himself into a clump of bushes. He knew they didn't exist but he could still feel them raking his legs. When he was sure he was out of sight, he stopped to catch his breath, wondering what had just happened. Whichever way he looked at it, it made no sense.

Feeling increasingly uneasy, Alex continued through the undergrowth and came out in a clearing surrounded by multicoloured mushrooms, each one about a metre high. He noticed a frog the size of a small dog squatting on the stump of a tree. It was an ugly thing, with a huge mouth that almost cut its entire head in half.

"You shouldn't have come here, Alex," the frog croaked. It blinked at him, its eyes a sickly shade of yellow.

"How do you know my name?" Alex demanded. It was impossible. When he had put on the haptic suit, he had left the security pass – along with all his ordinary clothes – in the locker room.

"We all know who you are," the frog replied. "Alex Rider. Teenage spy." It let out a loud belch. "I have to say you don't live up to your reputation, Alex. And quite soon it looks like you won't be living at all!"

Another figure approached. Another gamer, about twenty years old, with a wispy beard. He saw Alex and immediately raised his gun.

"You're not allowed to shoot—!" Alex began.

It was as if the gamer hadn't heard him. He pressed the

button and Alex saw a grinning skull materialize in the air. At the same time, he was punched in the chest – so hard that he thought his heart would explode. He let out a gasp and fell backwards into the long grass, then crawled away as quickly as he could. He knew now that it was the haptic suit he was wearing that was causing the agony. *You cannot get hurt. The sixty-eight haptic points built into your suit are kept at very low, safe settings*. He remembered what Rudolf Klein had said but knew now that the very opposite was true. Alex's suit had been turned to its very highest setting. It was lethal.

But why were the other gamers targeting him? Had the whole thing been a set-up? Had he been lured into the Arena deliberately along with thirty-nine killers, each one of them aiming for him? No. That was impossible. Nobody had any idea who he was. Jon Lucas had hacked into the entry system. They couldn't have known he was coming.

So what was going on?

There was no time to work it out. Alex made a decision. He had to get out of the Arena while he still could. If he was hit by too many more guns, his heart might not be able to take the strain. His haptic suit could quite easily kill him. He remembered something else Klein had said in the briefing. His suit had a built-in panic button. Still aching and breathless from the first two attacks, he staggered over to what might have been a shepherd's hut, half ruined, made of brick. He touched it. The building was real. He went inside.

The hut must have been used by the construction workers who had fitted out the Arena. They had left behind an electric kettle and half a dozen mugs, spread out on a table. Otherwise, it was empty apart from a sheep sitting in an old-fashioned armchair, reading a newspaper. It glanced at Alex and folded the paper.

"Have you read the ewes?" it asked.

Alex was in no mood for jokes.

"I would imagine you're looking for Shadrack," the sheep continued.

"Not really." Alex scowled. Shadrack was the Blind Hedgehog, but right now that was the last thing on Alex's mind.

"Victoria and Angel can help you. And as the French say ... shoot low!"

Alex was barely listening. He was examining his belt, searching for the panic button. At last he found it, round the side, moulded into the plastic. He pressed it and waited.

"I don't think it's working," the sheep muttered. "So it looks like you're dead meat."

It was right. Nothing had happened. Nobody had come to the rescue. The alarm had been deactivated. There was no way Alex was leaving this game. Not while he was still breathing, anyway.

Another explosion of pain. This time it hit him in the thigh. Alex spun round and half collapsed as his leg gave way beneath him. A third gamer – a boy only a year or two older than him – had appeared in the doorway of the hut. He had seen Alex and fired. He stood there, smiling, already taking aim.

Alex didn't want to hurt the boy but he had no choice.

He grabbed the steel kettle he had seen and threw it before the boy could fire a second time. The kettle flew across the room and made contact with the side of the boy's head. The boy swore and disappeared from sight. Alex stood there, trying to work out what to do next.

"Baaah!" the sheep muttered, in contempt.

Alex glanced at the kettle, lying on the floor. It was modern, bright silver ... and real! A thought occurred to him and with a sense of dread he went over to the door and picked it up. Holding it in front of him, he used it as a mirror, searching for his own face in the rounded surface. And there it was. Looking through the lenses of the headset, he saw exactly what he had expected. It wasn't his reflection that was looking back at him. Instead, there was a blue face with blazing eyes and horns, a razor cut of a mouth, a pointed beard. Now he knew why he was a target.

The augmented reality software had turned him into the Blue Devil that Klein had described before the game. *You will receive a reward of five magic apples if you manage to shoot him.* That was what Klein had said. Everyone else in the Arena was looking for him.

And all of them wanted him dead.

GAME OVER

Alex knew he had to get out of the Arena – fast. Everywhere he went, every move he made, the other players would see the Blue Devil and shoot at him without a second thought. Was there any way he could get out of the haptic suit that was causing him all this pain? He reached over his shoulder, searching for a buckle or a zip. Perhaps he could tear off the power pack that was charging it. But the suit had been designed in such a way that only a technician could remove it. He was stuck.

"You're toast!" the sheep remarked, watching him from the chair.

"And you're shepherd's pie," Alex growled moodily.

He went to the door. There was nobody looking his way at the moment and it occurred to him that he could stay inside the hut, simply hide there for the next forty or fifty minutes until the game was over. Maybe no one else would come in here and he would be safe.

He decided against it. There was the boy he had attacked. He might well tell some of the others and they'd all come looking. And then there was the stupid sheep with the newspaper. It knew who he was and it probably had a way of communicating. All it would take was another neon sign floating in the air – **THE BLUE DEVIL IS HERE** – and he'd be finished.

His only chance was to get back to the entrance without

being spotted – but he wondered if that was even possible. Alex could see the other players spread across the stadium and, despite its impressive size, there simply weren't enough trees and shrubs to hide behind. Klein and his technicians would be up in the observation box, watching his every move. Somehow, he had to take them all by surprise; he had to do something that nobody expected. Alex's eyes flicked from the hilltop to the river and the waterfall, the stretches of grass, the flowers, the various creatures on the ground and in the sky. He raised the headset and examined the grey reality that lay beneath the incredibly imagined world. And suddenly he knew exactly what he had to do. There was one way out. It had been in front of him all the time.

At once, he was running away from the hut, keeping low, hoping nobody would turn round and notice the Blue Devil trying to get away. Fortunately, his objective was right in front of him. He came to the edge of the river and jumped. It was an extraordinary experience as his feet broke through the surface, then the rest of his body. In a second, he was fully submerged in the water, plunging down two or three metres. His feet hit the riverbed and he stood there, trying to make sense of what was happening. He was soaking wet. He could feel the cold water against his skin and there was a gurgling sound in his ears. He should be drowning! But there was no water. It wasn't real! He had actually jumped into an artificial ditch and it was only the software, fed through the haptic suit and the headset, that made him feel like he had turned into a fish.

He was safe! The other gamers would be unable to see him now. The river would protect him. He could walk underwater all the way to the waterfall, and from there it wasn't too far to the exit. He would be out of here before anyone knew it. With fish swimming past his head, Alex set off upstream, wading through the current. Even knowing that the water wasn't real, he still found himself holding his breath. He could feel the pressure of the water trying to hold him back. The illusion was perfect.

Looking up, he saw a few indistinct figures shimmering on the edge of the river above him. But none of them noticed him – the Blue Devil under their feet. As he pressed forward, he heard a rushing sound and a series of soft explosions. Ahead of him, the river seemed to be in turmoil, with the surface above him a frothing white. He realized he had come to the waterfall but he didn't slow down. Instead, he walked right through it. For a moment, he was half blinded and deafened by the pounding water. Then he emerged on the other side to see a staircase ahead of him. It led into some sort of hollow. He climbed up.

Sure enough, there was a cave carved into the hillside behind the waterfall. Three of the walls were solid rock: the fourth was a curtain of water. A tiny home – like a hobbit hole – had been built inside the space. There were two armchairs, a sink piled with a stack of plates, a blazing stove, a bunk bed. A brown spiky creature was walking back and forth, wearing dark glasses and tapping its way with a stick. Quite by chance, Alex had stumbled across the Blind Hedgehog.

Despite himself, Alex couldn't help remembering what the sheep had told him. Victoria and Angel could help him. They were both names of waterfalls: Victoria Falls in southern Africa, Angel Falls in Venezuela. *And as the French say ... shoot low. La chute* was the French for fall and *l'eau* was water ... waterfall. That was what should have led him here.

"Congratulations! You win!" the hedgehog announced.

But Alex wasn't playing. He'd had enough of talking animals, and the last thing he needed in his life was a free Real Time AR Headset. There was a narrow gap between the waterfall and the rock face, with a path leading out. The exit was partly covered by a willow tree, presumably to make it more difficult for the gamers to find. The door to the changing room and the way out of the complex was just beyond, and Alex was in a hurry to reach it. Still wearing his headset, he set off, leaving the hedgehog and its prize to be discovered by somebody else.

There were no players in this part of the Arena. They had all moved further in, exploring the different sectors of the game. Another illumination – **WAY OUT** – hovered in the air above a sliding metal door but before Alex could reach it, a voice called out.

"Hello, Alex!"

He turned round, expecting to see another creature – but instead there were two girls standing in front of him. They had come from nowhere, one of them carrying a fake gun made of pink plastic. Alex knew them. The fair hair tied back like a Barbie doll; the pigtails and glasses. They had always hung out together at Kavos Bay, giggling and swapping stories about all the people they'd murdered. Numbers Twenty and Twenty-Three, recruited by Nightshade. It was impossible but somehow they had been allowed into the game and followed him here.

"What do you want?" Alex demanded. The girl with the gun was aiming directly at his head.

"What do you think we want?" Twenty said in a high-pitched voice. "We've been sent to kill you."

To kill you...

They were the words that saved Alex's life. He knew that the guns in the Arena could hurt him but so far none of them had been lethal. What was different now? In a flash, he remembered Steven Chan, the investigator found dead in Central Park. He heard Ben Daniels' words in the car. *They found pieces of black silicone inside the wound.* Alex had been given a black headset when he arrived at the Arena.

Only him.

The girls were smiling at him. They knew something he didn't.

There was something inside the headset. There had to be.

With a second to spare, he tore it off. He was holding it by the strap and he had already thrown it as far away from himself as he could when the tiny pipe bomb hidden in the plastic – activated by the radio signal transmitted from the gun – exploded. The headset shattered, pieces of plastic flying in all directions. The girls cried out. The headset had been nearer to them than to Alex at the moment of detonation and they had both been injured. Twenty-Three had blood running down the side of her face. Alex didn't hang around to apologize. He was already through the sliding door and on his way.

He was in a corridor and he was desperate to escape from the haptic suit but he knew that it was too dangerous to go straight to the changing room. That was the first place the two Numbers would look. And they were coming after him. He could hear their footsteps close behind. He turned a corner and came to a staircase with a door to one side. He opened it and looked into a storage cupboard. Perfect. He slipped inside, pulling the door shut.

The Numbers ran past a moment later. He heard them pause and exchange a few words. Then they turned and ran up the staircase. Alex looked around him, hoping for a pair of scissors or anything that might help him cut his way out of the haptic suit. There was nothing. He waited until he was sure he was on his own, then crept out again, making his way to the room where he had first got changed.

He went in – only to discover that he was not alone. The technician who had provided him with the deadly headset was standing there, presumably waiting for the game to end. Alex lashed out, gripping him by the throat and pinning him against the wall. The technician was older and larger than him but Alex's anger lent him strength. He was furious.

"You tried to kill me!" he snarled.

"What are you talking about?" The technician sounded genuinely shocked.

"You gave me the headset!"

Now the technician recognized him. "Yes. I was told to. One of the people in the observation room..."

"Which one?"

"I don't remember."

The name wouldn't have meant anything to Alex anyway and he realized that he was choking the technician, who looked terrified. He couldn't have been acting. He wasn't even trying to fight back.

Alex released him. "I'm sorry," he said. "The headset exploded."

"What? That's impossible."

"It's not impossible. It nearly killed me." Alex looked around him. "I have to get away from here. Can you help me out of this suit?"

The technician was rubbing his throat. "You attacked me!"

"Listen to me. I didn't mean to hurt you but someone just tried to kill me. If I'd been wearing the headset you gave me, I'd be dead now."

The technician didn't want to hear any more. He made a decision. "Turn round..."

Alex decided to trust him. He did as he was told and felt the technician's hands releasing the zip that ran all the way down his back. A moment later, the haptic suit fell away. "Thank you," he said. "Don't tell anyone about this. There are things happening here you don't want to know about."

"There's nothing happening here. You're just crazy!"

The technician was no longer a threat. He couldn't wait to get out of the room. Alex watched him leave, then hurried over to his locker.

Five minutes later, wearing his own clothes, he was on his way out of the building. He was keeping a lookout for Numbers Twenty and Twenty-Three and he was grateful that so far nobody had raised an alarm. He passed a TV monitor and saw the game still going on inside the Arena without him. It was very strange. Nobody seemed to have noticed that he had left – or if they had, they didn't care.

He went back through the main entrance hall and out into the open air. Almost at once, an electric buggy pulled up in front of him. This one was manned.

"Leaving already?" the driver asked.

"Yes."

"Want a lift to the main gate?"

"Sure..."

Alex had thought he was going to have to fight his way out of the Real Time headquarters or somehow get past the guards without being seen. Instead, he was being offered a lift! Feeling ever more confused, he climbed into the back seat and sat there as the driver hit the accelerator and they whirred through the now silent streets.

"You play the game?" the driver asked.

"Yeah." Alex was in no mood for a conversation.

"Pretty cool, isn't it!"

It was all wrong. The more he thought about it, the more he realized that nothing fitted together. Nightshade had been there, inside the Arena. The two girls had tried to kill him in exactly the same way they had killed Steven Chan. And someone inside Real Time had made sure he was wearing the headset that would have put a miniature bullet into his brain. But how had they even known he was coming when he'd actually been an uninvited guest, hacking his way on to the invitation list just one day before? And why weren't they coming after him now? The whole place should have been in lockdown with spotlights blazing and sirens screaming. Instead, he was being driven out in a buggy. The driver was whistling to himself, completely unconcerned. There were no guards in sight.

He remembered his meeting with Rudolf Klein. His first impression of the man behind Real Time hadn't been completely positive. Klein was not a pleasant man. His choice of clothes, his attempts to look younger and his perma-tan were all unattractive. But was he actually evil? In his time with MI6, Alex had met many people with plans to enrich themselves and destroy the world at the same time. He thought of Razim, the Grimaldi brothers, Damian Cray – they'd all had the same quality, a sort of intensity, a refusal to see that they were far less clever than they thought they were and that their plans were actually insane. By comparison, Klein had seemed almost ordinary. And now this – a free ride out! What was going on?

How had Nightshade known he was coming? Could they have seen his name on the security pass?

His name...

And then there was something else. When he was in the town of Orinda, just before the game, he and Ben Daniels had been in the café together and Ben had said something that had stuck in his mind, although he hadn't seen the significance until now.

Alex took out his phone and speed-dialled. Ben answered at once.

"Alex ... are you OK?"

"Ben? Are you near? I need to see you right now."

"Where are you?"

"I'm heading for the main gate."

"I'm on my way!"

Alex heard Ben's car engine start up. "Listen to me, Ben," he continued, urgently. "We've got it all wrong. All of it! You remember that poster we saw?"

"What poster?"

"In Orinda. It was an advert for orange juice." Alex was losing the signal. Ben must have driven into a dead spot. "Listen to me!" he shouted. "I know where Nightshade are hiding. It was what Freddy was trying to tell me. The answer's in the poster. Ben? Ben...?"

But there was no answer from the other end. Alex realized the connection had failed. He turned off the phone.

"We're here," the driver said. He slowed down and stopped.

The entrance gates were in front of them: six archways with separate lanes. It was well after five o'clock and the sun was getting lower in the sky, throwing dark red shadows across the surrounding hills. It was the end of another working day and some of the Real Time employees were on their way home, passing through the gates on the far side. Alex climbed down from the buggy.

"Take care!" the driver said.

"Thanks," Alex replied.

He went through one of the archways, handing his security pass back to one of the guards, who glanced at it, then dropped in into a tray. Nobody tried to stop him. He knew they wouldn't. He continued walking, leaving the Real Time headquarters behind him. In the distance, he saw a silver car racing towards him. He was relieved. Ben had arrived in record time. Once everything had been explained, he would take over. Alex would be back at Brookland without missing a single day of school.

The car skidded to a halt in a cloud of dust kicked up by the tyres.

It wasn't Ben.

Brother Mike got out, dressed in a suit, holding a gun. Number Thirteen, the boy who had driven the taxi to Tidworth Camp, was behind the wheel.

"Alex Rider," Brother Mike said. "Has anyone ever told you that you are extremely annoying?" He waved the gun. "Drop that phone and get in."

"No, thanks," Alex said. He was looking past the car, hoping to see Ben Daniels on his way.

"It's your choice. If you don't, I'll shoot you right here."

The road was empty. There was no sign of Ben.

Alex dropped his phone into the dust, hoping at least that Ben would find it and that he would work out what had happened. He got into the car.

EL DORADO

He could have stepped back in time. Or he could have been on the set of a Hollywood film. As Alex stepped out of the car and began to walk down the main street – the only street – of the town in which he now found himself, it was as if he had been transported to the Wild West. After the afternoon he had spent in the world of *Eden Fall*, he was beginning to wonder if he had finally lost touch with reality. Every detail was perfect: the wooden sidewalks, the lettering on the El Dorado Hotel, the wanted posters plastered on the jail wall, even the cactus sprouting next to the well. It was a rich man's toy, brilliantly conceived.

"This town goes all the way back to the 1870s," Brother Mike said. "Its name was El Dorado and it's still called that now. Of course, most of it has been reconstructed. Our host enjoys playing the cowboy. I think you'll find he has a part for you, too."

Alex didn't like the sound of that.

Brother Mike had put his gun away. He no longer had any need of it. Alex knew that he was in the middle of nowhere, miles from the nearest town. Even if he could escape, he had nowhere to go and no way to get there. He had also clocked half a dozen guards who must have been provided by Nightshade as part of their security package. They were wearing dirty jeans and cowboy hats and looked like outlaws, some of them with rifles resting lazily on their shoulders, all of them with pistols hanging from their belts. He had seen some of the other Numbers, similarly dressed, sitting on the wooden steps outside the El Dorado Hotel and the El Dorado post office, watching him with hostile eyes. The sun had almost set and gas lights had been turned on behind the windows of the hotel and the saloon. A church stood at the very end of the street. Alex noticed the gravestones and the recently dug grave.

"I imagine you're keen to know the identity of our host," Brother Mike said.

"I know already," Alex said.

"Really?"

"I know everything, Brother Mike. And so does MI6. You failed with 'Leap of Faith' and you're going to fail again. That's the trouble with Nightshade. You never get it right."

"You're lying. You don't know anything."

"We're in El Dorado, it's a ranch about fifty miles south of San Francisco. As for our host, it looks like he's come out to meet us. Surprise! Surprise!"

But Alex didn't sound surprised. He sounded bored.

A man was walking towards them with the dying sun behind him. His face was in shadow but Alex didn't need to see it to know who it was.

"Hi, Alex," Jon Lucas said.

The head of Vision-X, the man Edward Pleasure had interviewed, was also dressed cowboy-style with a scarf around his neck and a Stetson hat. He had been barefoot in his office but now he was wearing calf-length boots made of brown leather. His modern glasses were still in place, slightly at odds with the rest of his image.

"Nice to see you again, Mr Lucas."

"Is it?" Lucas was surprised.

"Not really. But I was talking to Ben Daniels about you this morning. We both know what you're doing. You're working with Nightshade."

"He's bluffing," Brother Mike muttered. "We should kill him."

"No, no." Lucas smiled. "I've got some entertaining ideas for Alex Rider. Bring him inside."

Brother Mike gestured and they followed Lucas into the courthouse, an imposing red-and-white brick building with pillars in front of the entrance. It stood in the middle of the street, next to the jail. Lucas stopped by the main door. There was an electronic keypad in the wall and he pressed in a code. Well, that was certainly something they'd never had in the Wild West. Alex heard a click and the door swung open.

The interior of the courthouse had been transformed into a hi-tech workspace. The original features were still there, with the judge's chair dominating the far end, the witness stand and the jury box to one side. But the spectators' area – which once would have had lines of wooden benches – had been taken over by interlocking white tables and swivel chairs with industrial-sized computers, monitors, processors and other machinery that could have belonged to some future world. The room was cold with a sophisticated air-conditioning system that not just lowered the temperature of the air but sanitized it.

A small office had been arranged in one corner with

a desk, a sofa and a fridge. Lucas took a carton of sparkling cucumber water out of the fridge and sat down, gesturing for Alex to do the same. Brother Mike perched on the edge of one of the tables. He didn't look pleased. Alex guessed that he didn't want any of this. If things had gone his way, Alex would already be dead.

Jon Lucas had come to the same conclusion. "Well, Alex, I never expected you to get out of the Arena alive," he said. "I was sure the haptic suit would kill you. And if that didn't work, Brother Mike had his two little girls waiting to put a bullet in your head. I said it was a waste of talent and we could find a better use for you. I'm glad I'm going to get the chance."

"So what do you want?" Alex asked.

"Well, first of all" – Lucas waved a hand lazily – "I need to find out how much you know and all the rest of it. As it happens, tomorrow is a big day for me. I just want to be sure it's going to go ahead smoothly."

"You're going to kill another teenager?"

Lucas blinked. For a moment, he looked genuinely amused. "Is that what you think this is all about?" he asked.

"You want to destroy Real Time."

"That's absolutely right, Alex. But I'm not going to kill one teenager. I'm going to kill hundreds of them – and it all starts at ten o'clock tomorrow."

Alex stared at him. "Why?"

Lucas flicked open the carton and took a sip. "It looks as if I may have overestimated you," he said. "You really don't know anything at all. But since you're here, I might as well explain it to you. Not that there's anything you can do." He smiled. "This is all about augmented reality, a technology that's going to be bigger than the Internet, that will change the world. Whoever controls augmented reality will have more power and wealth than Steve Jobs, Bill Gates and Elon Musk put together! I want that person to be me, Alex – and that's what I'm going to achieve with a little help from my friends at Nightshade. When Real Time collapses, I'll pay them fifty million dollars. Does that sound like a lot to you? It's peanuts compared to how much I'm going to earn."

He leaned forward across the desk, jabbing a finger in Alex's direction. "I'm afraid I rather misled you when you first came to my office," he went on. "I worked with Rudolf for ten years. That bit was true. But those accidents that happened at the Arena? The safety problems I told you about? I'm afraid that was all my fault. Yes! I cut corners. I didn't listen to advice. But so what? He still had no right to fire me. I had designed the first dedicated e-sports arena in America! It was a masterpiece and of course I wanted to see it up and running. Did it really matter if a kid broke his leg or some rookie soldier got blinded by a laser beam? I was thinking about the bigger picture. We needed to get the game started. We had to keep moving.

"But, as I told you, Klein letting me go was the best thing that ever happened to me. Once I was on my own, I was free to set up Vision-X, my own company, and since then I haven't looked back. But it's like I said when I met you that first time with Ed. Despite all my hard work, we're still number two in the market. We're tiny compared to

Real Time. We don't have the political contacts. We don't sell to the police or the army. We're developing games but we don't have the finance or the resources to create anything in the same league as *Eden Fall*. That game is genius! I know because I worked on it. Half the ideas that are out there now are mine. And I want it! I want the kids in every country in the world who will one day play it. You can forget everything else about augmented reality. The games industry alone is worth billions. And very soon it will be mine.

"How am I going to get it? Very simple. I already control the game, Alex. Before I left the company, I slipped some very special malware into the system: different viruses, worms, Trojan horses that actually give me complete control of everything that happens in the game. You'll have seen that for yourself when you were at the Arena. I turned you into the Blue Devil. I cranked up the pain sensors in the bodysuit you were wearing. I was able to watch what you were doing on a screen right here and I even talked to you. That fat green frog you met in the mushroom field? That was me."

"It suited you," Alex said.

"Wow! It's going to be fun watching you die. But let me finish. I control the newest level of *Eden Fall* – from this very room. Ever since it was released, I've been able to manipulate things so that players can get hurt ... or killed. We did a few tests just to make sure it worked. So, for example, that kid in Amsterdam. What was her name? I can't remember. But it was easy enough to change what she was seeing so that when she crossed the road, she thought it was empty because her headset didn't show her the tram heading towards her at thirty miles per hour. Then there was that boy in London, Brendan Connor. We laid a path across an electric railway line and then added a neon sign telling him to walk over it. And Colin White! That was the easiest. We led him into an empty building and then sent him across a bridge that didn't actually exist.

"To be honest, Colin was a mistake. That was me cutting corners again. I just get too excited for my own good! I should have realized that he had a wealthy father who'd spend a lot of money trying to find out what had really happened. Wilbur White was becoming quite a problem for me – but in the end we were able to turn the situation to our advantage. It was lucky I had Nightshade on-hand to sort out any problems. First they tracked down the detective and killed him and anyone he'd spoken to, including my old friend Paul Shaffer in New York. He'd designed *Eden Fall* and had discovered something was wrong. Then they took out Wilbur White. That was an expensive operation but it was worth it because by the end of it everyone was quite certain that it was Rudolf Klein trying to protect himself. He was the one who was killing everyone! Nobody suspects us!

"As you know, Real Time is introducing two new characters to *Eden Fall* tomorrow, which means there will be a huge amount of interest in the game with record numbers of players logging in. I'm afraid it's not going to be a very happy day for Rudolf Klein. The accidents won't begin straight away but by lunchtime the casualty departments of hospitals all over the world will find themselves rushed off their feet. It's going to get worse and worse and if they try to shut down the game, they'll find that something's gone wrong and they don't have control. That's because I do! I'll be controlling everything from here. And will be watching the bodies pile up.

"Real Time have already paid off the families in Amsterdam and London, but what will they do when they're confronted with dozens of accidents and fatalities happening in a single day? Lawyers will be chasing them from every direction. They'll find themselves buried in lawsuits. The police will get involved. Rudolf Klein will almost certainly end up in jail. What's certain is that his company will collapse. And that's when I'll move in. I'll take over the personnel, the programmes, the technology, the contacts. Vision-X will become the number one augmented reality company in the world. And all of it will be mine!"

Jon Lucas stopped. He was breathing heavily and, despite the chill in the room, there was a sheen of sweat on his forehead. Alex looked from him to Brother Mike, and at that moment he wasn't sure which of the two of them was the most evil. They were both mad in their own way and, for all its genius, *Eden Fall* hadn't managed to come up with a devil that was more dangerous than either of them.

"It won't work," he said simply.

"I'm sorry?" Lucas looked puzzled.

"Your plan won't work because the police and the intelligence services will know it was you who caused the accidents."

"And how will they find out?"

"My friend, Ben Daniels, will tell them." Alex went on quickly before he was interrupted. "The thing is, you see, I'd already guessed what you were doing. And I'd already told Ben when Brother Mike picked me up."

"He's lying," Brother Mike said in a flat voice.

"How did you know?" Lucas asked.

"You made a stupid mistake."

"Tell me." The smile was still there on Lucas's face but it had frozen. He was holding his drink so tightly that the carton had crumpled.

Alex shrugged. "You sent over a security pass to get me into the Arena. It had a photograph you'd taken in your office and also my name underneath."

"Yes." Lucas shrugged. "I said I'd do that for you. So what's the deal?"

"I never told you my full name. When you first saw me, you asked if I was Edward Pleasure's son. He told you I was called Alex but that was all he said. You must have known who I was the moment I walked in. That told me you were lying to me."

"There are a hundred ways I could have found out who you were."

"But you were the only person who knew I was going to the Arena. Somehow, Nightshade followed me there. More than that, you boasted how you'd hacked into the ticketing and entry systems. So when Numbers Twenty and Twenty-Three turned up and tried to kill me, it was pretty obvious that it must have been you who'd managed to get them in."

"What are you saying...?"

"You can cause as many so-called accidents as you want tomorrow, but everyone will know it was you. Ben will make sure of that. Nobody's going to sue Real Time. They're going to come after you."

"Just ignore him, Mr Lucas," Brother Mike said. "He didn't have time to tell his friend very much. The rest of it he's only worked out from what he's seen and what you've told him. If the authorities knew we were here, they'd have already sent in the army."

"I'd like to see them try!" Lucas scowled. He turned to Alex. "You might have noticed that I'm well protected here. This place may look old but it's got quite a few tricks up its sleeve."

"Nobody's coming anywhere near El Dorado," Brother Mike assured him. "The plan will work and you'll have everything you ever wanted. Alex Rider is trying to make you doubt yourself. I did advise against bringing him here. Now, if you'll listen to me, you'll get rid of him as soon as possible."

"Yes." Lucas nodded slowly. "I think that's exactly what we should do."

"The others are waiting for us outside."

Lucas got to his feet. Alex stayed where he was, refusing to play along. Brother Mike leaned forward and swung a hand, hitting him on the side of his head. "Get up!" he commanded.

Alex did as he was told. There was no point taking any more punishment. He needed his strength. Part of him was shocked that he'd been unable to persuade Jon Lucas to give up his plan. But more worryingly, there was a part of him that wondered – how much had Ben Daniels heard on the phone? Did he have any idea where Alex was? It was a horrible thought, but Brother Mike could be right. He could be on his own.

They left the courthouse and went back out into the open. Four people were waiting in the fast-fading light – and armed guards watched with ugly eyes from the other side of the street.

Brother Lamar, Sister Jeanne and Sister Krysten, all of them in their grey robes, were standing in front of him. Freddy Grey was in the middle, dressed in jeans and checked shirt, his hands hanging by his sides. Alex felt a jolt of sadness on seeing him. For the first time in his life, Freddy looked like an ordinary boy. Somehow, the Teachers must have discovered that he had tricked them, that Tom Harris hadn't been killed and that Freddy had been helping Alex from the very start. What must it have been like for him, being dragged back into this madness, having his life stolen from him for a second time? And what must he be thinking now? Alex was meant to have come and rescued him. Instead, he was a prisoner too.

"So this is where it ends!" It was Brother Lamar who had spoken. He was looking at Alex with hatred flickering in his eyes. "If I had my way, I'd shoot you now – or hang you. That's what they used to do to outlaws in the Wild West. But our generous host has other ideas and we must give him what he wants."

Jon Lucas stepped forward. "I want a duel," he said. "That's the one thing we've never had in El Dorado. A proper, old-fashioned shootout." He smiled. "You guys are probably too young to have seen all the Clint Eastwood movies but there's one I always liked. There's a shootout with the bad guy and there's a pocket watch that plays a tune." He took an old-fashioned gold watch out of his pocket and held it up, dangling it on a chain. "One like this. And these are the rules. Nobody says anything. The music gets slower and slower until it finally stops and that's when the two cowboys are allowed to shoot. That's exactly what will happen at ten thirty tomorrow morning. We're going to give both of you guns – one bullet each – and you're going to face each other right here."

"Why should we do that?" Alex demanded. Even as he spoke, he was looking at Freddy, trying to read him. He had no need to remind himself that Freddy was a trained killer, that there was no question which of the two of them would be faster and more accurate with a gun. But would Freddy accept the challenge? After all, he was different now. He had already proved that. He and Alex were friends.

It was impossible to say. Freddy's face was empty. He looked defeated.

"I could shoot Freddy," Alex went on. "He could shoot me. What's the point? You're going to kill both of us anyway. So why play your dirty little game?"

"That's a good question," Brother Lamar said. "And I'll give you the answer. One of you lives. One of you dies. If it's Number Nine who shoots you, we'll take that as evidence that he's learned the error of his ways and we'll take him back into the fold. Do you understand that, Number Nine? This is your last chance for salvation."

Freddy nodded slightly but said nothing.

"And if I kill Number Nine?"

"We can't let you go, Alex. But we can let you live. We'll find a role for you here in El Dorado. Maybe you can join the cleaning staff or work in the stables. I agree it's not much to look forward to, but it's probably better than an early grave."

"Or you can both refuse and we will hang both of you," Brother Mike added helpfully.

"You have the night to think about it," Brother Lamar said. He rapped out an order. "Take them both to the cells. Keep them separated. We don't want them talking to each other. And make sure they're both watched until we're ready for them. Numbers Four and Twelve can take the first shift."

The guards moved in to take Freddy and Alex away. The two boys looked at each other but said nothing. What were they both thinking? What were they going to do when they faced up to each other in the duel? They would have to wait until the next day to find out.

NIGHTFALL

The building was just off Union Square in the heart of San Francisco, surrounded by some of the most expensive shops, the smartest hotels, and the most famous museums in the city. It was in a narrow, tree-lined street with buildings either side and it would have been easy to walk past without noticing it. There was a single door, a video entry system and a sign that read: CROWN INTERNATIONAL ACCOUNTANTS. The company initials might have provided a clue as to the organization that was actually based here.

Ben Daniels had called Alex. He had spent twenty minutes looking for him outside the Real Time complex. Then he had called him again and this time he had heard the sound of Alex's mobile, buzzing in the dust. Feeling sick at heart, he had picked it up and that was when he had realized what must have happened. Somebody had snatched Alex moments before he arrived.

He had come straight to the CIA office in Maiden Lane, knowing that he had no choice, that there was nowhere else he could go. A young woman had led him up to the top floor and along a corridor to a room with a door that had been specially widened to allow a wheelchair user to enter and leave without difficulty. Dwain Garfield was waiting for him inside, along with two of his agents who didn't speak but who listened carefully as Ben explained why he was there. Garfield didn't say a word either. His face gave nothing away.

"I think Alex is in trouble. I know where he is but I can't reach him on my own. I'm hoping you'll agree to help."

Ben had been talking for about five minutes. Finally, he came to a halt.

Garfield nodded slowly, weighing up what he had just heard. His hands were folded in front of him and Ben noticed that, even indoors, he was wearing his leather gloves. "I thought I told you to leave town," he muttered, finally.

It was the last thing Ben had expected to hear. He struggled to hold down his anger. "Perhaps you didn't hear me," he growled. "We've done your job for you. We've found Nightshade. Alex worked it all out."

"Because he saw a name in an advertisement."

"That's right." Ben took a breath. "When Alex was taken prisoner in England, he met Freddy Grey, and Freddy said something very strange. *Revenge is golden.* Those were his exact words."

"You weren't there!"

"No. I wasn't there right then. But we discussed it later. Everyone thought Freddy was just talking about California. The Golden State. But we were wrong. It turns out that Jon Lucas has a ranch called El Dorado, and when we were in Orinda we saw a poster advertising a soft drink in Spanish. It had the same word. Golden. I translated it and that was how Alex guessed."

"How did he know the name of the ranch?"

"Edward Pleasure mentioned it when Alex was staying with him in Presidio Heights." Ben couldn't hide his frustration. "I've already told you all this!" he said. "And while we're sitting here talking, Alex could be fighting for his life."

Dwain Garfield didn't look even slightly concerned. He turned to one of his agents. "What do we know about El Dorado?" he asked.

The agent was holding an iPad. He referred to the screen. "It's a huge ranch," he said. "The main house has twenty-seven bedrooms, two swimming pools, a helipad ... that's where Jon Lucas lives. But he's surrounded by thirty-five thousand acres of land – that's more than fifty square miles. He keeps horses and cattle, and there are a whole load of different crops plus orchards and vineyards. There's a Wild West town in the middle of the property. Lucas had it completely restored. It's not open to the public. In fact, the whole place is off-limits and heavily protected, and there are rumours he put in a complete defence system including electric fences, mines, underground bunkers, surface-to-air guided missiles ... the works."

"Jon Lucas used to work for Real Time. Why would he want to do them harm?"

"I don't know the answer to that," Ben replied. "But looking at the evidence, I'd say it's highly likely that he's got a grudge against them. After all, Klein fired him. When Alex was with him, Lucas told all sorts of lies about Rudolf Klein. How he had horrible parents who died in an accident, how everyone was afraid of him, how he cut corners and didn't care about safety. But I've checked it out and none of it's true."

"And what do you expect us to do, Mr Daniels?"

"Well, we've got to raid the place, find Alex and get him out."

"That may be easier said than done. Electric fences ... missiles? We go busting in there, it could turn into a war!"

"You said you wanted to find Nightshade."

"I said I wanted to wipe them off the face of the Earth – and maybe I can do just that!"

The agent with the iPad spoke again. "We've got satellite pictures that have just come in, sir," he announced. He handed the machine to his boss.

Without asking permission, Ben got up and went behind the desk so that he could look at the images too. He already knew that American spy satellites could read the front page of a newspaper from outer space, but even so he was impressed by the quality of the images, taken when the sun was setting and the light was poor. He saw a long street with a church at one end and what looked like a courthouse in the middle. A Wild West town. Several people were visible and he recognized Alex and Jon Lucas at once. There was a third man with them. Ben had never met him but he guessed this must be Brother Mike.

"That's him!" Ben exclaimed. "When was this taken?"

Garfield glanced at the agent, giving him permission to answer. "Ninety-eight minutes ago," the agent said.

"Alex is their prisoner. That's all the proof you need. There's Jon Lucas and the man who's with them is one of the leaders of Nightshade."

"We know who he is," Garfield said. "His real name is Lenny Michelangelo but he calls himself Brother Mike. He used to be a heavy hitter with the Mob. He dropped out of sight ten years ago ... and now we know why."

"So what exactly are you waiting for, Mr Garfield? He's a sitting duck. You've got them all!"

"Why don't you go back to your seat, Mr Daniels?"

Ben did as he was told while Garfield examined the information on the iPad. Another minute passed. Then the CIA chief spoke again.

"We're not going in there," he said. "It would be crazy ... suicidal. We know about Nightshade. They're like the worst terrorist organization on the planet. They don't give a damn about their own lives and they'll kill anyone who even looks at them the wrong way without a second thought. They're not even human beings. They're monsters! I heard what happened in Rio de Janeiro. The toughest police force in South America and they suffered multiple casualties! That's not going to happen to my people. Not on my watch."

"Then what—?" Ben began.

Garfield held up a hand for silence. "We'll get more intel from our satellite system," he said. "But you're right about one thing. We've got Nightshade exactly where we want them. They're on their own in the middle of nowhere and nobody's ever going to know what happened to them."

"What do you mean?"

"I mean, we're going to wipe them out with a single air strike. We've got Edwards Air Force Base just three hundred and fifty miles south of here. We can mobilize a convoy of fighter aircraft and in just five minutes the ranch and half the surrounding countryside won't exist. We don't need to argue with these people. We just want them terminated. This is the easiest way."

"But, with respect, sir ... these are children! They didn't ask to work for Nightshade. They were brainwashed!"

"Nothing I can do about that, Mr Daniels. Anyway, I don't see them the same way you do. You say they're children but what sort of child plans to drop a deadly chemical weapon on two thousand people in a holy place, a cathedral? I'd say you'd have to be some kind of devil to want to do that but it very nearly happened in your home city. Are you really saying you won't be glad to see the back of them?"

"You've seen the satellite images. You know Alex is there. If you send in attack aircraft, he's going to get killed."

Garfield handed the iPad back to the agent. "Get on to Edwards," he said. "And connect me with the Pentagon. I want this assault to be arranged and authorized as soon as possible. We may need to talk to the White House too, although the less the President knows about this, the better."

He turned back to Ben.

"I'm sorry about your friend, Mr Daniels. But I'm not going to risk the lives of my people for the sake of a single kid ... and one who isn't even American." He shrugged. "In a way, it's your own fault. I told you both to leave San Francisco. You should have done it while you still had the chance."

The jail block in the old town of El Dorado was a single corridor that stretched out behind the sheriff's office. There were six cells in total, each one a square box with three brick walls and a fourth made entirely of bars. Inside each cell, there was a slab of wood to be used as both a bed and somewhere to sit. A bucket stood in place of a toilet.

Freddy Grey was lying on his back, his head resting on a soiled pillow, his body covered by a horsehair blanket. He was unable to sleep. For the past hour he had been thinking about Alex Rider, unable to get him out of his head. He had felt a surge of hope when he had first seen Alex outside the courthouse. The plan that he had improvised at the airfield had worked! Alex had understood the clue that Freddy had given him moments before he had pretended to kill Tom Harris. Alex had found his way to El Dorado.

That was what he had thought. But all his hopes had vanished when he realized that Alex was on his own, a prisoner like him. He hadn't brought any back-up. There were just the two of them and in a few hours' time, one of them was going to be forced to kill the other. There was no way out. Freddy had listened in silence as Jon Lucas had outlined what was going to happen: the pocket watch, the tune, the shootout.

And then there was Brother Lamar. *If it's Number Nine who shoots you, we'll take that as evidence that he's learned the error of his ways and we'll take him back into the fold.* That was what he had said and Freddy replayed the words now. He had killed many, many people in his short life. Would one more make any difference? He liked Alex but if he wanted to save himself, he knew what he had to do.

Nightshade had deliberately kept them apart. They were occupying cells at the far ends of the corridor. They couldn't speak to each other. They couldn't call out. One of the Numbers was sitting in a wooden chair in front of the barred door and Freddy knew that there would be another watching over Alex. They weren't going to be allowed to come to any sort of agreement or decide on a strategy. Freddy had never felt more alone. In England, he'd been given a glimpse of some sort of future, with a home and parents, a normal life. That had been brutally snatched away and now he had a long night stretching ahead of him and, in the morning, either murder or suicide. That was the brutal choice.

He heard the flap of sandals on the wooden floor as someone approached his cell and knew at once what to expect. He looked up and saw Brother Mike, dressed in his grey robes with a golden disc around his neck. Number Four – who had been guarding him – stood up respectfully.

"You can go to bed," Brother Mike told him. "Number Seventeen has the next watch. I want to talk to Number Nine."

"Yes, Brother Mike." Number Four nodded his head and left.

Freddy watched him go. All the Numbers had ignored him since he'd been exposed as a traitor. As far as he could see, they were going about their business as usual. But was that completely true? He had seen it even now... Number Four seemingly awkward and unhappy. He knew something had gone badly wrong. Perhaps the others did too. Was it possible that the power of the Teachers was slipping away?

Brother Mike sat down in the empty seat.

"How are you feeling, Number Nine?" he asked.

"Why do you care?" Freddy replied.

"I care about all the Numbers. I'd like to think I've been a father to you all your life."

"You stole me from my real father."

Brother Mike looked pained. "I'm the only father you've ever had, Number Nine. I helped make you what you are. You were the very best of all the Numbers – the fastest, the strongest. You can be again."

"I've had enough of killing."

"Really?" Brother Mike smiled sadly. "I don't hold you responsible for what happened, letting yourself get captured in London. And I have a good idea what British intelligence have tried to do to you. But I'm here to tell you that it's not too late. What Brother Lamar said, in the street, is true. We want you back. We want you to be one of us again. Do you honestly think there's any alternative? Imagine we were all killed. Imagine Nightshade ceased to exist. What would happen to you? After all the things you've done since you were five years old, do you think you have any chance of a normal life? Your so-called parents are already disgusted by the many crimes you've committed. How long will it be before they hate you? And is there any real chance you'll survive in an ordinary school? The first kid who calls you names in the schoolyard will end up with a broken neck before you even realize what you've done. Girls will be scared of you. You'll never have any friends.

"Like it or not, you are what we've made you. And your only hope is to embrace it, to recognize your unique talents and to continue to work with us. All of this unpleasantness can be over. The past can be forgotten. There's just one thing you have to do."

"Kill Alex Rider."

"Exactly. This shootout was Lucas's idea, not ours. But actually, it's perfect! You're ten times faster and more accurate than Rider. He doesn't have a chance. You can shoot him with your eyes shut – and all the Numbers will be watching. In a single moment, you'll prove to them that you're one of us again. Lucas will be happy. The operation will go ahead. Nightshade will be richer than ever and maybe we'll promote you – a sign of how much we value you. You could become an Assistant Teacher. You could help with our future planning and share in our profits. How would you like that? You've grown up very quickly, Number Nine. It's time we treated you as one of us."

Brother Mike got to his feet.

"I'll leave you to get some sleep. I just wanted you to know that you can turn this situation to your advantage. I'm confident you'll do the right thing. The simple truth is that Alex Rider has done you nothing but harm. It's time you got him out of your life."

Alex Rider had heard the muttered conversation but Brother Mike had been too far away for him to make out any of the words. Now he heard him walking back down the corridor and a moment later his shadowy figure passed the bars at the front of the cell. He didn't even glance in Alex's direction, which wasn't a surprise. He had only ever had contempt for Alex. His business had been with Freddy. Alex shuddered to think what the two of them might have agreed.

There had been two Numbers on guard all evening but

it was time for a new shift. Moments after Brother Mike had left, a girl walked down to the wooden chair at the far end while a boy took his place next to Alex's cell. Alex recognized him at once.

The boy was Number Seven. William Jones.

Alex waited until William had sat down and he was sure that Brother Mike had left the cell block. He knew that the other Number was at the end of the corridor but she was far enough away that she wouldn't be able to hear what he was about to say.

"Number Seven," he muttered.

William ignored him.

"Number Seven...!" Louder this time – but not so loud that the girl at the other end of the corridor would hear.

"What?"

"I'm glad to see you."

"Shut up and go to sleep. I don't want to talk to you."

"Really? I saved your life, remember? I climbed out of a plane..."

"I don't care what you did," William snapped. "Don't pretend you're my friend. You're nothing to me – and tomorrow you're going to be dead."

"That's not very nice," Alex said. "As a matter of fact, you're the main reason I'm here."

"Why?"

"Your mother sent me to find you."

William fell silent but Alex was sure that his last words had found their target. William was sitting very straight in his chair on the other side of the bars. He was breathing heavily. This was the moment. Alex might never have another chance. "She asked me to give you something," he said.

He had been carrying it ever since he left England. It had been with him when he went to the Arena and it had been in his back pocket when Brother Mike had forced him into the car. He took it out now: the photograph of William on his first day at school that Mrs Jones had given him and which he had examined on the way to the airport. Alex rolled off the bunk and went over to the bars. He held it out for William to take. But William didn't move.

"It's a picture of your first school – St Leonard's," Alex explained. "There's a wooden elephant in the playground. Do you remember it? You used to play on it all the time."

Still William was silent. He was sitting there, as rigid as a statue, and Alex was afraid that this last gamble had failed.

"Aren't you going to look at it?" he asked. "Don't you want to see your mother?"

William had been holding his breath. But now he let it out with an almost inaudible sigh. He got up and went over to the bars. "Show me," he said.

Alex handed him the photograph.

William looked at it for a long time. "This could be anyone," he muttered.

"It's you. You know it's you. And look at the woman. Look how similar she is to you. And why don't you talk to Freddy? He's actually met his parents. He knows the truth. Why else do you think he's been trying to help me?"

"This is a lie. You and Number Nine are in it together. You're both trying to trick me!"

"Why would we do that? I saved your life, William! If it wasn't for me, you'd have died on that plane and you'd be buried in Greece. I came to America to find you, to take you home."

William was still holding the photograph, staring at it – and suddenly Alex knew that his appearance in the jail had been no coincidence. He had already had his doubts. He'd wanted to see Alex again.

"You know I'm telling the truth!" Alex went on. "Your mother's waiting for you. This is your one chance to end all this."

"No!"

William had shouted out the word and the other Number must have heard him. He moved closer to Alex and his face looked contorted, furious in the shadows of the jail block. "You say one more word to me and I'll call the Teachers," he whispered. "Tomorrow morning you're going to shoot Number Nine or he's going to shoot you. I don't care what happens. But you leave me alone. I don't want to hear any more."

He went back to his chair and sat there, staring into the darkness. His head didn't move. He didn't even glance in Alex's direction and it was clear that he had nothing more to say.

But he had kept the photograph.

SHOOTOUT

9.36 a.m. – El Dorado Ranch, California, USA

Sitting on his own in the enormous kitchen of his ranch house, Jon Lucas enjoyed a healthy breakfast. Today his butler had served him smoked oats with soya milk yoghurt and organic blueberries followed by a tofu omelette with boiled spinach, all washed down by several cups of caffeine-free lemon balm tea. He was feeling excited. In exactly twenty-four minutes he was going to activate the hidden software inside *Eden Fall* that would turn the game into a minefield for anyone unlucky enough to be playing it. He had told Alex that hundreds of gamers were going to die but it occurred to him that it could quite possibly be thousands. After all, *Eden Fall* was sold in over thirty countries. By the end of the day, the entire world would have turned against Real Time. The company would collapse and Vision-X would be there to pick up the pieces.

"Can I get you anything else, sir?" the butler asked.

"No, thank you, Jetson. And you can have the rest of the day off. Tell the chef I won't be needing lunch."

"Very good, sir."

The shootout was timed for ten thirty and Lucas was impatient for it. It was one thing to own a perfect replica of a Wild West town but what was the point if you couldn't enjoy the traditions that had once been common all over the American frontier? In the old days, outlaws had been chased down by posses. When they were caught, they'd been strung up from the nearest tree. There had been bar-room brawls, poker games that had ended with an explosion of gunfire. Cowboys wouldn't drink a glass of whisky; they'd down the whole bottle. The town of El Dorado was perfect in many ways but it never felt completely real. Well, today, in less than an hour's time, two boys would stare into each other's eyes in Main Street and one of them would die. You couldn't get more real than that.

But first he had work to do.

He left the ranch house, the spurs on his leather boots clanking as he walked down the stairs. Lucas had put on his best cowboy outfit today. Starting from the feet up, that meant boots, jeans with leather chaps, a belt with a huge buckle, a denim shirt, a cotton scarf and, finally, a ten-gallon hat. His stableman was waiting outside with Lucas's favourite horse, a beautiful black stallion called Indio. Quickly, he mounted and then set off at a trot, through the neighbouring fields, past the apple orchard and down into the valley where the town of El Dorado was laid out. He slowed down when he reached Main Street, nodding at the armed guards who were standing at intervals, also dressed as cowboys, then dismounted outside the courthouse and tied the horse to a hitching post. The door to the courthouse was locked but Lucas entered a six-digit code into the keypad and there was an electronic buzz. He pushed the door open and went in.

His eyes settled briefly on the judge's chair, raised up at the far end of the courtroom. That was where he should be sitting, because he was making a judgement on the world. He was about to make himself more money than anyone who had ever lived. But for that to happen, he had to pass a sentence of death. In a way, it was a shame. Jon Lucas did not think of himself as a bad man. But as every businessman knew, you can't get rich without making difficult decisions.

He went over to the main console and sat down with a keyboard in front of him. He glanced at his watch, then allowed his fingers to dance over the keys. On the screen, dozens of lines of computer code appeared in luminous green and began to scroll down. He tapped the ENTER key – not once but several times. One after another, new pages of data appeared in front of him, the entire screen filled with letters, numbers and different symbols. His eyes travelled rapidly down, missing nothing, devouring it all. ENTER/ENTER/ENTER. Finally, a single box appeared in front of him. ACTIVATE: YES/NO?

It was exactly ten o'clock.

Jon Lucas pressed YES. It was done. The malware inside *Eden Fall* had come to evil life. And there was nothing anyone – at Real Time or anywhere else – could do.

10.01 a.m. – Jailhouse, El Dorado

Alex looked at his breakfast, sitting on a tin plate: a pile of beans and biscuits covered in beef fat with a tin mug of black tea next to it on the tray. It had been brought in by one of the Numbers an hour ago, but he hadn't touched any of it. It wasn't just that the food revolted him. He had no appetite. He hadn't slept. He had been thinking, endlessly, about what the day was going to bring.

He could only assume that Ben Daniels had no idea where he was, that the connection had been lost on his mobile phone before he could explain what he had worked out. William Jones had left the cell block some time during the night and hadn't reappeared so it looked as if the school photograph hadn't affected him after all. He had failed. Alex had heard the church bell toll and knew that it was already ten o'clock and that Lucas would have activated the death-traps concealed in *Eden Fall*. How long before the first death took place? It could already have happened.

And then there was the shootout.

Alex couldn't beat Freddy Grey. If the contest went ahead and they both played by the rules, Freddy was faster, more experienced and would simply gun him down. Not that it made any difference. In his heart, Alex knew that he would never be able to kill Freddy in cold blood, not even to save his own life. The question was: did Freddy feel the same way?

Alex had made his decision.

Back in England, when the two of them had broken out of Tidworth Camp, he had been unsure about the other boy. He really had believed that Freddy had killed Tom Harris. But he had been wrong. It wasn't a mistake he was going to make twice. Freddy had tricked everyone and given Alex the vital clue that had brought him here. He had deliberately put his own life on the line. So no matter what happened, Alex wasn't going to shoot at him. He was going to trust him.

With his own life.

Alex had just one small hope. Perhaps even at this late

stage, Freddy would find a way to send him a sign, some indication of what he was planning to do. It wouldn't be easy. The two of them would be surrounded. The Teachers, the guards, the Numbers – everyone would be watching. But all it would take was a blink of an eye, a nod of the head and he would know.

He heard the door of the jailhouse crash open. Suddenly, Brother Mike was in front of him.

"It's time," he said.

Meaning there was no time left.

6.17 p.m. – East Sussex, UK

There were rumours that the Blue Devil was about to visit Camber Sands on the south coast of England and even though the sun was already setting, that was enough to bring out gamers from many of the surrounding towns. They came from as far afield as Hastings and Rye, parked their cars and bikes on the Old Lydd Road, then chose one of the many sandy paths that cut through the undergrowth and brought them down to the beach itself. Two of them were schoolfriends, fifteen years old. The oldest was twenty-four, a student nurse. She'd left her boyfriend at home, watching TV. They all knew each other. They'd often met, playing *Eden Fall*, and they'd texted each other before coming out tonight.

Camber Sands provided a wonderful landscape for the game. In the summer, the beach would attract huge crowds of visitors. It stretched out, uninterrupted, for almost two miles, with perfect sand, one of the longest dune systems in Europe, great conditions for kitesurfing and even areas that welcomed dogs. But on this cool spring evening with the water dark grey and clouds twisting towards the horizon, there was a wildness about it, a sense almost of desolation. To the gamers, this was part of the attraction. They hadn't come for deckchairs and ice creams. The adventure was all the more enjoyable when it had a sense of danger.

Wearing their headsets and with their smartphones at hand, they greeted each other and spread out along the shoreline where the waves crashed down. One gamer shouted and pointed to a school of dolphins that were obviously part of the game. They were wearing school ties. A spaceship lowered itself out of the darkness and hovered over the surface of the water. Huge worms burrowed in and out of the sand.

The gamers had all forgotten that Camber Sands is also a dangerous place. The wind will occasionally push huge torrents of water onto the beach and they can be accompanied by vicious riptides. This happens very quickly and visitors are advised to keep an eye on the weather charts, particularly if they're walking alone, out of season. For all its beauty, the area has seen many deaths.

There were plenty of warning signs on the beach that evening but the gamers didn't see any of them. There was a simple reason. The software in their headsets had simply erased them, removing them from sight. The student nurse had been sensible enough to check the weather conditions but the game had fooled her. **LOW TIDE. CONDITION GREEN. BEACH OPEN.** The notices were all around them, encouraging them to carry on the game.

As they continued to search for the creatures from *Eden*

Fall, none of them were aware of the surge of ice-cold, dark water racing towards them, urged on by the wind. The ocean was gathering its strength, waiting for its moment. Very soon it would rush in and then it would kill them all.

10.26 a.m. – Main Street, El Dorado

Alex stood outside the jail, blinking in the morning light. It was going to be a hot day. The sun was already beating down on the long, sand-covered street with its collection of wooden-fronted bars, hotels and stores standing in two long lines. All the Numbers had assembled for the shootout, by the side of the street or slouching on the sidewalks with their thumbs hooked into their gun belts. Alex saw William Jones – Number Seven – just a few steps away, leaning against one of the hitching posts. His face showed nothing. It was as if the conversation between them had never happened.

The armed guards had positioned themselves all around. They were keeping themselves to themselves, away from the Numbers, covering every angle. Some had climbed up to the balconies of the hotel and the saloon. Others stood in the doorways of the various buildings. He saw one of them raise his eyes as a small, single-engine plane passed overhead. Otherwise the sky was clear.

Brother Lamar, Sister Jeanne and Sister Krysten were sitting on a wooden bench outside the courthouse. They alone had refused to change into cowboy gear and they looked slightly ridiculous: the bald man, the ageing supermodel and the witch in their flowing grey robes and gold discs. The length of the street was empty. This was where Alex would face Freddy. Like Alex, Freddy had been made to dress in jeans and a cowboy shirt with an empty gun belt dangling low on his hip. He was standing some distance away, his face very pale, his eyes giving nothing away.

A killer or a friend? The next minutes would show which of the two he had decided to be.

Jon Lucas stepped forward, carrying the gold pocket watch that he had shown Alex the day before. "So this is the big moment," he exclaimed. "It's all being filmed, by the way, so when one of you boys bites the dust, at least you'll have the consolation of knowing the moment's been captured for ever."

Freddy hadn't spoken. His face was utterly blank.

"And what if we refuse to play?" Alex asked.

"Then I guess we'll film a hanging instead." He smiled. "In a minute, you're both going to be given a gun. It has just one bullet, so don't even think of trying anything fancy. There are a dozen armed guards watching every move you make and they'll gun you down before you can blink. Remember the rules. You fire when the music stops. No cheating! The watch plays a tune you may recognize by the way. 'Twinkle, Twinkle, Little Star.' It's not exactly appropriate for a shootout but the watch was my grandpa's and he used to play it to me when he was trying to get me to sleep. Are you ready, Alex?"

"The CIA know I'm here," Alex said. "They know about your plan. You're doing all this for nothing and you're going to end up in jail for ever."

Jon Lucas laughed. "You never give up, do you? A shame,

really. I was hoping you'd be a bit more like Clint Eastwood. Mean and moody." He pointed at the centre of the street. "Would you mind moving into position?"

Alex weighed up his options. Right now, he didn't have any. He did as Lucas had commanded, walking into the centre of the street so that he was face to face with Freddy, about ten steps apart.

"Remember, neither of you are to speak. Not one word. If you do, you'll be disqualified, and I don't need to tell you what that will mean. Do you understand?"

Alex was waiting for Freddy to meet his eyes, to give some indication of what he was planning. But he was staring at the ground, his face blank.

"OK ... give them their guns."

Two of the Numbers moved forward, their feet making no sound on the soft sand. One of them slipped a loaded gun into Alex's holster. Alex felt the weight of it, dragging him down. One bullet.

The other did the same for Freddy. Freddy lowered his hands, his fingers curving towards his thighs.

Jon Lucas stepped out with the pocket watch. There was complete silence in the little town.

He lifted the lid and the music began to play.

1.27 p.m. – Philadelphia, Pennsylvania, USA

The Philadelphia Schools District workers were on strike and all the schools were closed for the day so there were more children than usual out in the streets and open spaces of the city. Many of them were wearing Real Time headsets.

A group of them had found their way to the railroad facility on the other side of Clarissa Street, in the shadow of the Roosevelt Freeway. The area was off-limits, of course, but part of the fence on the edge of the complex had rusted away and, according to the Real Time software, a three-headed dog had been seen here, meaning that there would be plenty of other characters from *Eden Fall*, maybe even a blue demon or the famous Blind Hedgehog.

There was a major railway network on the other side of the fence. Passenger trains rattled past constantly and to one side a rail yard stretched out, full of trucks and containers where goods trains loaded and unloaded. Colourful signs, hanging in the sky, urged the gamers on.

THIS WAY.
SHOOT THE BLUE DEVIL.
WIN MAGIC APPLES.
UNLOCK THE NEXT LEVEL.

The railway lines were straight ahead of them but seemed to be deserted. None of the gamers had any idea that a huge electric train with nine carriages had just left the station at 17th Street and was thundering towards them. The headsets made it vanish just as the earpieces cancelled any sound.

12.28 p.m. – Mexico City, Mexico

Everyone knew the old apartment complex known as the Condominio Insurgentes. It stood on the corner of a wide intersection in the Roma district, just south-west of the city centre, and it had been abandoned ever since an earthquake in 1985 had made it unsafe. It was hard to believe that wealthy business people and lawyers had once lived here and that there had even been a private helipad on the roof. Over the years, the walls had mouldered, the paint had peeled away, many of the windows had been smashed and the building had been occupied by squatters, drug addicts and petty criminals.

But now it seemed that the condominio had a new resident.

Shadrack, the Blind Hedgehog, had moved in.

There were plenty of young gamers living in the Roma neighbourhood and as the word spread, they quickly gathered their Real Time headsets, which directed them to the broken door at the back of the building. Urged on by birds and butterflies, with neon arrows lighting the way, they climbed up to the twelfth floor.

There was no twelfth floor. It had rotted away years ago. But it was only when the gamers attempted to cross the black-and-white surface stretching out from the stairwell that they would find there was nothing beneath their feet ... just a slab of solid concrete, coils of barbed wire and broken pieces of rubble waiting for them far below.

10.29 a.m. – Whistler, British Columbia, Canada

It was the latest extreme sport. Not just snowboarding – but snowboarding off-piste, wearing an augmented reality headset at the same time. You got the speed, the exhilaration of a black run, the powder snow, the sunshine ... and you also had a host of weird creatures to cheer you on your way.

The group of English and Italian friends had travelled

all the way from Europe for a week in the Whistler and Blackcomb Mountains – eight thousand acres of trails and terrain parks, sixteen alpine bowls and three glaciers. It was one of the most challenging ski resorts in the world and they planned to enjoy it in a unique way.

Tom Harris had said that his brother was a fan of *Eden Fall* and here he was, chasing down the side of the mountain on his Nidecker Mosquito snowboard with the snow whipping up behind him and the Blue Devil just in front of him, desperately trying to get away.

The piste continued for another half-mile. Jerry could see it quite clearly through his Real Time goggles. He had missed all the warning signs. DANGER. DO NOT PROCEED. Nor would he see the edge of the precipice with the one-thousand-metre drop into nothing that was getting closer by the second. His friends were behind him, but Jerry was way ahead.

The void was waiting for him. He would be the first to reach it...

10.30 a.m. – Main Street, El Dorado

The pocket watch was still playing its tinkly tune. The music hadn't yet begun to slow down.

With the seconds ticking away, Alex examined Freddy one last time, trying to work out what the other boy was planning to do. But Freddy was deliberately hiding any emotion. His face could have been a frozen photograph of itself.

Alex made his final calculations. He had to live. Somehow, he had to close down the computer programme that Jon Lucas had launched from the control room inside the courthouse. It was well past ten o'clock. All over the world, the traps had already been set and gamers would be cheerfully heading to their deaths. Jon Lucas was the only man who could stop it. Alex had to reach him and force him to undo what he'd done. It might already be too late. He needed Freddy on his side, but if that wasn't possible, then he would have no choice but to shoot.

No, he told himself. *Freddy gave you the clue. Golden. He brought you here. He's not going to hurt you.*

But when Brother Lamar was telling them the plan, about the duel that the two of them had to fight, Freddy hadn't argued. In fact, he'd nodded. Suppose the Teachers had managed to brainwash him again after he was brought here? Suppose they had turned him back into a killer?

Alex noticed Brother Lamar smiling and, with a jolt, realized that the music being played by the pocket watch was slowing down. How many more seconds did it have to run? The tune was repeating itself.

Twinkle, twinkle, little star,
How I wonder what you are...

The childish words and the tune were horribly inappropriate. Did the watch have enough power in its spring to reach the end of the verse? He doubted it. There could only be ten or fifteen seconds remaining.

Desperately, he looked around him. There was no way out of this. Jon Lucas was standing in front of the courthouse. The two female Teachers were still sitting on the wooden bench, but Brother Lamar had got to his feet to gain a better view. Where was Brother Mike? Alex checked over his shoulder and saw the last Teacher smiling at him unpleasantly, and aiming a pistol at his back. That was bad news. If Alex did anything except shoot Freddy, Brother Mike would gun him down. If he tried to run, he would be dead before he could take a step.

The music was still slowing down, struggling to continue.

Alex returned his gaze to Freddy, who was standing there, exactly as he had been all along, his eyes fixed on Alex, his hands hanging low, ready to grab hold of the pistol that hung in its holster, flat against his thigh. *He won't kill me,* Alex told himself. *He won't. He can't.* Alex wanted to call out to him but knew that he couldn't. It was against the rules and anyway his mouth was too dry. He could feel his heart pounding. He glanced at the guards, up on the rooftops. They were all peering down, fascinated. None of them had ever seen anything like this before. Not in real life.

Slower and slower...

Alex knew what he had to do.

The music stopped.

10.30 a.m. – Edwards Air Force Base, California

The F-16 Fighting Falcon had reached the end of the runway at Edwards Air Force Base and was preparing for take-off. The single-engine, supersonic, multi-role fighter aircraft was one of the most famous in the world, instantly recognizable with its triangular aluminium-alloy wings set well back and its cockpit positioned high up, with the bubble canopy giving the pilot a unique, unobstructed view. The plane looked deadly – even without the six AGM-65 Maverick air-to-ground missiles it was carrying, along with two 2,000-pound bombs and a 20mm multi-barrel cannon with 500 rounds. To the pilots it was known as the Viper – there was something about the shape of the plane that reminded them of the lethal snake. It had a range of 2,425 miles, but today its target was much closer. Just three hundred miles to the north.

Sitting in the control tower, the chief of the CIA Covert Action Division watched the plane manoeuvre itself into position. Dwain Garfield was wearing sunglasses that blocked out much of his face. Certainly nobody could see the excitement in his eyes. In a few minutes' time, Nightshade would no longer exist. He would have taken out one of the most dangerous terrorist organizations in the world and he alone would get the credit. In fact, apart from the pilots themselves, there were only a handful of officers at the base who knew the nature of the mission that was about to be launched. And nobody had been told about the English agent who would also die in the bombardment. Even when he had spoken to the Pentagon, Garfield had been careful not to mention Alex Rider's name. He was a necessary sacrifice, and anyway, it didn't matter. When this was all over, there would be no evidence he had ever been there. He would have been vaporized.

"Runway two-one right at Echo. Wind three four zero at three. Clear for take-off."

Garfield heard the master controller communicating directly with the pilot and saw the blaze of fire exploding out of the rear of the F-16 as the General Electric turbofan engine urged it on with 25,000 pounds of thrust. The plane hurtled down the runway and soared into the air.

Behind it, five more F-16s rolled out, getting ready to follow.

10.31 a.m. – Main Street, El Dorado

Freddy fired first, Alex a second later.

Alex was certain that Freddy had aimed at him. He had whipped his gun out of his belt so fast that the whole thing had been a blur and when he had pulled the trigger, it had been pointing directly at his head. Or so it seemed. For a fraction of that second, Alex thought he had miscalculated, that he was dead.

But then he realized that Freddy's bullet had passed over his shoulder, close to his neck. He turned round and saw that Brother Mike had been hit exactly between the eyes. He was still standing up but he was already dead and, as Alex watched, he dropped his pistol and collapsed to the ground.

His own shot had gone nowhere near Freddy. His target was Jon Lucas. Alex had decided that whatever happened, the chief of Vision-X couldn't get away. He might be the only person in El Dorado who could turn off the deadly version of *Eden Fall*. After all, he was the one who had created it. Alex needed Jon Lucas alive and had used his single bullet to shoot him in the leg, spinning the man round and throwing him into the dust.

So far, so good. Alex was still alive. Freddy had made the right choice. Brother Mike was finished. Jon Lucas was neutralized.

The next ten seconds would make all the difference. Alex had already worked it out in his own mind. Snatch Brother Mike's pistol. Somehow get to the other Teachers without being taken out by the guards or by the Numbers. The Teachers didn't seem to be armed, so once he'd reached them, he would be safe. Hold them at gunpoint and force them into the courthouse along with Lucas. Lock the door. Turn off *Eden Fall* and smash the controls. Hope for the best. Alex would be trapped. But at least he would have saved all the gamers whose lives had been in danger.

With a bit of luck, Freddy would have had the same idea. It would help if there were two of them. Two against thirty-five. Better than one!

Alex was already moving. He had grabbed Brother Mike's pistol before anyone else in El Dorado had fired a single shot and he was racing towards Brother Lamar, who was staring at him with a look of growing horror. *Get to Lamar before the shooting starts. Get to Lamar and I will be safe.* That was all Alex could think.

He was so close. But he had been too slow.

Despite the monk's outfit he was wearing, Brother Lamar had been armed all along. His hand ducked inside his grey robes and when it came out, it was clutching a huge gun, a Magnum or something similar. It was pointing directly at Alex and it was obvious that there were to be no second chances. Alex didn't have time to take aim. This was the end.

There were three shots.

Alex braced himself, expecting to feel the impact of three bullets. But he hadn't been touched. As he stared in disbelief, Brother Lamar crumpled to the ground. Sisters Krysten and Jeanne hadn't even made it to their feet and were sprawled sideways. All three had been shot dead.

But who had fired?

Then Alex saw William Jones, also holding a gun, and knew at once that, after all, the photograph Mrs Jones had given him had worked. William had remembered who he was – or who he had been. He had switched sides. There was a part of Alex that was shocked. A boy his own age had just killed three adults right in front of his eyes. But then he had to remind himself: this was no ordinary teenager and the Teachers were utterly evil. The world would be a better place without them.

Alex hadn't stopped moving. He realized now that Freddy had caught up with him.

"What's the plan?" Freddy shouted, and there was a certain joy in his voice, as if he had finally broken free.

"Jon Lucas! We have to stop the game!"

Alex had barely got the words out when the whole world exploded around him.

The guards had come to their senses and opened fire, aiming at the two boys who had only made it halfway to the courtroom entrance. If they had been on their own, both Alex and Freddy would have been cut down already. But with a jolt of relief, Alex saw that all the Numbers were firing back, blasting away at the guards, who were diving for cover. William must have spoken to them during the night and persuaded them that the Teachers had been lying to them. The Teachers were now dead. The Numbers had taken control. And they, too, had chosen to give Alex their support.

The guards had stopped shooting, forced to find cover. Several of them were too slow. Alex saw the two girls – Numbers Twenty and Twenty-Three – spraying the hotel balcony with bullets, shooting with deadly accuracy. One guard somersaulted over the edge and crashed into the sidewalk below. Another was slammed into the wall behind him and slid down, his legs stretched out, his eyes empty.

But there were other guards who were still alive and who were determined to take back the advantage. Alex heard more shots and the sand close to his feet suddenly spat upwards, stinging his ankles. William was standing in the same spot, pivoting left and right, firing with each turn. Another guard cried out and clutched his arm, his gun falling away.

With the gun battle raging around them, Alex and Freddy reached Jon Lucas, who was cowering on the floor, blood oozing out of the wound in his leg. Just a few minutes ago, the millionaire had been full of himself, boasting of his plans to take over the world. Now he looked pathetic. His hat had been knocked to the side of his head and his cheeks were dusty and streaked with tears.

"You've hurt me!" he whimpered.

"You have no idea what we're going to do if you don't come with us!" Freddy said.

They pulled him to his feet, using him as a shield from the bullets that were still raining down.

Alex saw one of the Numbers get hit by a bullet and fall forward. Suddenly he was nervous. The Numbers outnumbered the guards, but they were out in the open whilst the guards had the best positions, higher up, protected by the wooden railings at the front of the balconies. Alex had to remind himself that he hadn't come here to kill anybody and that the Numbers weren't really his enemies – they never had been. This was all the fault of the Teachers and they had already paid for what they had done. He needed to get all these teenagers to safety.

How?

Even as he was trying to work out an answer, he was aware of a shadow sliding across his face as something plunged towards him. There was a deafening burst of machine-gun fire and, at the same time, the wooden walls of the hotel, the general store and the funeral parlour were turned into matchwood. What was going on? Alex looked up and saw a single man falling out of the sky, suspended underneath a parachute. He was holding a machine gun, firing as he went. A moment later, he hit the ground in the middle of the street. He rolled over and got to his feet again, firing a second burst.

Alex remembered the plane he had seen flying over El Dorado even as he recognized Ben Daniels. He couldn't help smiling. Ben had obviously improved his parachuting technique since the days when they had first met. But why had he come alone? Where was the CIA?

Ben saw him. "Alex!" he shouted.

"We need to get everyone inside!" Alex called back.

Freddy had grabbed hold of Jon Lucas's shoulder and swung him round, crashing him into the keypad beside the door. "Open it!" he shouted.

Jon Lucas didn't argue. Wincing in pain, he pressed the six-figure combination and the door swung open.

"Get in!" Alex shouted. "Everyone inside!

Still firing at the remaining guards, the Numbers swarmed up the stairs and into the courtroom. William

Jones was the first to arrive. He grinned at Alex but said nothing. More bullets slammed into the walls close to the door and Alex saw Freddy suddenly jerk as if something had stung him.

"Are you OK?" Alex was terrified that Freddy had been hit.

"Yeah. It was close!" Freddy pushed Jon Lucas into the room.

He and Alex went in.

The space was crowded. Several of the Numbers had been wounded, but they had all made it inside. Freddy slammed his fist against a button set in the wall and the door swung closed again. For the moment, they were safe.

Ben Daniels had been the last to enter, freeing himself from his parachute before following the others in. He had no real idea what was going on, but he could see that Alex and Freddy were both still alive and that they had persuaded the other Numbers to come over to their side. Now he pushed his way through the crowd to find Alex.

"We have to get out of here – now!"

Alex looked at him. "Where's the CIA?"

"That's the point. Garfield has given orders to bomb the place. They could be minutes away!"

Alex let out a deep breath. To have come so far, to have achieved so much and then, at the very last minute, be bombed out of existence? It didn't seem fair.

Jon Lucas had overheard. "There's a way out of here!" he rasped. "I can show you..."

"What do you mean, a way out?"

"An underground passage. An escape hatch. If you don't hurt me, I'll take you!"

Was he imagining it or could Alex hear a sound outside the courtroom? The scream of a distant engine. An approaching plane.

But he couldn't leave yet.

He grabbed Lucas and led him over to the main console where a single chair had been placed in front of a triple-sized computer screen. This had to be the master control. He forced Lucas to sit down. "Close down *Eden Fall*," he commanded.

Lucas looked at him as if he couldn't believe what he had just heard. "What?"

"You heard me. Close down the game."

"We don't have time." The sound of the jet fighters was getting louder. There was more than one of them. Closing in.

"None of us are leaving here until you've done it!" Alex was holding the man with one hand, his gun hanging loose in the other.

"I can't!"

"Then we all die."

Lucas let out a sob and began to strike the keys. The twenty-one Numbers watched what was happening. None of them seemed afraid, but then they had spent their entire lives in a ringside seat to death. William Jones was standing next to Ben Daniels. He was observing Jon Lucas carefully and Alex didn't like to think what he would have done if Lucas had refused a second time. It was impossible to tell if the guards were still shooting at the courtroom. The scream of the F-16s was consuming everything.

Alex saw Lucas's fingers travelling over the keyboard.

On the screen, line after line of programming poured down in an everlasting stream. How long was this going to take? Did they have enough time? The Vision-X boss was trembling in pain. One mistake and he might have to start the whole thing again.

"Have you done it?" Ben Daniels growled.

"I'm trying!" Jon Lucas was close to tears.

Frantically, he punched in commands. The screen flickered. One bank of data was swept away to be replaced by a second, a box asking YES/NO? then another demanding more information. Finally, a single command. DEACTIVATE.

Jon Lucas slumped in his chair, exhausted.

Alex leaned forward and pressed the ENTER key.

It was done.

The fighter jets were directly overhead. From the howl of their engines, they could have been in the room.

Lucas's leg was covered with blood where he had been shot. There was a pool of blood beneath his feet. But Ben showed him no mercy, pulling him roughly to his feet. "Which way?" he shouted.

"The jury room!"

Alex set off first. Freddy was next to him, looking pale and exhausted. He was moving slowly, as if in pain. Alex was worried, but there was no time to do anything now. The first missiles could strike at any moment. Ben was manhandling Jon Lucas into a room next to the jury box. When the building had been a courthouse, this would have been where the jury met to discuss the trial.

There was a spiral staircase in the middle of the floor, leading underground.

"Down there!" Lucas mumbled.

"Thanks!" Ben Daniels pushed Lucas ahead of them, and first Alex, then Freddy and William Jones, and finally all the other Numbers followed. It was a crush going down, but the further they went, the more hopeful Alex became. Perhaps there was some sort of bomb shelter at the bottom. It would be typical of a man like Lucas that he would have somewhere to hide and make sure he was safe.

Nothing could have prepared Alex for what he discovered when they finally reached the bottom. Electric lights had come on automatically to reveal a long, narrow space covered in white tiles with a curving roof and a platform taking up one side. It was a subway station with an electric train; two sleek silver carriages shaped like bullets were waiting to carry them into a tunnel stretching underneath the town of El Dorado and on into the countryside. It must have cost millions to build.

"Where's the driver?" Ben demanded.

"You are!" Lucas whimpered. "It's automatic. Just press the green button."

"Get in then!"

"No!" Lucas shook his head. The tears were flowing faster now. He must have made up his mind on the way down. "I'm not coming with you! I don't want to go to jail."

"Suit yourself." Ben pushed him away. "Everyone in!" he shouted to the others.

High above them, on the surface and some distance away, they heard the first explosion. The whole station shook.

The attack had begun and suddenly everyone was

surging forward, making their way onto the train. There was a second blast and dust came spewing out of the tunnel mouth, rushing into the station. Ben was at the front of the train. There were four or five buttons, a dial, a lever ... almost no controls. He found the green button and pressed it.

The doors hissed shut. For a moment, nothing happened. Then, slowly, the train began to glide towards the tunnel. Alex looked out of the window and saw the platform slipping past. Jon Lucas was sitting on the floor in his cowboy costume but without his hat. He was resting his back against the wall, still crying. And then he was gone.

The train picked up speed and plunged into the tunnel as the first missiles found their target, utterly destroying the town of El Dorado and laying waste to the countryside for a mile around.

10.51 a.m. – California State Highway 84

The train took fifteen minutes to reach its destination. It was a long, wooden construction standing next to a hillside, surrounded by dense woodland. The train slowed and stopped automatically and the Numbers hurried out into the fresh air. There was a river beyond and another hill covered in pine and redwood.

Anyone driving past would have been surprised to see so many people pouring out of what looked like a deserted barn. It had been cleverly designed, making it impossible to guess that it was actually the exit from a tunnel that burrowed deep into the rocks behind. They might also have been puzzled by the plume of smoke rising into the sky in the far distance. Later, the news would report that a local ranch had caught fire at the same time as a training exercise had been taking place at the Edwards Air Force Base. The two events were, of course, unconnected.

Alex and Ben Daniels had been the first off the train. They wanted to be sure that none of the guards had been sent ahead to ambush them. But the area was clear. A gravel path led down to the highway and Alex guessed that Lucas would have used this "back door" as a way to slip in and out of El Dorado without being seen. It felt strange to be surrounded by the Numbers who, only a short while ago, would have been happy to kill him. Twenty and Twenty-Three – both of them unharmed – were actually smiling at him ... in a non-lethal way.

He didn't know if he wanted to talk to them or not, but suddenly Number Seven, William Jones, was standing next to him. Looking at him, Alex knew at once that he was about to hear bad news.

It came. One word.

"Freddy..."

Alex rushed back into the barn and onto the train. He had seen Freddy Grey – Number Nine – as they pulled in. He had been sitting in a corner, not speaking, and Alex had assumed he was exhausted. Now he saw that it was much worse than that. Freddy's shirt and the seat around him were both covered with blood. Alex remembered the moment outside the courthouse when Freddy had twitched as if something had stung him. That was when he had been hit by a bullet. Freddy had pretended he hadn't been hurt.

But the wound was a vicious one. Without help, Freddy wouldn't live long.

He felt a hand on his shoulder. Ben had followed him in and quickly examined the other boy. When he straightened up, his face was grave. "I'll call an ambulance," he said. "You stay with him. I'll be right back..."

He hurried out to make the call. Alex and Freddy were left alone.

"I'm sorry..." Freddy muttered.

"You're going to be fine," Alex said. There was a tightness in his throat that made it hard to speak the words. He hoped his face wasn't giving away what he was thinking.

"You don't need to lie to me, Alex," Freddy said. "I'm not going anywhere."

"No, Freddy. We're calling for help. You just need to hang on..."

Freddy smiled. "Brother Mike came to see me last night," he said. He was finding it difficult to talk, but he went on without pausing. "He wanted me to come back into Nightshade. He said there was no chance I could ever have a normal life in the real world."

"He was lying."

"He was right. I've done too many bad things, Alex. I know it wasn't my fault and I would never do any of it again. I hope the others will manage ... the Numbers. They're going to need a lot of help ... to become human again."

"Freddy..."

Freddy held up a hand to stop Alex interrupting. "It's too late for me. But I'm not sorry. That's what I want you to know. I'm glad you were my friend. You know, in my whole life, I never had a proper friend. That only changed when I met you and all that time we spent together – escaping from prison, Greece, even Tidworth Camp – I liked being with you. I think that was the only time I was ever alive."

He coughed and Alex saw blood on his lips.

"Can you say sorry to my mother and father? They thought I was dead for all those years and now they're going to have to get used to it again. But tell them that I wasn't sad at the end. You were here. We beat the Teachers. We saved all those people when we shut down the game. You and me together. We did it!"

Ben Daniels appeared in the doorway, holding his mobile phone. "I've spoken to the paramedics," he said. "They'll be ten minutes. They're on their way."

"They're already too late," Alex said.

Freddy Grey, Number Nine, had died.

RESIGNATION

Two weeks later, Alex walked down Liverpool Street in the City of London and stopped outside the elegant, old-fashioned building that advertised itself as the home of the Royal and General Bank. It was nothing of the sort, of course. In fact, this was the main office of the Special Operations Division of MI6. Alex had been just fourteen years old when he had first come here following the sudden death of his uncle, Ian Rider. It felt like a lifetime ago. That was when he had been recruited by Alan Blunt, who had recognized that a fit and intelligent teenager who spoke several languages and who had learned judo and karate from the age of six could be incredibly useful to the organization. Alex had been sent to investigate a Lebanese billionaire called Herod Sayle and that had been the start of a series of adventures that had taken him all over the world. Once they'd got hold of him, MI6 had been reluctant to let him go.

And here he still was, more than two years later. However, he hadn't come alone. Jack Starbright and Tom Harris had insisted on joining him, even though it was early morning and they should have been at work, or school. "I just want to see you walk out of there," Jack had said to him. "Blink, and the next thing I know, you'll be in Russia or Afghanistan or outer space ..."

"... or dead," Tom added gloomily.

Alex knew he had to go in alone. Jack and Tom were going to have to wait for him at a nearby Starbucks, but it would help him knowing they were close.

"Just don't let Mrs Jones talk you into doing anything else for her," Jack warned him. "I don't even know why she wants to see you."

"She said she had something to tell me," Alex said.

"She could have sent you an email!"

"I'll be twenty minutes. Maximum."

"We'll be waiting!"

"Hot chocolate's on me," Tom said.

Alex smiled and went into the building, stopping in the reception area with its row of lifts, its multiple clocks and drab brown marble floor. There was a receptionist waiting for him, but before he could introduce himself, one of the lift doors opened and John Crawley stepped out. He came straight over and Alex guessed that he must have been watching Alex's arrival on CCTV.

"Good morning, Alex."

"Hello, Mr Crawley."

The last time the two of them had met had been at the Lower Wick Airfield.

"I'll take him up, Svetlana," Crawley called to the receptionist.

"Svetlana?" Alex was surprised.

"Yes. It's a Russian name, I think. A bit worrying..."

They got into the lift and Crawley pressed the button for the sixteenth floor. As always, Mrs Jones's deputy had the look of someone who had just got out of bed – and who hadn't slept well to begin with.

"So it seems we have to congratulate you once again, Alex," he said. "First Scorpia, now Nightshade. There really is no stopping you."

"I think I do want to stop, Mr Crawley," Alex said.

"Yes. I can understand that. I heard this adventure didn't end altogether happily for you. I'm sorry about Freddy Grey."

"How are his parents?"

"Sir Christopher and Lady Grey are devastated, as you'd expect. To lose a child once is bad enough – but twice?" He sighed. "However, there was some consolation knowing that Freddy was a hero. He saved Tom Harris's life. He gave you the clue that helped you find Nightshade. He went back into the organization at great risk to himself. And there's no question that he helped persuade William Jones – Number Seven as he was – to change sides. The boy was a true hero, as brave as any soldier I've ever met. That may not mean much to you, Alex. But I was in the army myself. That sort of courage is remarkable. Freddy will never be forgotten."

The lift had arrived. The doors opened and they stepped out into the corridor.

"Why does Mrs Jones want to see me?" Alex asked.

"That's for her to tell you." Crawley hesitated. "But it may be that she wants to say goodbye."

They came to the office that had once been occupied by Alan Blunt but which had been assigned to Mrs Jones when she took over as head of MI6 Special Operations. Crawley held out a hand. "She wants to see you alone," he said. "So I'll say goodbye for now. I do hope we meet again, Alex.

You really are a remarkable young man and we owe you a great deal."

They shook hands. Alex knocked and went into the office alone.

He saw at once that things had changed. Mrs Jones was sitting behind a completely empty desk. The books had disappeared from her shelves. It was as if she no longer belonged here.

She waved Alex to a second chair. He sat down opposite her.

"How are you?" she asked.

"I'm OK."

"Really? I know this last mission was very tough."

"Jack's looking after me."

"You're very lucky to have her." Suddenly, Mrs Jones was business-like. "There are a few things I wanted to tell you. I'll start with the fact that the King has awarded Freddy Grey a posthumous medal – the George Cross. It's the very highest award for courage in the face of the enemy."

"I'm sure Freddy would like that," Alex said, although he sounded unconvinced.

"Well, it brought some comfort to his parents. Nightshade, of course, is finished. Jon Lucas died in the missile strike launched by the Americans, and you'll be glad to hear that not one single player was hurt or killed by the various traps hidden inside *Eden Fall*. The game was deactivated just in time." She paused. "I've had a full briefing from Ben Daniels. He filled me in on everything that happened in San Francisco…"

"Where is Ben?"

"He's on active service. I'm afraid I can't tell you where. But he asked me to give you his best wishes."

Mrs Jones got up and perched on the corner of the desk.

"I was horrified that Dwain Garfield was prepared to sacrifice you to destroy Nightshade," she continued. "You might like to know that last week Mr Garfield was found in a Washington motel, sound asleep, with an empty bottle of whisky and half a million dollars stolen from the CIA concealed in his wheelchair. He has been suspended and is currently in jail."

"Did Crawley have anything to do with that?" Alex asked.

Mrs Jones blinked. "He may have been involved."

There was another pause. It was as if Mrs Jones was reluctant to come to the point. Alex helped her. "How is William?" he asked.

She smiled. "That's why I asked you to come here. First of all, I want you to know the children who were stolen from their parents by Nightshade and who thought of themselves as Numbers are being looked after by the Americans. No charges are being brought against them. Quite the opposite. The CIA are searching for their parents and families. At the same time, they are being given psychiatric counselling. They have an awful lot to learn ... and even more to forget. It's going to take a long time, but we have every hope that one day they'll be able to lead a normal life."

Alex remembered what Freddy had said. He had died believing that a normal life would never be possible for him.

"I was able to extract William and he's here with his sister in Britain. He knows that the Teachers lied to him all his life and that he was made to do terrible things that were never in his nature." She faltered for a moment and right then she looked more vulnerable than Alex had ever seen her. "He has accepted that I'm his mother."

"I'm very glad to hear it," Alex said.

"Freddy had already gone some way to persuading him. But in the end, it was you who turned him round. Showing him the photograph I gave you unlocked memories that had been inside his head for twelve years. And he was upset that the Teachers had turned on Freddy. On that last night, while you were in the cell, William spoke to the other Numbers and convinced them to help you. That last gunfight smashed the hold that Nightshade had over them. It was violent and horrible. But it helped them find themselves."

Mrs Jones took a little plastic box of peppermints out of her pocket and slipped one into her mouth. It was an old habit of hers. She always sweetened her breath when she had something difficult to say.

"I lost my two children a long, long time ago," she went on. "You know all about that. And now, thanks to you, I have both of them back. You have no idea how much that means to me, Alex. You have utterly changed my life. I will never forget you."

"You're leaving," Alex said.

Mrs Jones nodded. "Yes. I have to give all my time to William and Sofia, and help them get over what was done to them. You know, from the very first day I met you, there was something about you that reminded me of them. It won't mean very much coming from me now, but I always knew it was wrong of us to use you the way we did and I worried about you more than you may believe. Anyway, I've resigned from MI6. Today is my last day. I'm not going to say goodbye to you, because I hope we'll meet each other again, but I do want to thank you for everything you've done, especially for me."

"Is Mr Crawley taking over?" Alex asked.

"No. We're recruiting from outside. Should the new chief decide to contact you, Alex, I hope you won't take the call. I hear you got top marks in your mock GCSEs. That's brilliant, especially considering how much school you missed. You should follow your plans of sixth form and university. I think that's a good idea."

"Can I use you as a reference?"

"I don't exist."

"I'd forgotten."

Alex got up and the two of them shook hands. "Say hello to William from me," he said.

"Maybe you'll come and see him."

"Maybe."

But as he emerged into Liverpool Street a few minutes later, Alex knew it was unlikely. Mrs Jones needed to be alone with her two children. It wasn't a very pleasant thought, but from now on he knew that he would be nothing more than a bad memory. It would be better for her to leave MI6 and everything that it represented behind her.

He found the coffee shop and saw Jack and Tom through the window, sitting together, laughing. He still had the rest of the term and the summer holidays with Tom, who was already talking about another trip to Italy, hiking and camping with Jerry, who was just back from Canada. And Sabina would be returning to London in a few months. She'd already messaged him several times, full of excitement about the fact that they would soon be together.

Alex was not the sort to think too much about past sadness. He had the whole summer ahead of him and it was looking good.

He opened the door and went in.

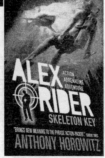

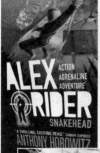

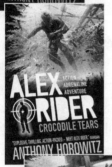
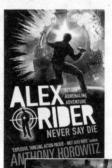
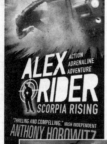

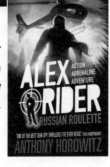
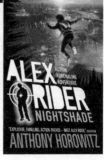

Photograph © Jon Cartwright

Anthony Horowitz is one of the most prolific writers working in the UK, and is unique for working in so many areas – juggling books, TV series, films, plays and journalism. Anthony has written over 50 books, including the bestselling Alex Rider teen spy series, which is estimated to have sold 21 million copies worldwide and has been filmed for TV, and the thrilling fantasy-adventure series, The Power of Five.

Anthony is also an acclaimed writer for adults, and was commissioned to write new novels for the Sherlock Holmes and James Bond franchises. His adult crime fiction includes *Magpie Murders* and *Moonflower Murders* and the Hawthorne series, and his TV work includes the award-winning *Foyle's War*, *Midsomer Murders*, *Collision* and *Injustice*. He adapted his own novel *Magpie Murders* with Lesley Manville in the lead role.

Anthony is proud to be a patron of the charity Suffolk Home-Start. He has been awarded a CBE for services to literature.

You can find out more about Anthony and his work at:
www.alexrider.com
@AnthonyHorowitz